FANTAGRAPHICS BOOKS

*Edited by Eric Reynolds . Designed by Jacob Covey*
*Production by Paul Baresh . Promoted by Jacq Cohen*
*Published by Gary Groth*

*Fantagraphics Books Inc.*
*7563 Lake City Way NE, Seattle, WA 98115*
*www.fantagraphics.com*


*Subscribe to* NOW*: Visit www.fantagraphics.com/now for details.*

*ISBN 978-1-68396-256-4*
*Library of Congress Control Number: 2018949686*
*Printed in Korea*

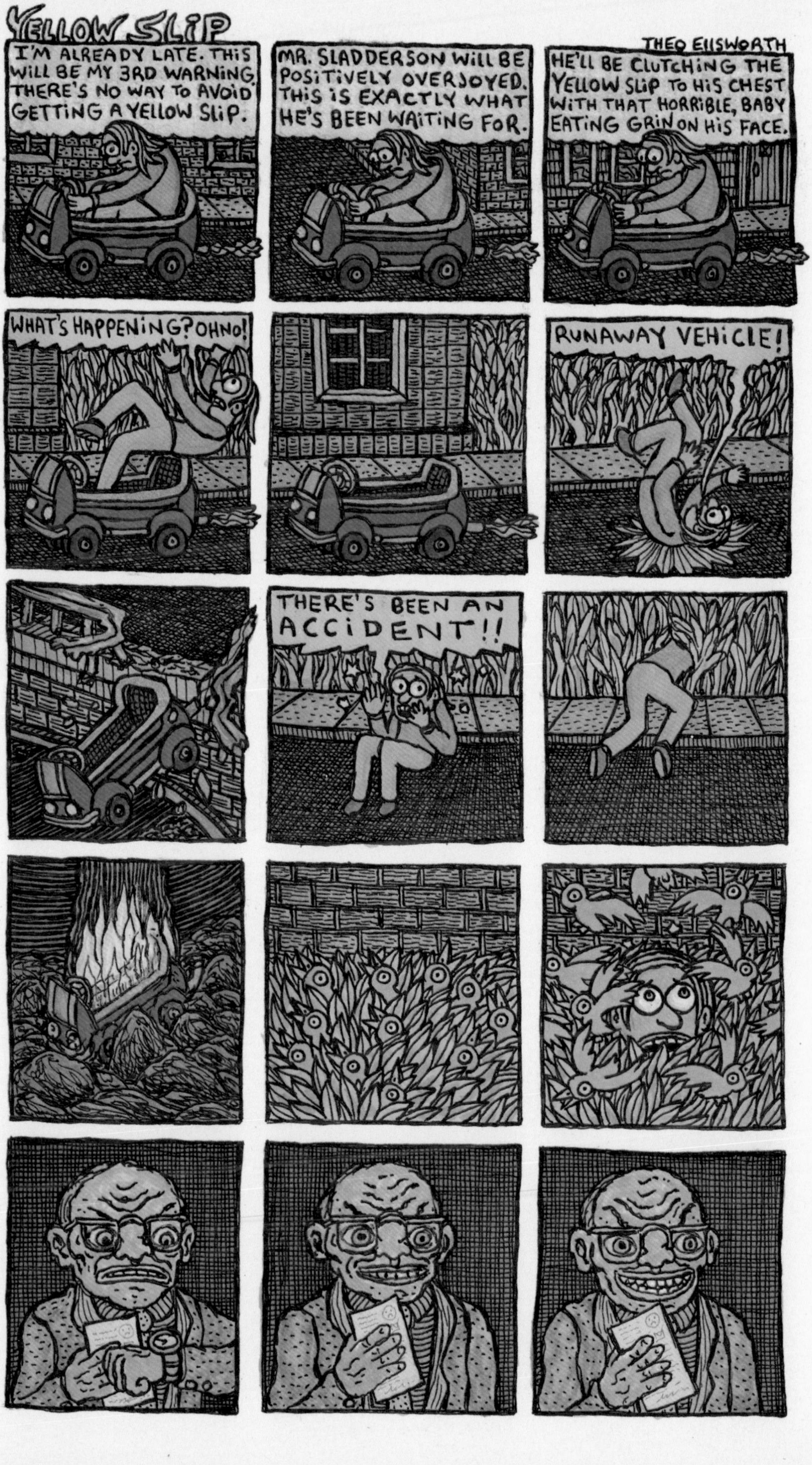

YELLOW SLIP
THEO ELLSWORTH
I'M ALREADY LATE. THIS WILL BE MY 3RD WARNING. THERE'S NO WAY TO AVOID GETTING A YELLOW SLIP.
MR. SLADDERSON WILL BE POSITIVELY OVERJOYED. THIS IS EXACTLY WHAT HE'S BEEN WAITING FOR.
HE'LL BE CLUTCHING THE YELLOW SLIP TO HIS CHEST WITH THAT HORRIBLE, BABY EATING GRIN ON HIS FACE.
WHAT'S HAPPENING? OH NO!
RUNAWAY VEHICLE!
THERE'S BEEN AN ACCIDENT!!

# Further Reading:

**WILL SWEENEY:** http://willsweeney.co.uk/

**THEO ELLSWORTH:** http://thoughtcloudfactory.com/

**TOMMI PARRISH:** @tommi_pg

**EL DON GUILLERMO:** https://eldonguillermo.com/

**JAMES ROMBERGER:** https://jamesromberger.com/

**CHRIS WRIGHT:** http://www.hoboink.com/

**KURT ANKENY:** http://kurtankeny.com/

**MARÍA MEDEM:** @mariamedem

**KATE LACOUR:** https://www.katelacour.com/

**KEREN KATZ:** https://kerenkatz.carbonmade.com/

**NICK THORBURN:** @nickfromislands

**NOAH VAN SCIVER:** @noahvscomics

**NATHAN COWDRY:** @stinkstagram

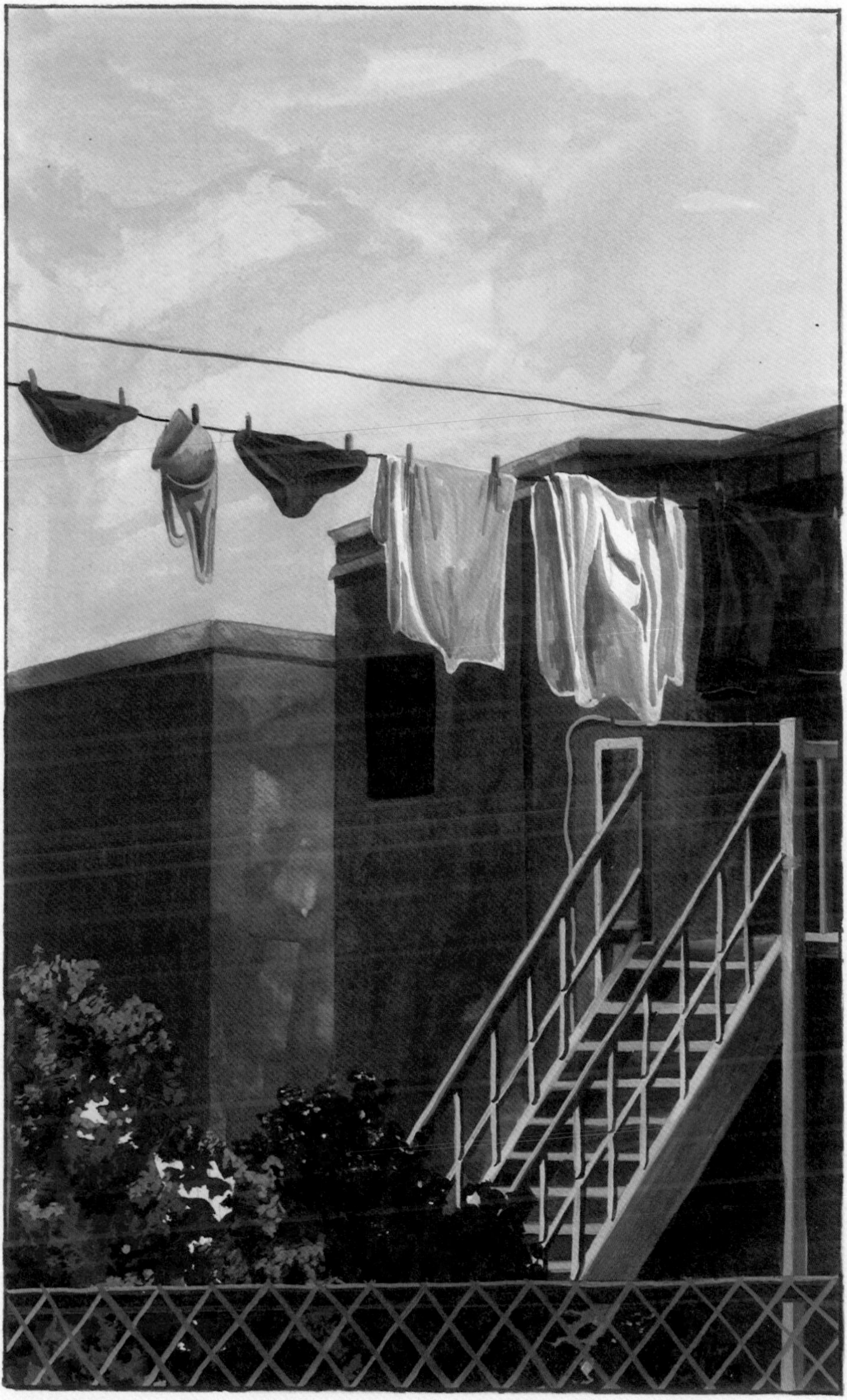

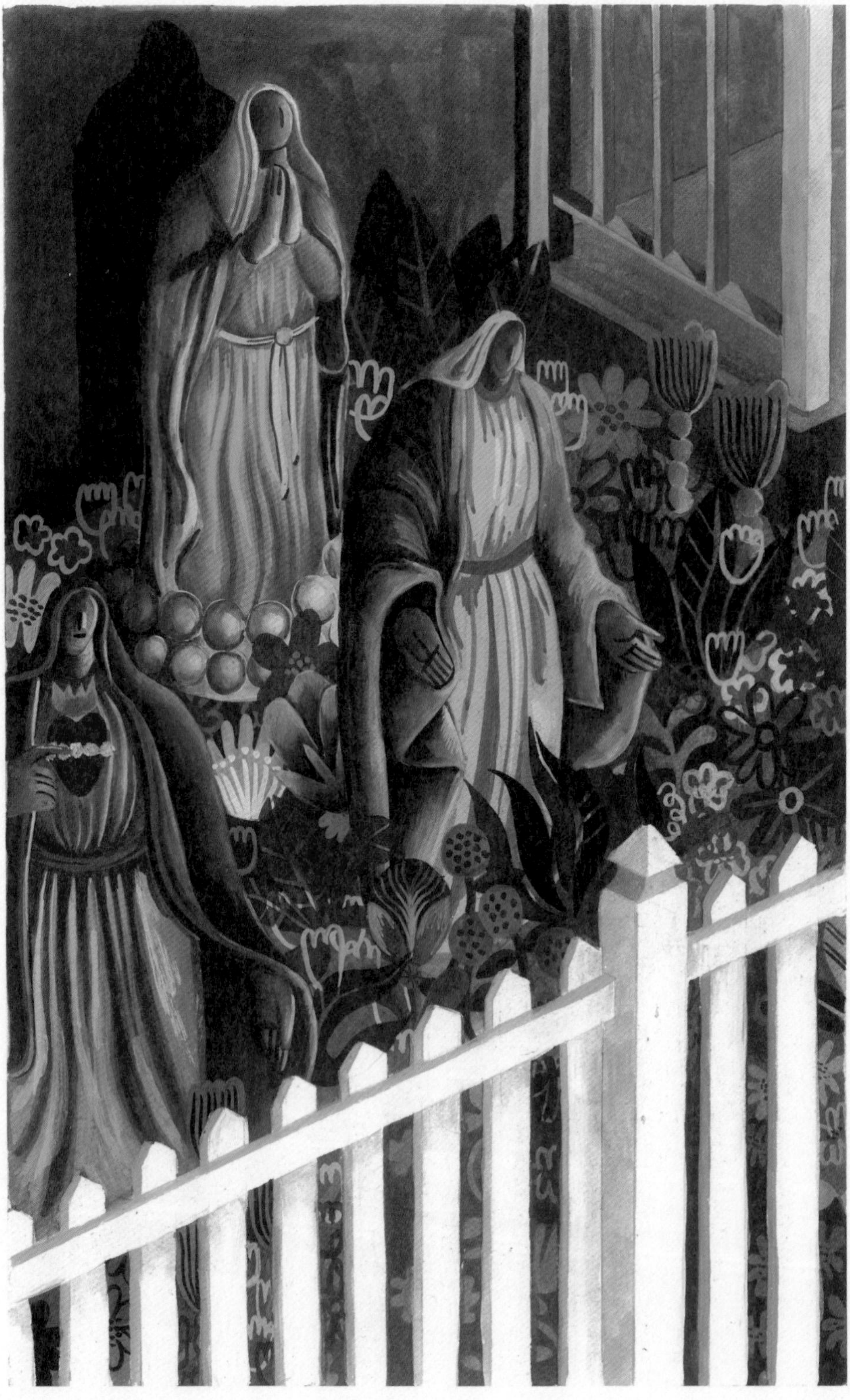

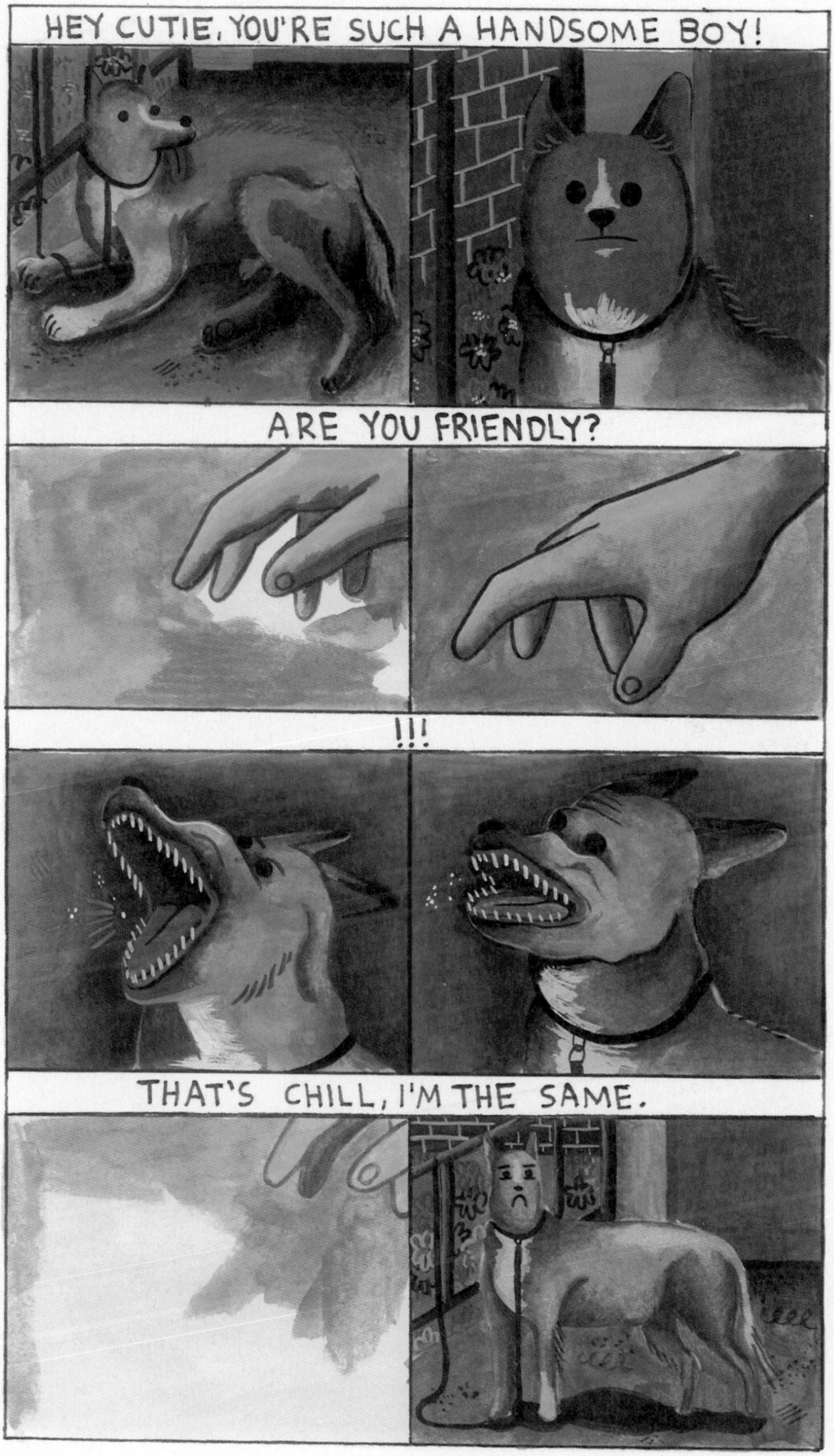
HEY CUTIE, YOU'RE SUCH A HANDSOME BOY!
ARE YOU FRIENDLY?
!!!
THAT'S CHILL, I'M THE SAME.

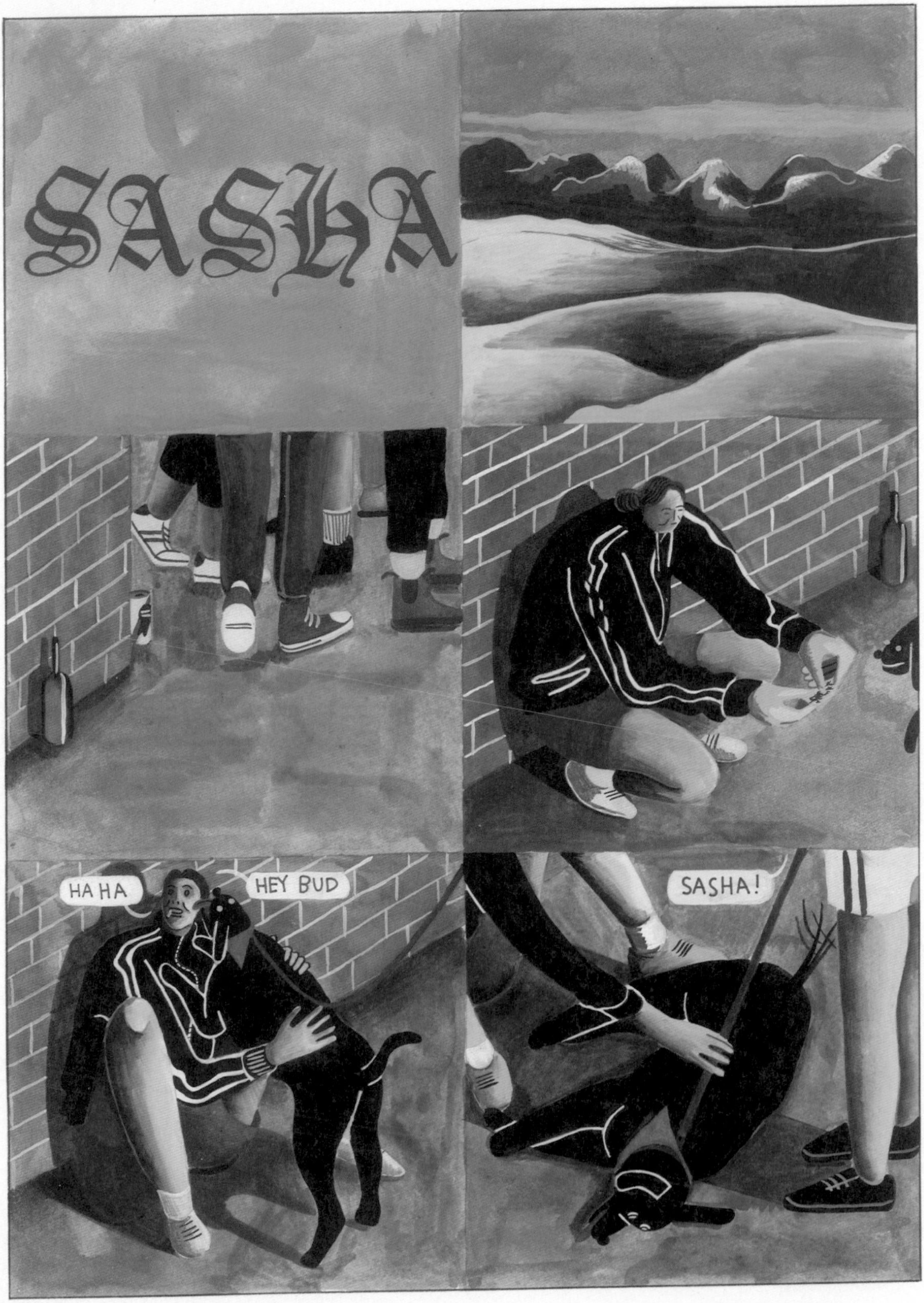
SASHA
HA HA
HEY BUD
SASHA!

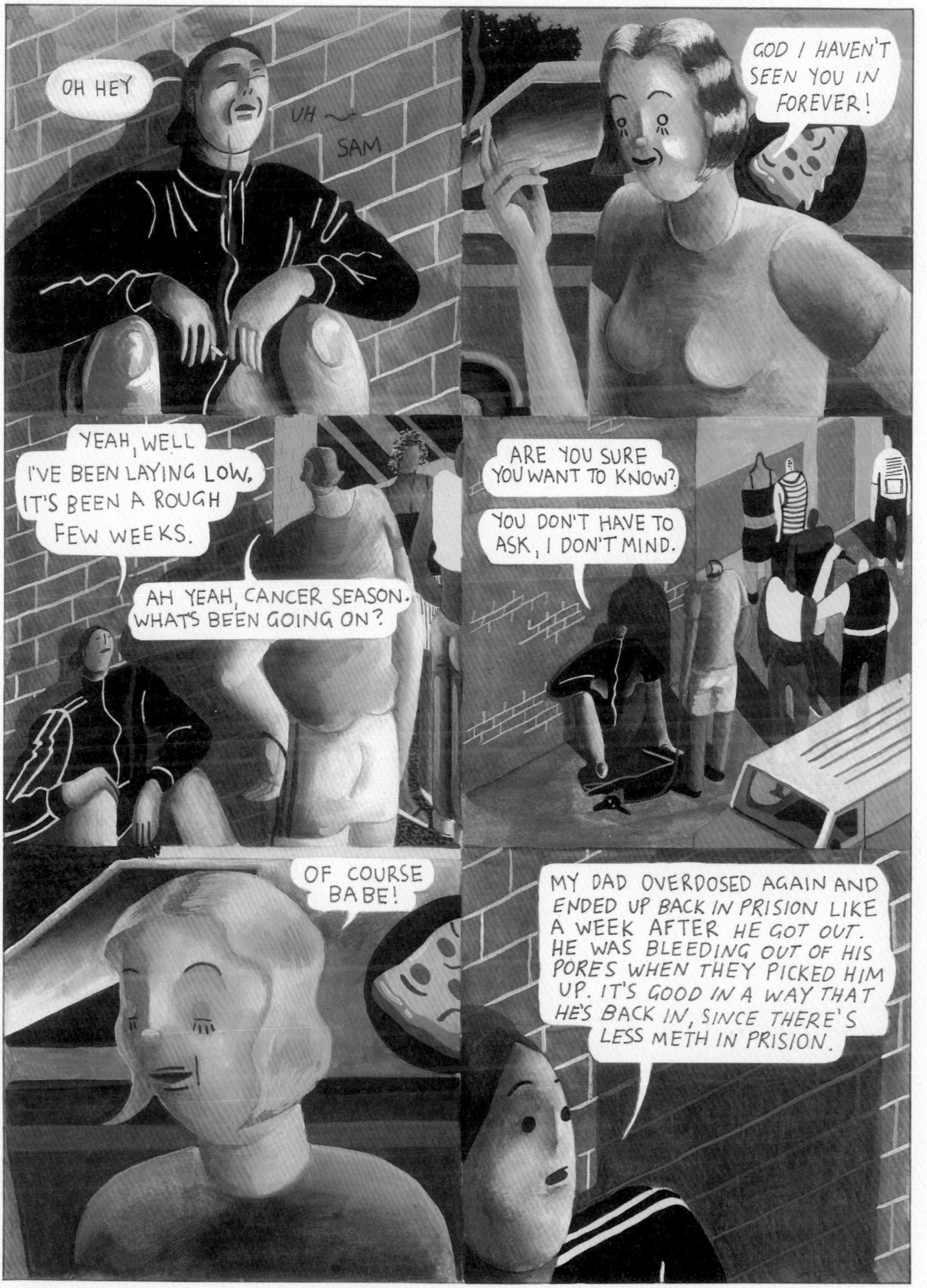
OH HEY
UH ~ SAM
GOD I HAVEN'T SEEN YOU IN FOREVER!
YEAH, WELL I'VE BEEN LAYING LOW, IT'S BEEN A ROUGH FEW WEEKS.
AH YEAH, CANCER SEASON. WHAT'S BEEN GOING ON?
ARE YOU SURE YOU WANT TO KNOW?
YOU DON'T HAVE TO ASK, I DON'T MIND.
OF COURSE BABE!
MY DAD OVERDOSED AGAIN AND ENDED UP BACK IN PRISION LIKE A WEEK AFTER HE GOT OUT. HE WAS BLEEDING OUT OF HIS PORES WHEN THEY PICKED HIM UP. IT'S GOOD IN A WAY THAT HE'S BACK IN, SINCE THERE'S LESS METH IN PRISION.

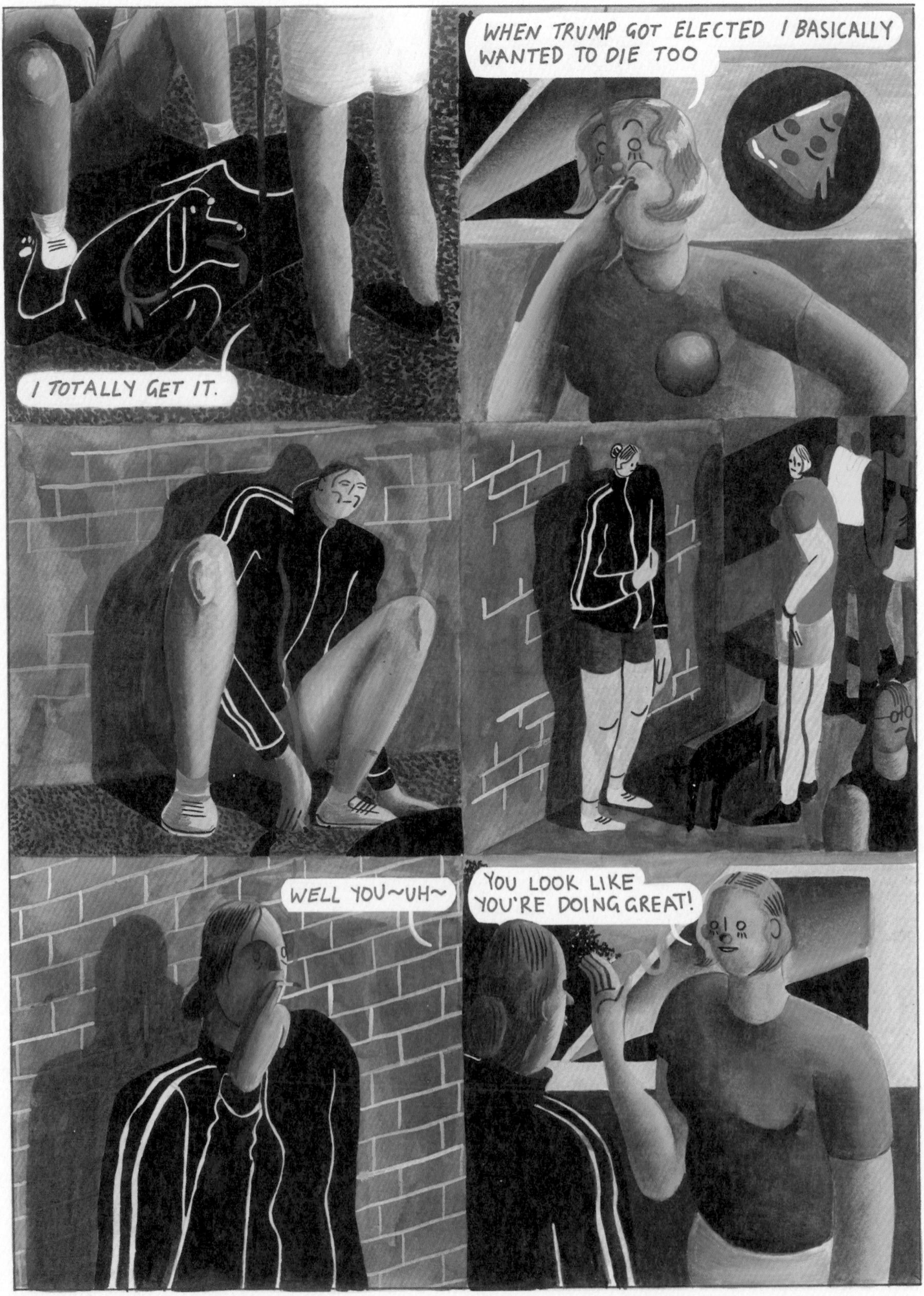
I TOTALLY GET IT.
WHEN TRUMP GOT ELECTED I BASICALLY WANTED TO DIE TOO
WELL YOU~UH~
YOU LOOK LIKE YOU'RE DOING GREAT!

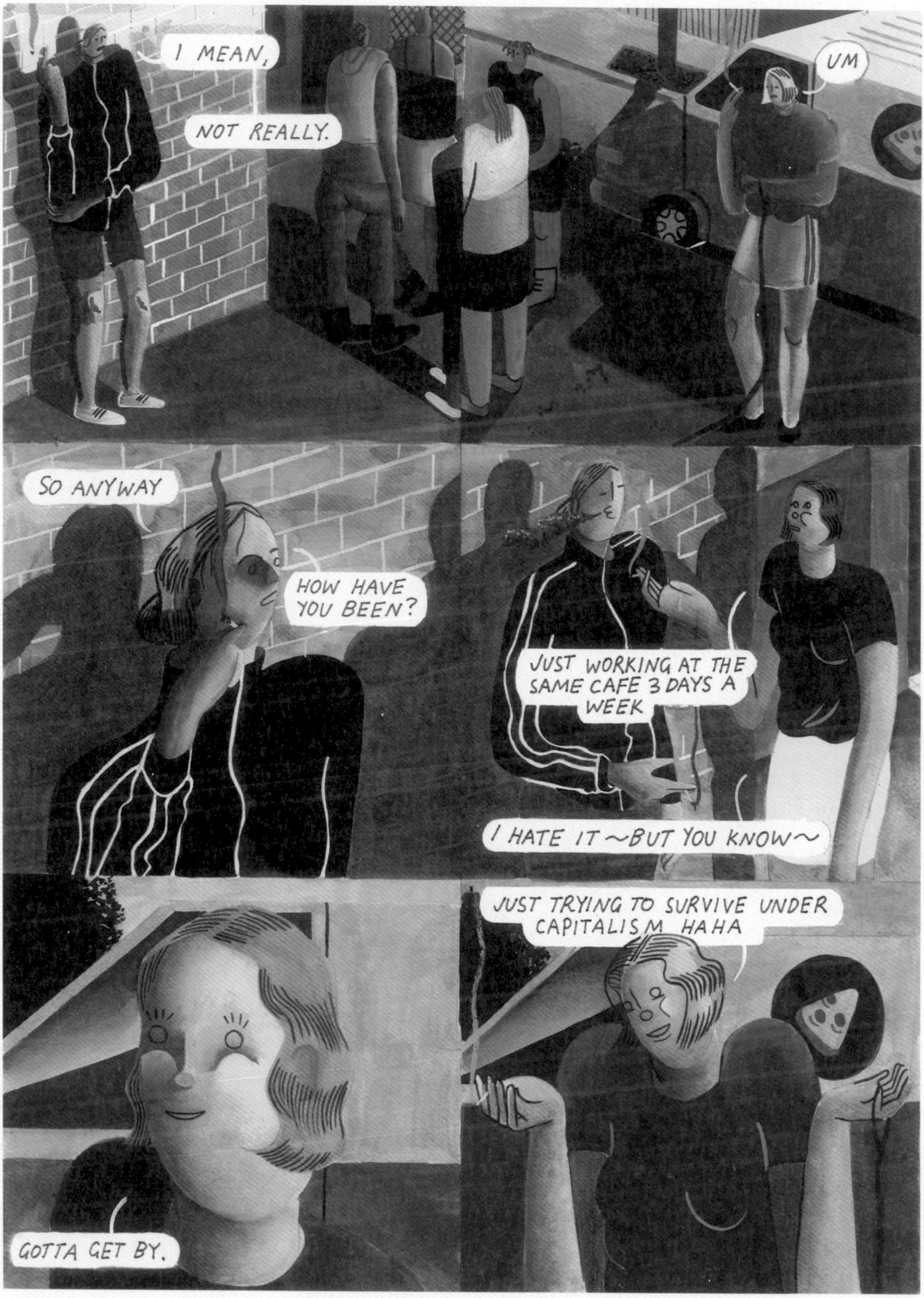
I MEAN,
NOT REALLY.
UM
SO ANYWAY
HOW HAVE YOU BEEN?
JUST WORKING AT THE SAME CAFE 3 DAYS A WEEK
I HATE IT ~ BUT YOU KNOW ~
GOTTA GET BY.
JUST TRYING TO SURVIVE UNDER CAPITALISM HAHA

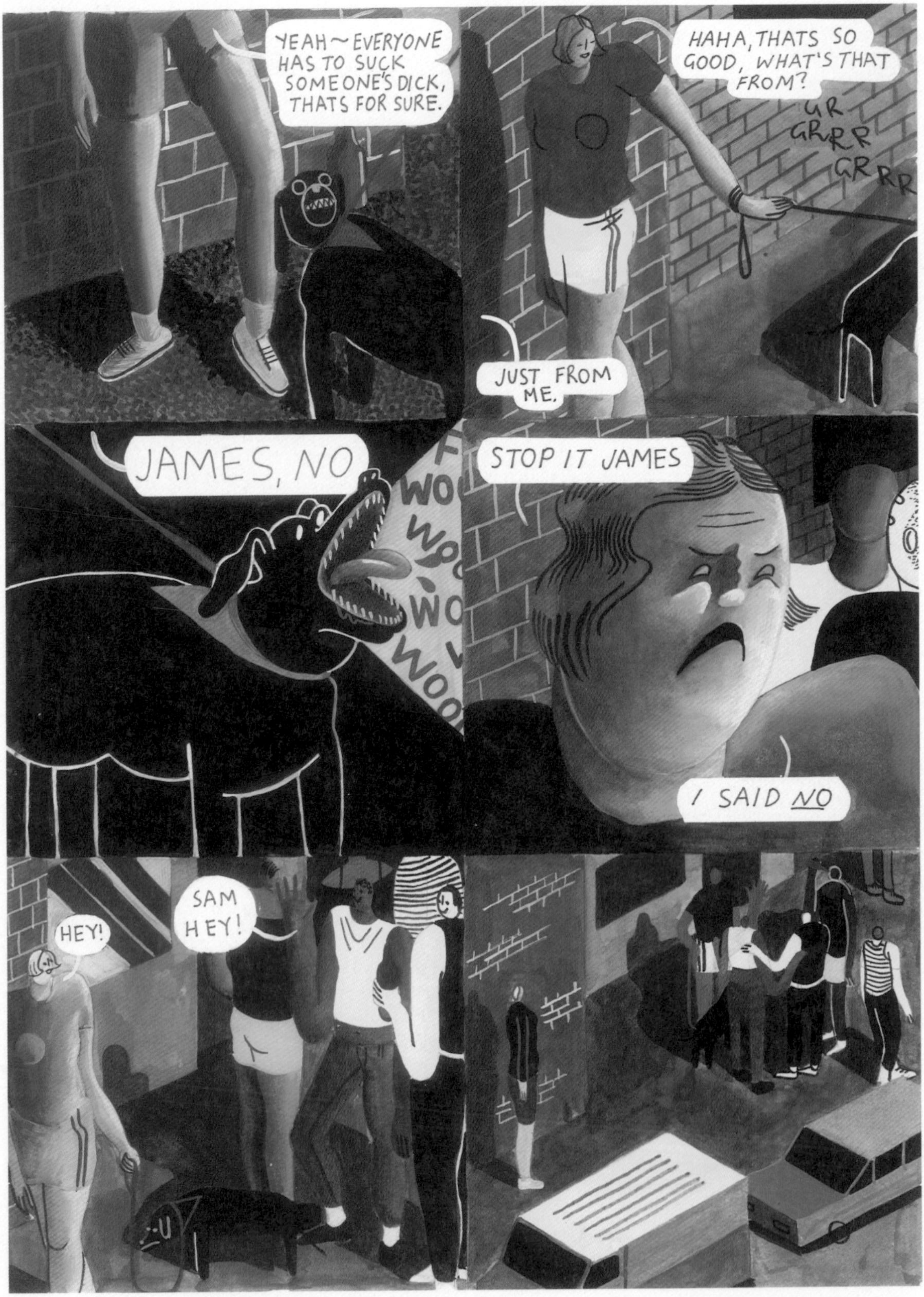
YEAH ~ EVERYONE HAS TO SUCK SOMEONE'S DICK, THATS FOR SURE.
HAHA, THATS SO GOOD, WHAT'S THAT FROM?
GR
GRRR
GRRR
JUST FROM ME.
JAMES, NO
STOP IT JAMES
I SAID NO
HEY!
SAM HEY!

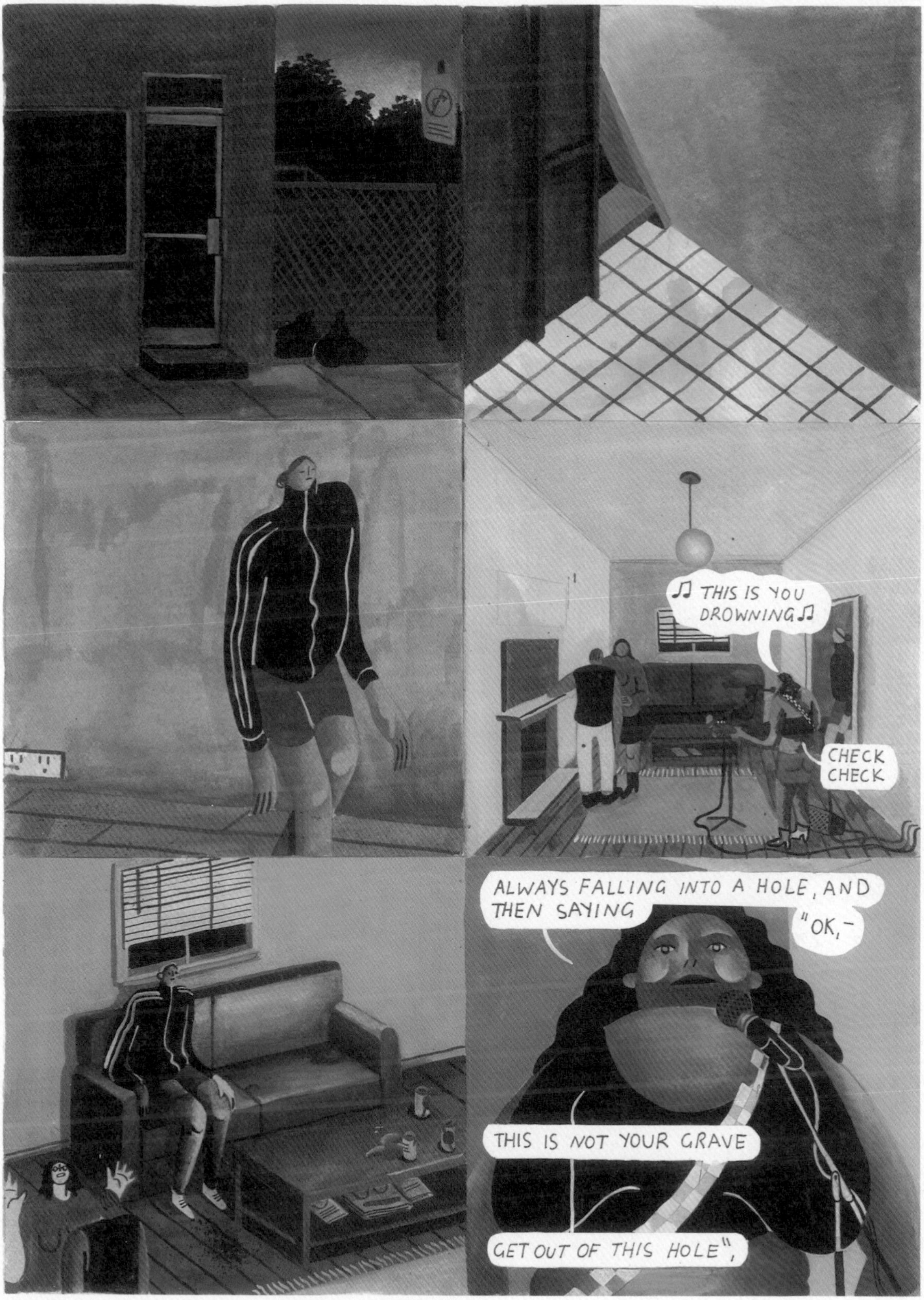
♫ THIS IS YOU DROWNING ♫
CHECK CHECK
ALWAYS FALLING INTO A HOLE, AND THEN SAYING
"OK, -
THIS IS NOT YOUR GRAVE
GET OUT OF THIS HOLE",

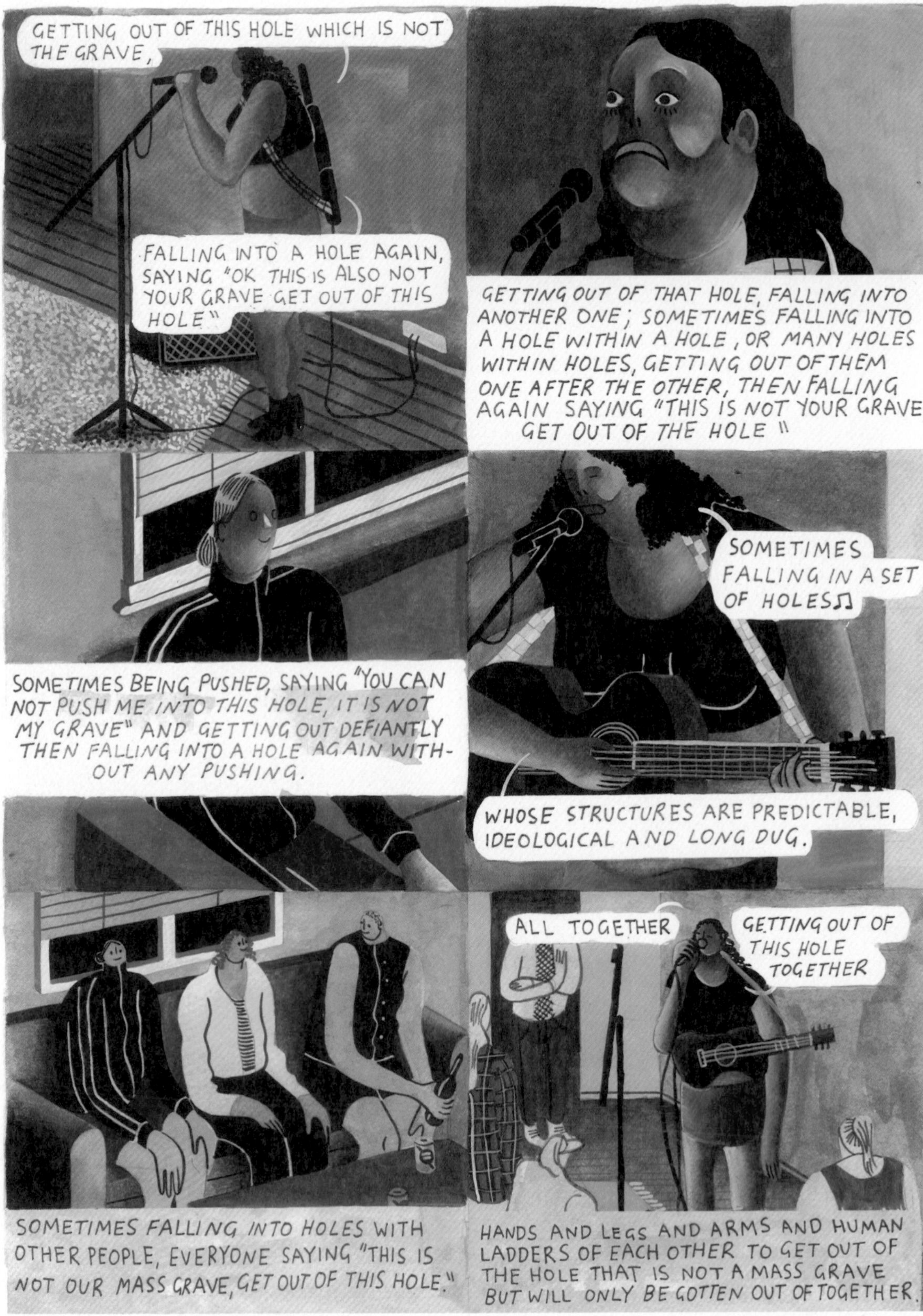
GETTING OUT OF THIS HOLE WHICH IS NOT THE GRAVE,
FALLING INTO A HOLE AGAIN, SAYING "OK THIS IS ALSO NOT YOUR GRAVE GET OUT OF THIS HOLE"
GETTING OUT OF THAT HOLE, FALLING INTO ANOTHER ONE; SOMETIMES FALLING INTO A HOLE WITHIN A HOLE, OR MANY HOLES WITHIN HOLES, GETTING OUT OF THEM ONE AFTER THE OTHER, THEN FALLING AGAIN SAYING "THIS IS NOT YOUR GRAVE, GET OUT OF THE HOLE"
SOMETIMES BEING PUSHED, SAYING "YOU CAN NOT PUSH ME INTO THIS HOLE, IT IS NOT MY GRAVE" AND GETTING OUT DEFIANTLY THEN FALLING INTO A HOLE AGAIN WITHOUT ANY PUSHING.
SOMETIMES FALLING IN A SET OF HOLES♫
WHOSE STRUCTURES ARE PREDICTABLE, IDEOLOGICAL AND LONG DUG.
SOMETIMES FALLING INTO HOLES WITH OTHER PEOPLE, EVERYONE SAYING "THIS IS NOT OUR MASS GRAVE, GET OUT OF THIS HOLE."
ALL TOGETHER
GETTING OUT OF THIS HOLE TOGETHER
HANDS AND LEGS AND ARMS AND HUMAN LADDERS OF EACH OTHER TO GET OUT OF THE HOLE THAT IS NOT A MASS GRAVE BUT WILL ONLY BE GOTTEN OUT OF TOGETHER.

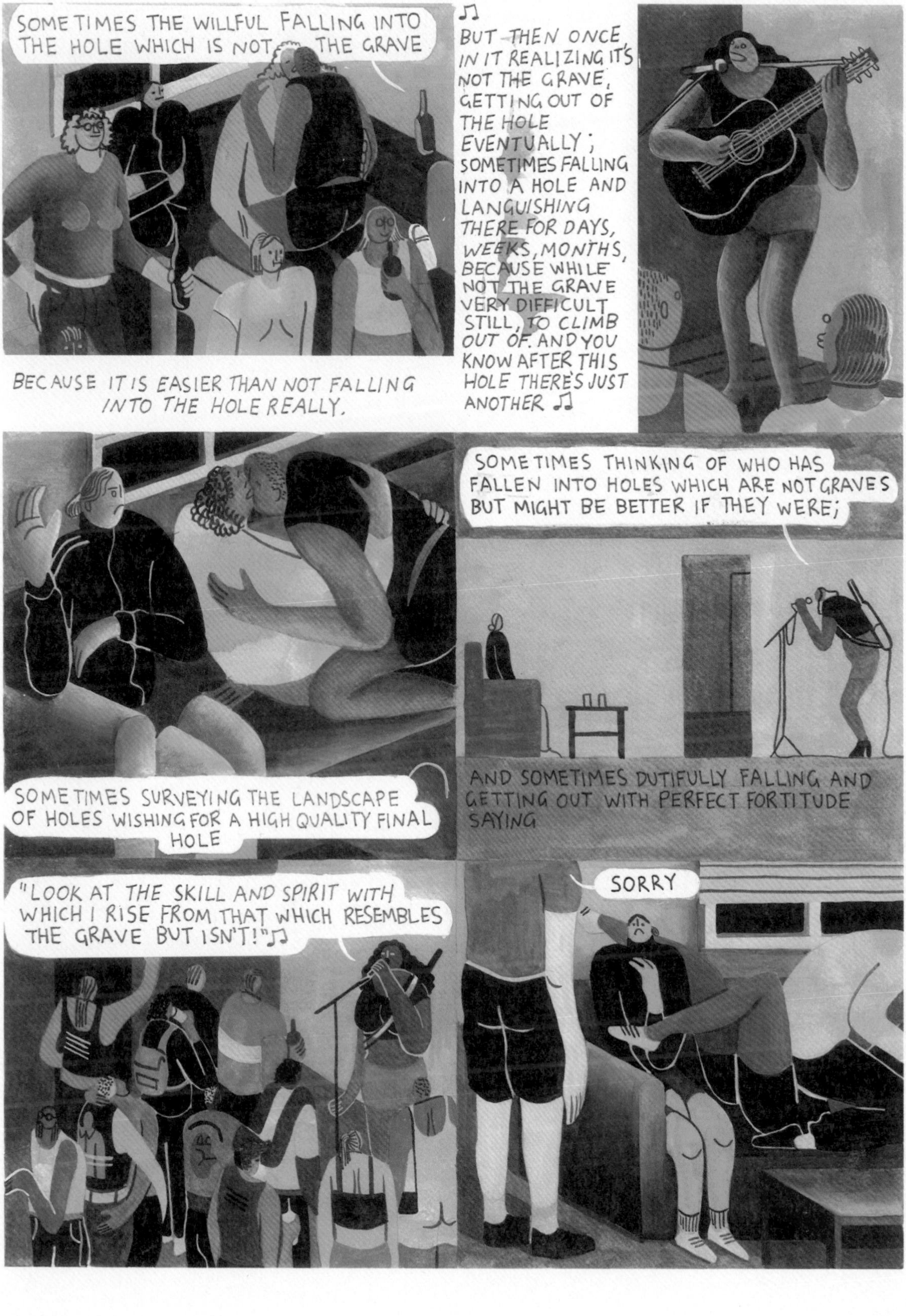
SOMETIMES THE WILLFUL FALLING INTO THE HOLE WHICH IS NOT THE GRAVE
BECAUSE IT IS EASIER THAN NOT FALLING INTO THE HOLE REALLY.
♫ BUT THEN ONCE IN IT REALIZING IT'S NOT THE GRAVE, GETTING OUT OF THE HOLE EVENTUALLY; SOMETIMES FALLING INTO A HOLE AND LANGUISHING THERE FOR DAYS, WEEKS, MONTHS, BECAUSE WHILE NOT THE GRAVE VERY DIFFICULT STILL, TO CLIMB OUT OF. AND YOU KNOW AFTER THIS HOLE THERE'S JUST ANOTHER ♫
SOMETIMES SURVEYING THE LANDSCAPE OF HOLES WISHING FOR A HIGH QUALITY FINAL HOLE
SOMETIMES THINKING OF WHO HAS FALLEN INTO HOLES WHICH ARE NOT GRAVES BUT MIGHT BE BETTER IF THEY WERE;
AND SOMETIMES DUTIFULLY FALLING AND GETTING OUT WITH PERFECT FORTITUDE SAYING
"LOOK AT THE SKILL AND SPIRIT WITH WHICH I RISE FROM THAT WHICH RESEMBLES THE GRAVE BUT ISN'T!"♫
SORRY

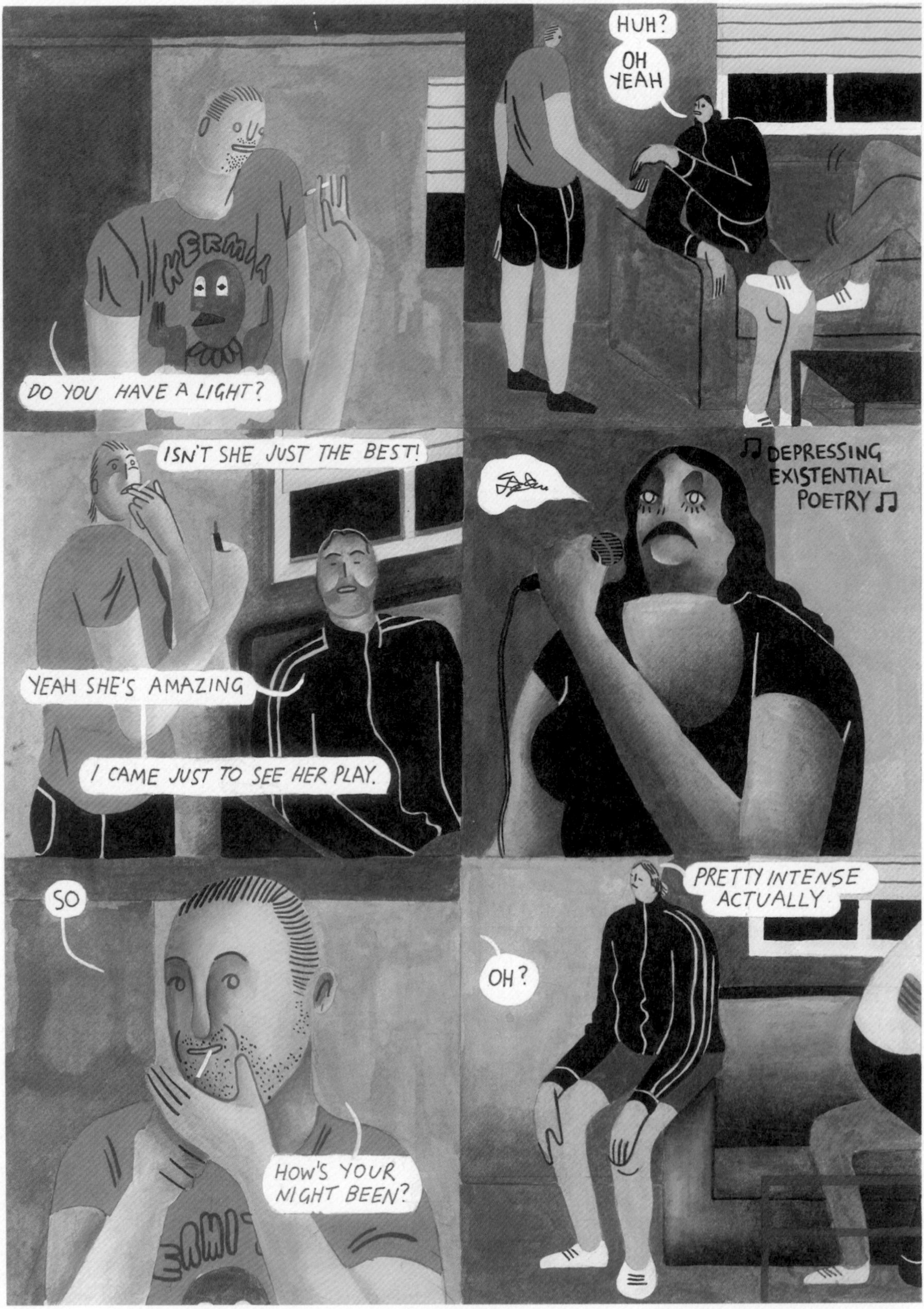
DO YOU HAVE A LIGHT?
HUH?
OH YEAH
ISN'T SHE JUST THE BEST!
YEAH SHE'S AMAZING
I CAME JUST TO SEE HER PLAY.
DEPRESSING EXISTENTIAL POETRY
SO
HOW'S YOUR NIGHT BEEN?
PRETTY INTENSE ACTUALLY
OH?

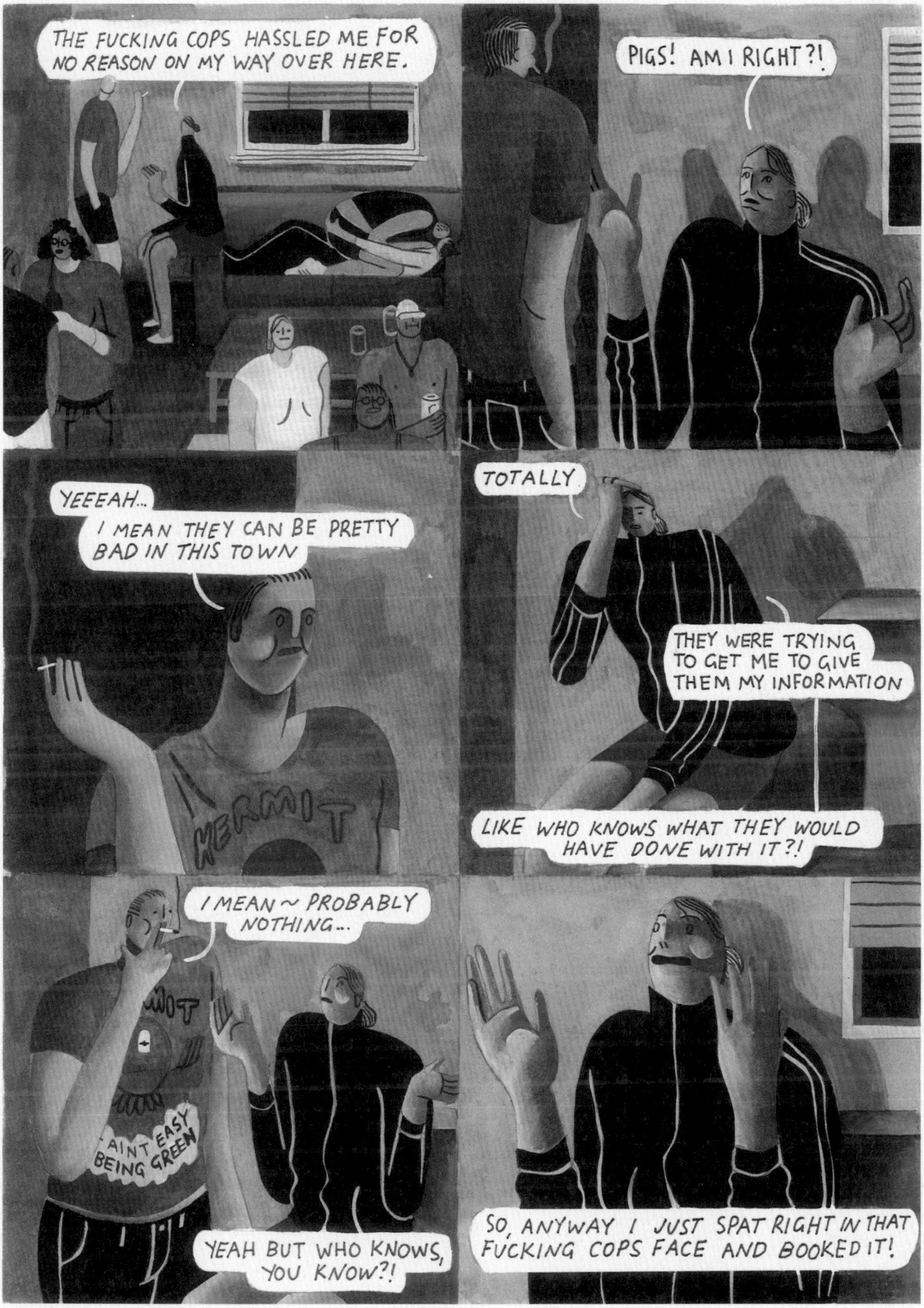
THE FUCKING COPS HASSLED ME FOR NO REASON ON MY WAY OVER HERE.
PIGS! AM I RIGHT?!
YEEEAH...
I MEAN THEY CAN BE PRETTY BAD IN THIS TOWN
HERMIT
TOTALLY
THEY WERE TRYING TO GET ME TO GIVE THEM MY INFORMATION
LIKE WHO KNOWS WHAT THEY WOULD HAVE DONE WITH IT?!
I MEAN ~ PROBABLY NOTHING...
AINT EASY BEING GREEN
YEAH BUT WHO KNOWS, YOU KNOW?!
SO, ANYWAY I JUST SPAT RIGHT IN THAT FUCKING COPS FACE AND BOOKED IT!

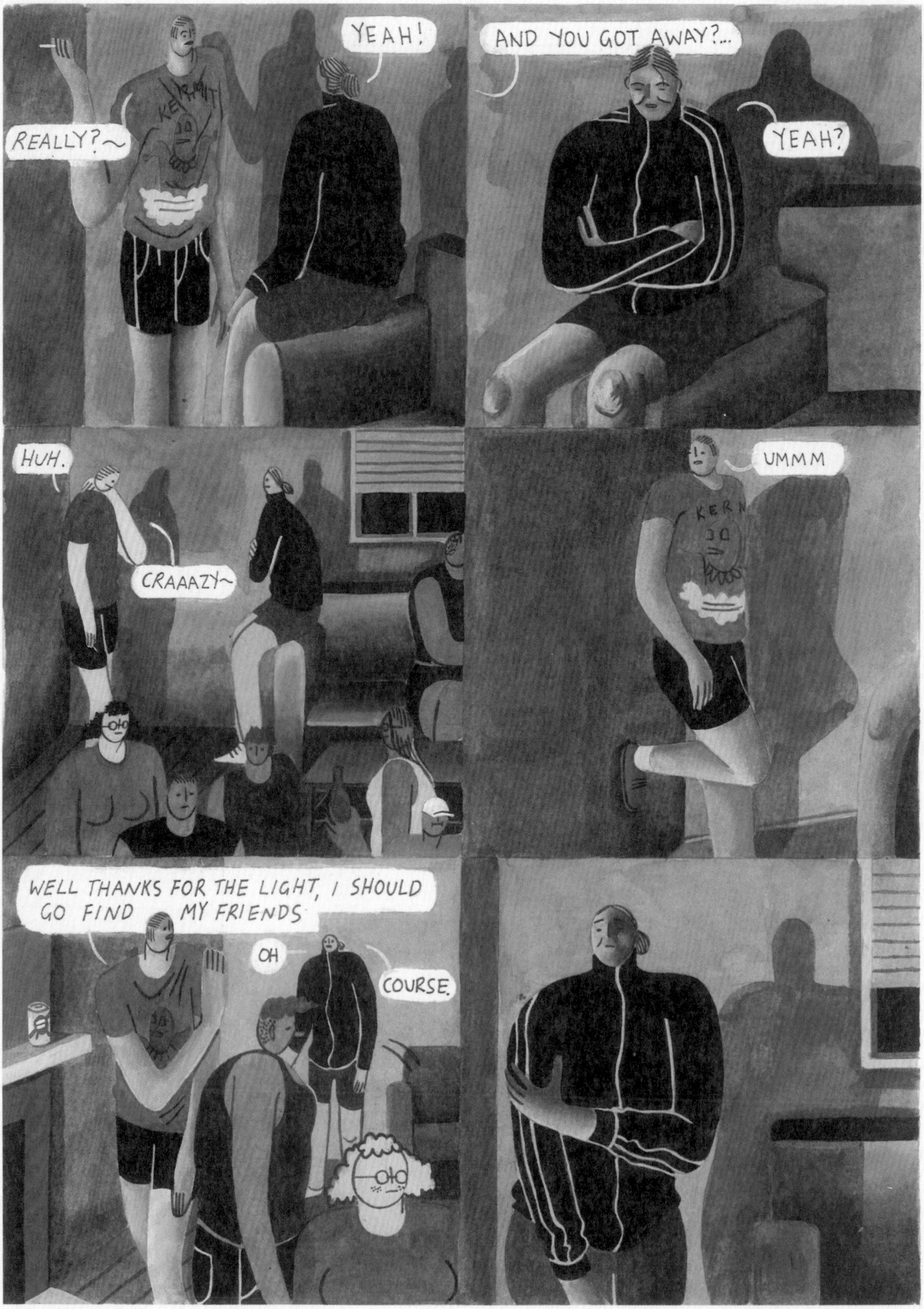
YEAH!
REALLY?~
AND YOU GOT AWAY?...
YEAH?
HUH.
CRAAAZY~
UMMM
WELL THANKS FOR THE LIGHT, I SHOULD GO FIND MY FRIENDS
OH
COURSE.

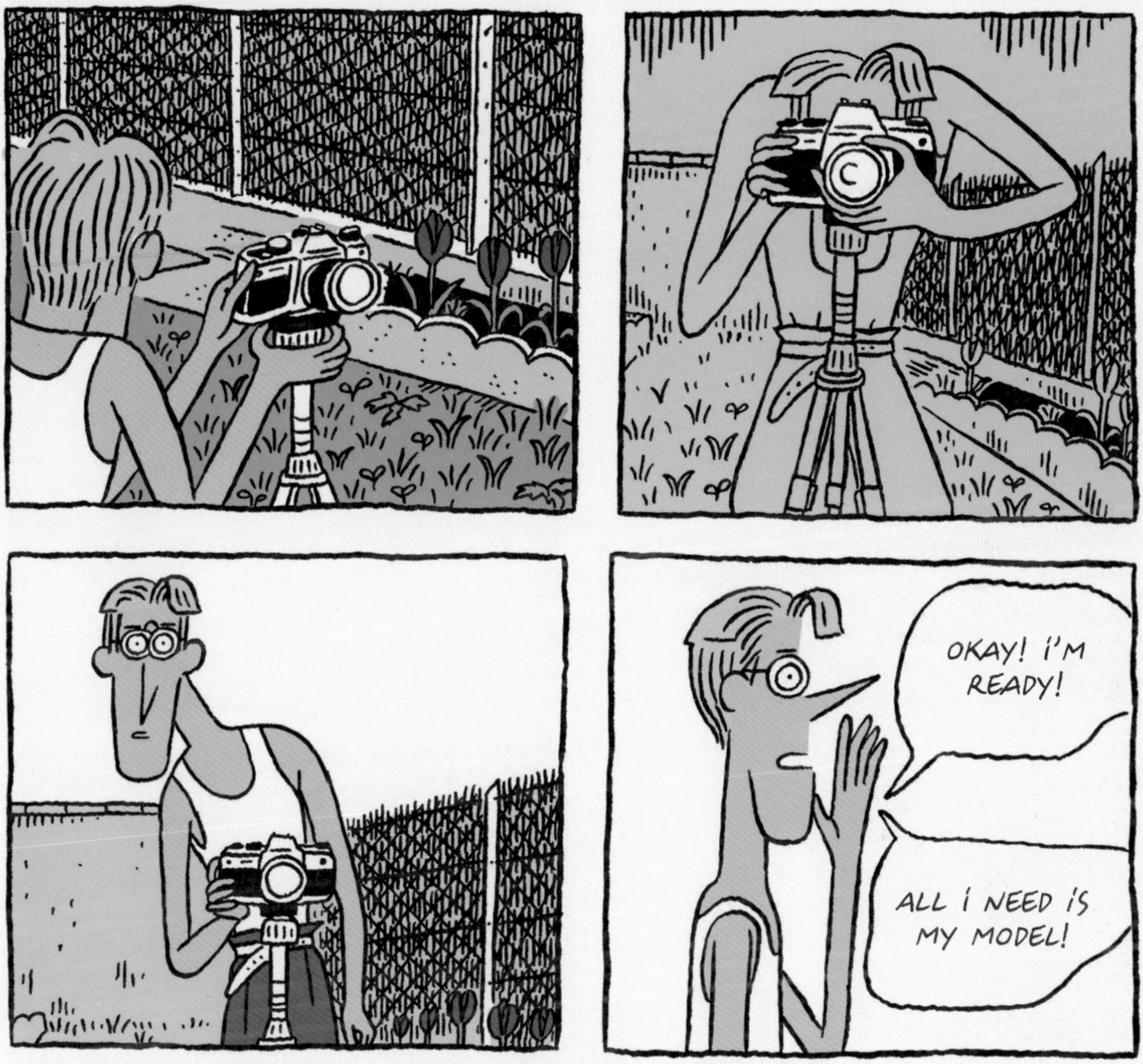
OKAY! I'M READY!
ALL I NEED IS MY MODEL!

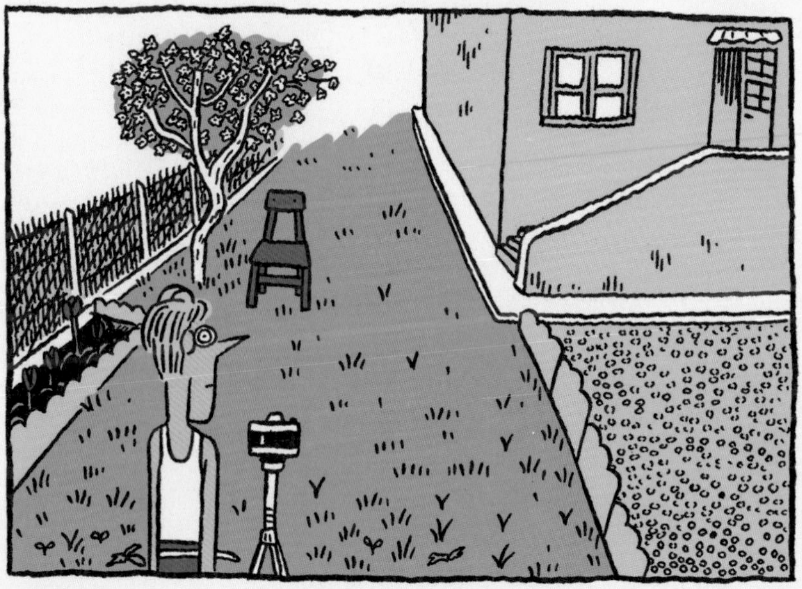

# THE CHERRY SEASON

EL DON GUILLERMO

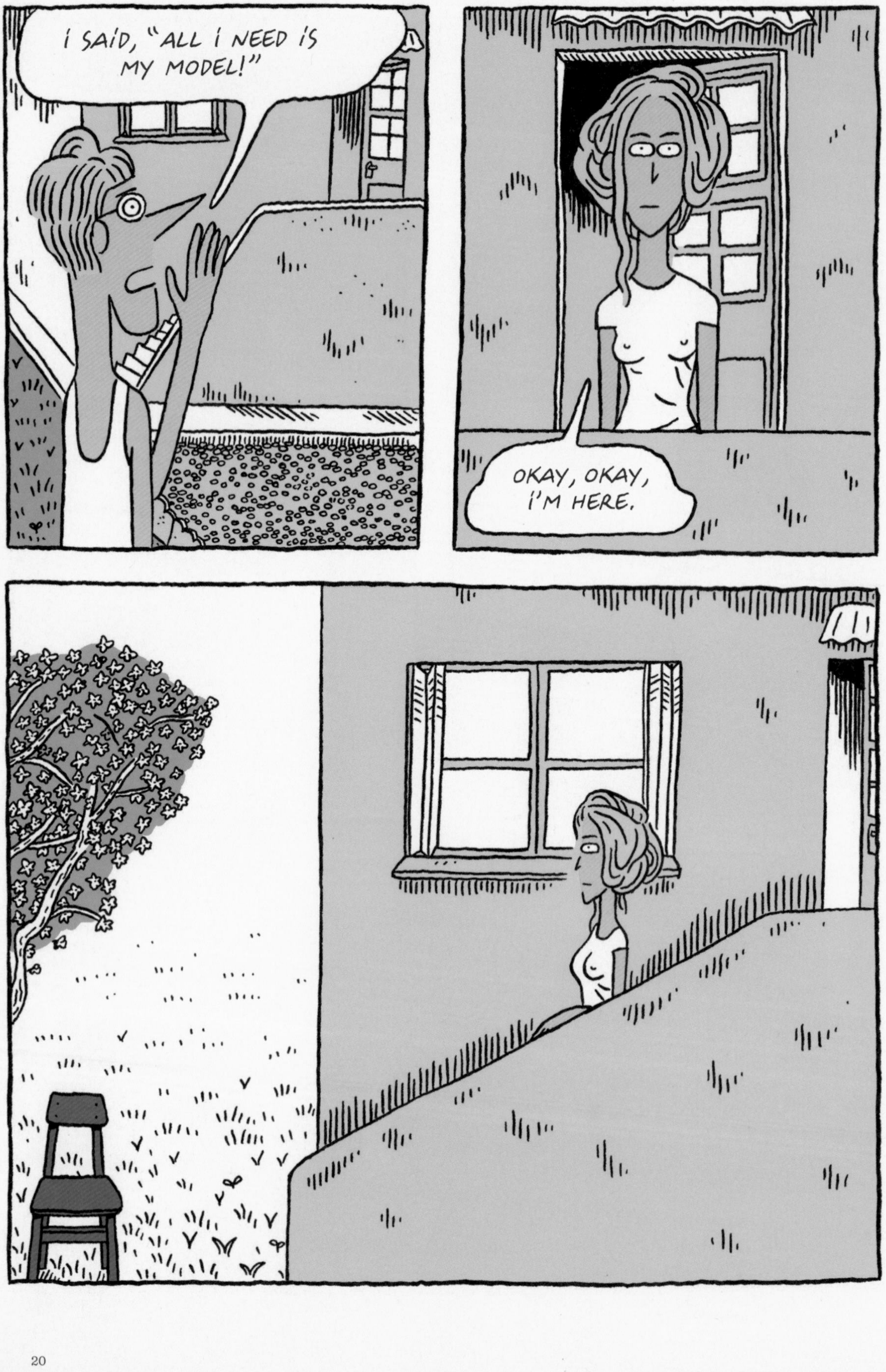
i SAiD, "ALL i NEED iS MY MODEL!"
OKAY, OKAY, i'M HERE.

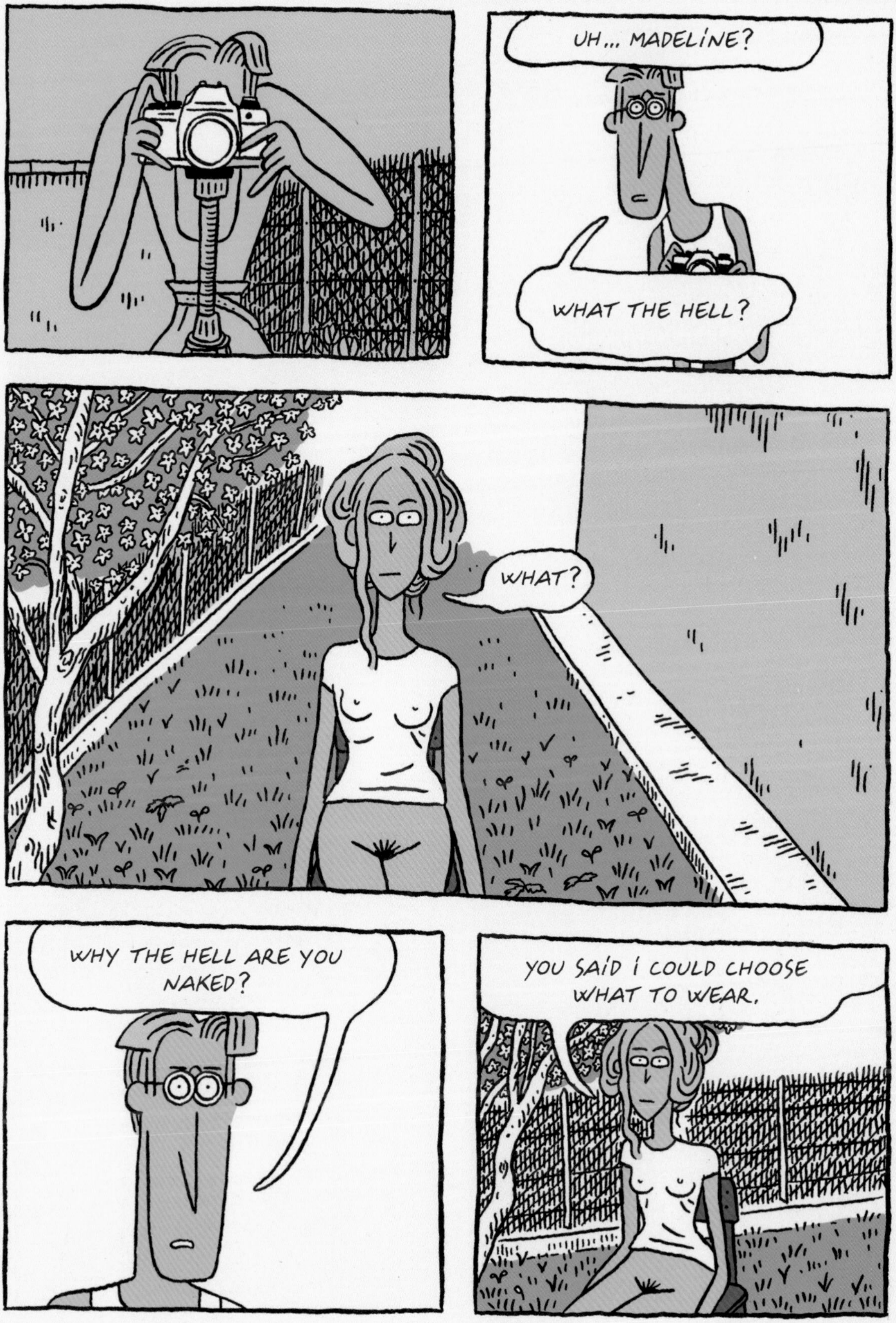
UH... MADELINE?
WHAT THE HELL?
WHAT?
WHY THE HELL ARE YOU NAKED?
YOU SAID I COULD CHOOSE WHAT TO WEAR.

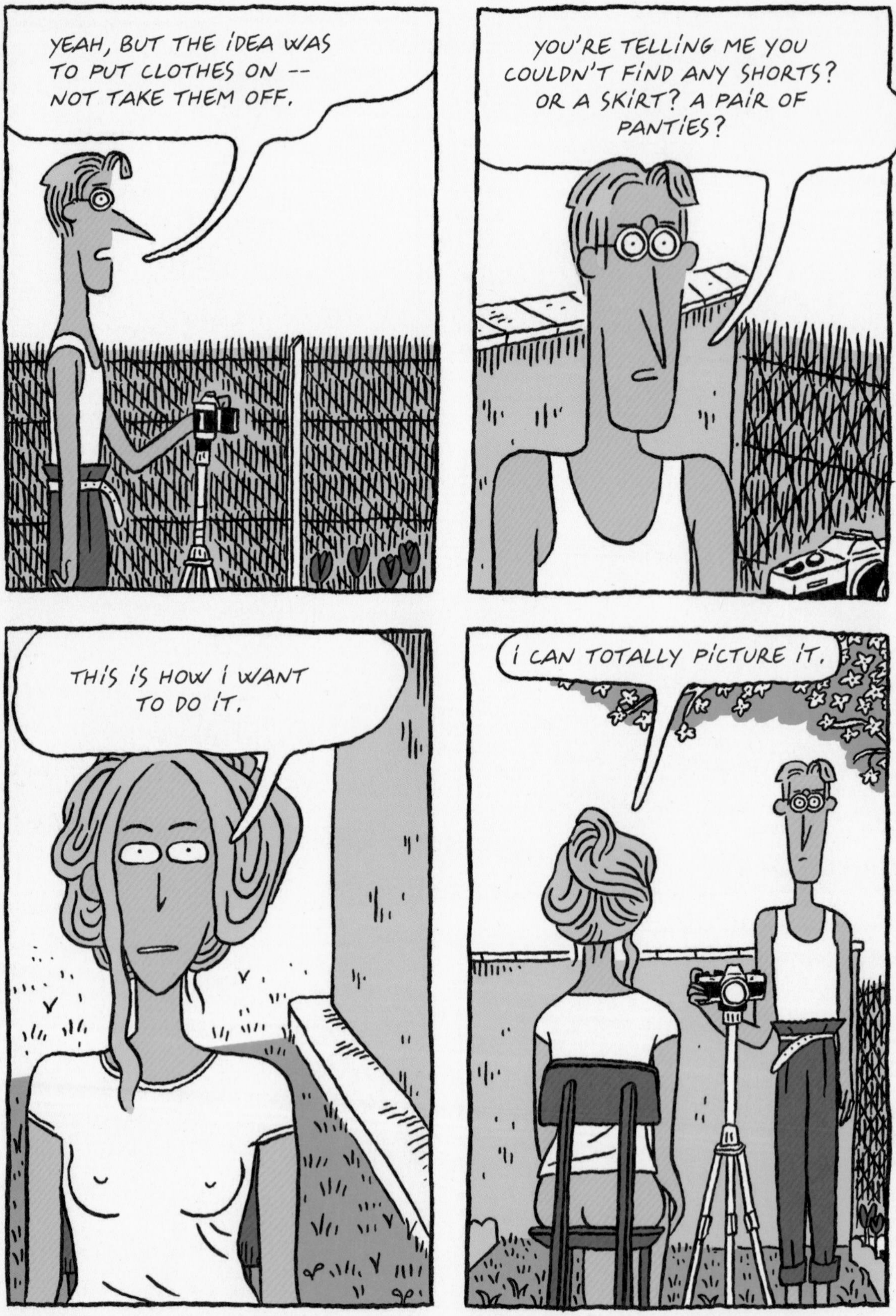
YEAH, BUT THE IDEA WAS TO PUT CLOTHES ON -- NOT TAKE THEM OFF.
YOU'RE TELLING ME YOU COULDN'T FIND ANY SHORTS? OR A SKIRT? A PAIR OF PANTIES?
THIS IS HOW I WANT TO DO IT.
I CAN TOTALLY PICTURE IT.

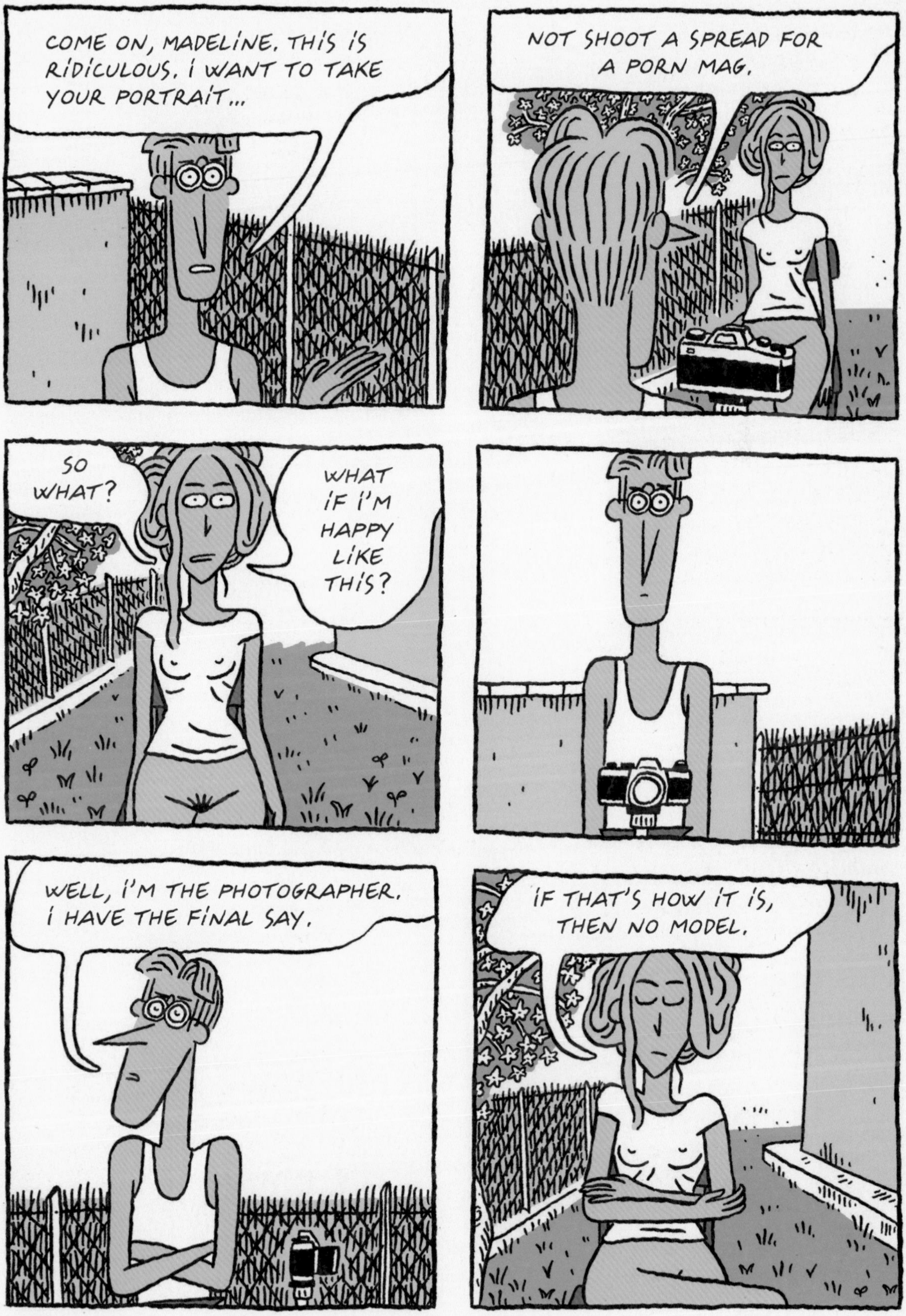
COME ON, MADELINE. THIS IS RIDICULOUS. I WANT TO TAKE YOUR PORTRAIT...
NOT SHOOT A SPREAD FOR A PORN MAG.
SO WHAT?
WHAT IF I'M HAPPY LIKE THIS?
WELL, I'M THE PHOTOGRAPHER. I HAVE THE FINAL SAY.
IF THAT'S HOW IT IS, THEN NO MODEL.

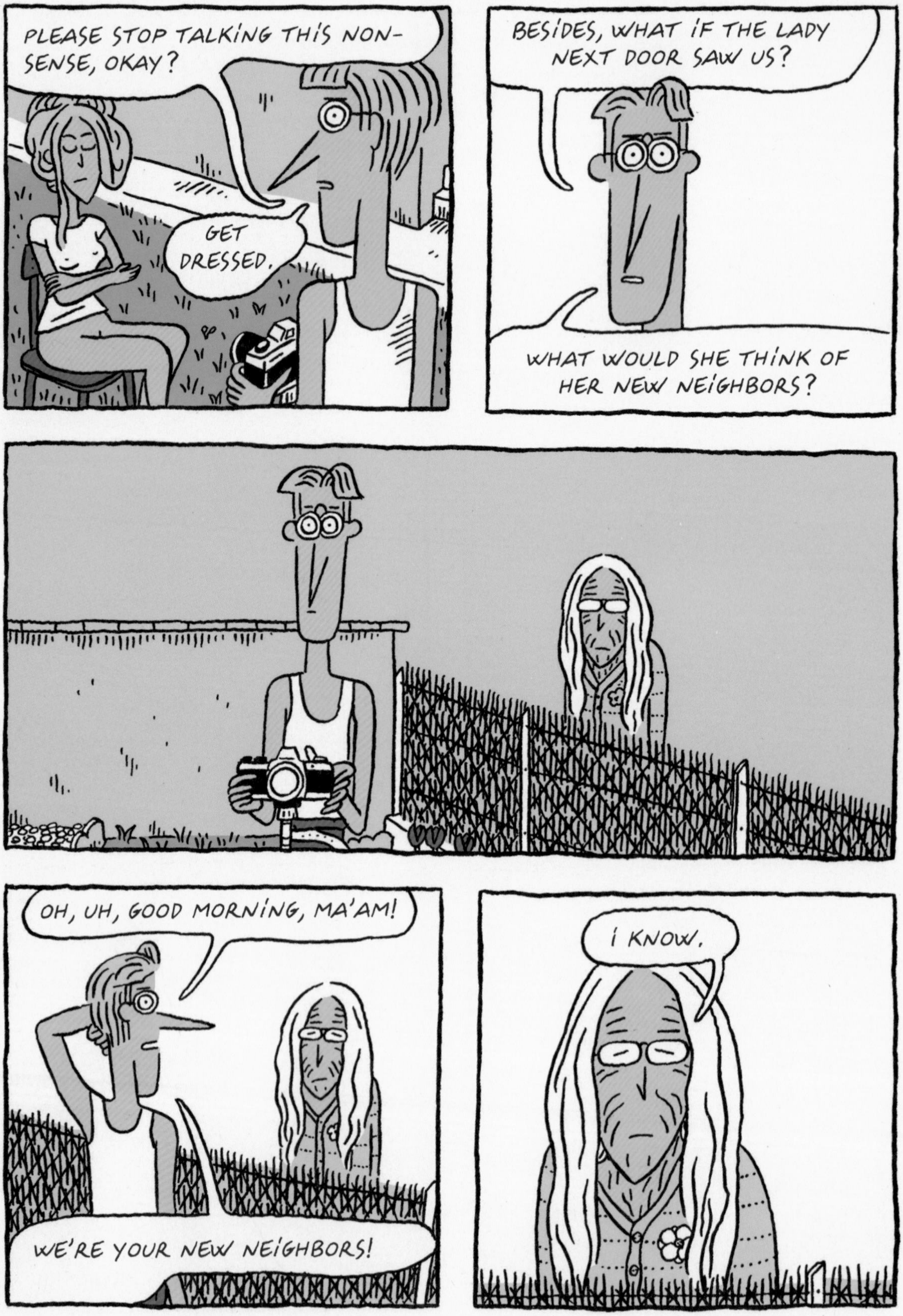
PLEASE STOP TALKING THIS NON-SENSE, OKAY?
GET DRESSED.
BESIDES, WHAT IF THE LADY NEXT DOOR SAW US?
WHAT WOULD SHE THINK OF HER NEW NEIGHBORS?
OH, UH, GOOD MORNING, MA'AM!
WE'RE YOUR NEW NEIGHBORS!
I KNOW.

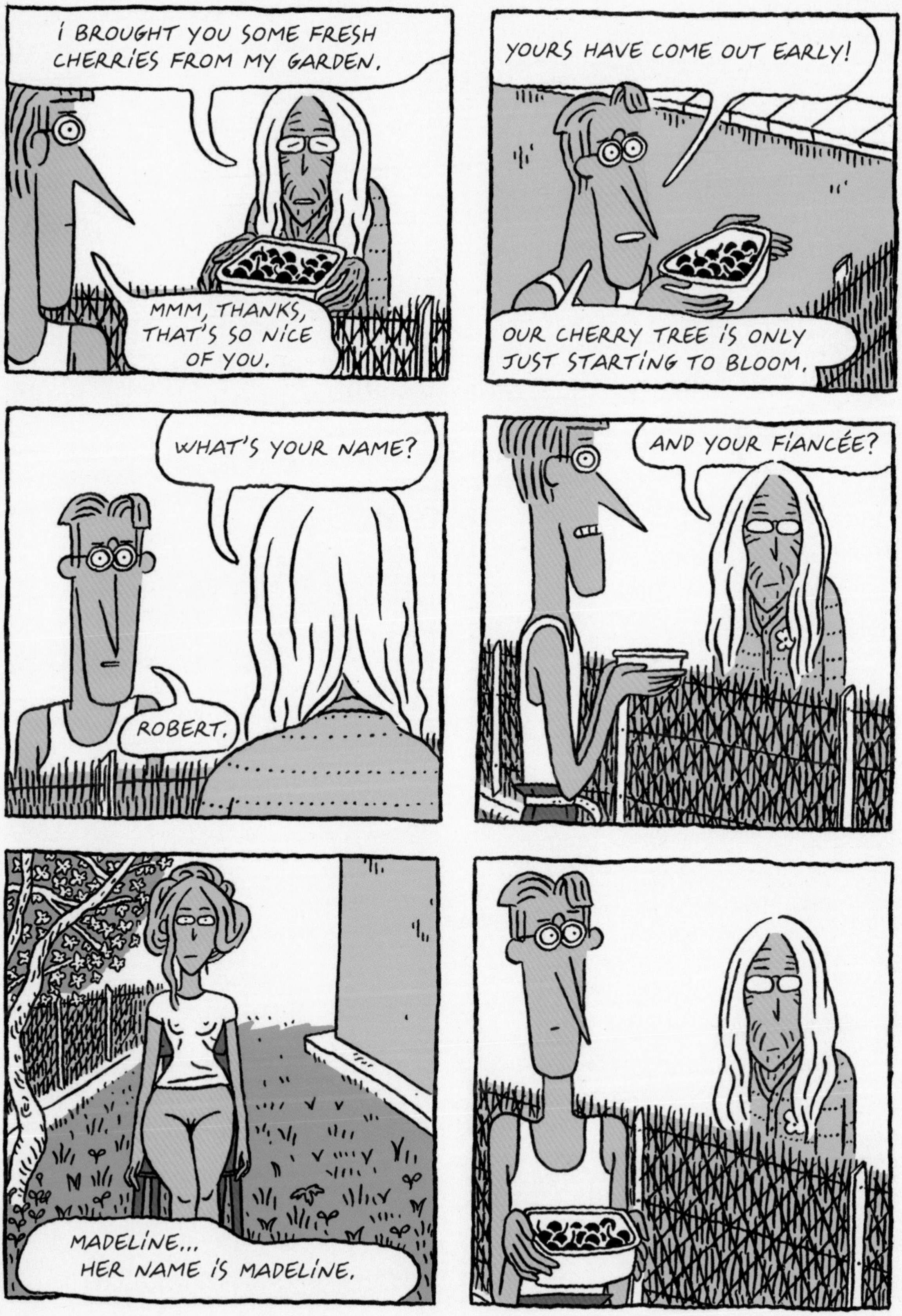
I BROUGHT YOU SOME FRESH CHERRIES FROM MY GARDEN.
MMM, THANKS, THAT'S SO NICE OF YOU.
YOURS HAVE COME OUT EARLY!
OUR CHERRY TREE IS ONLY JUST STARTING TO BLOOM.
WHAT'S YOUR NAME?
ROBERT.
AND YOUR FIANCÉE?
MADELINE...
HER NAME IS MADELINE.

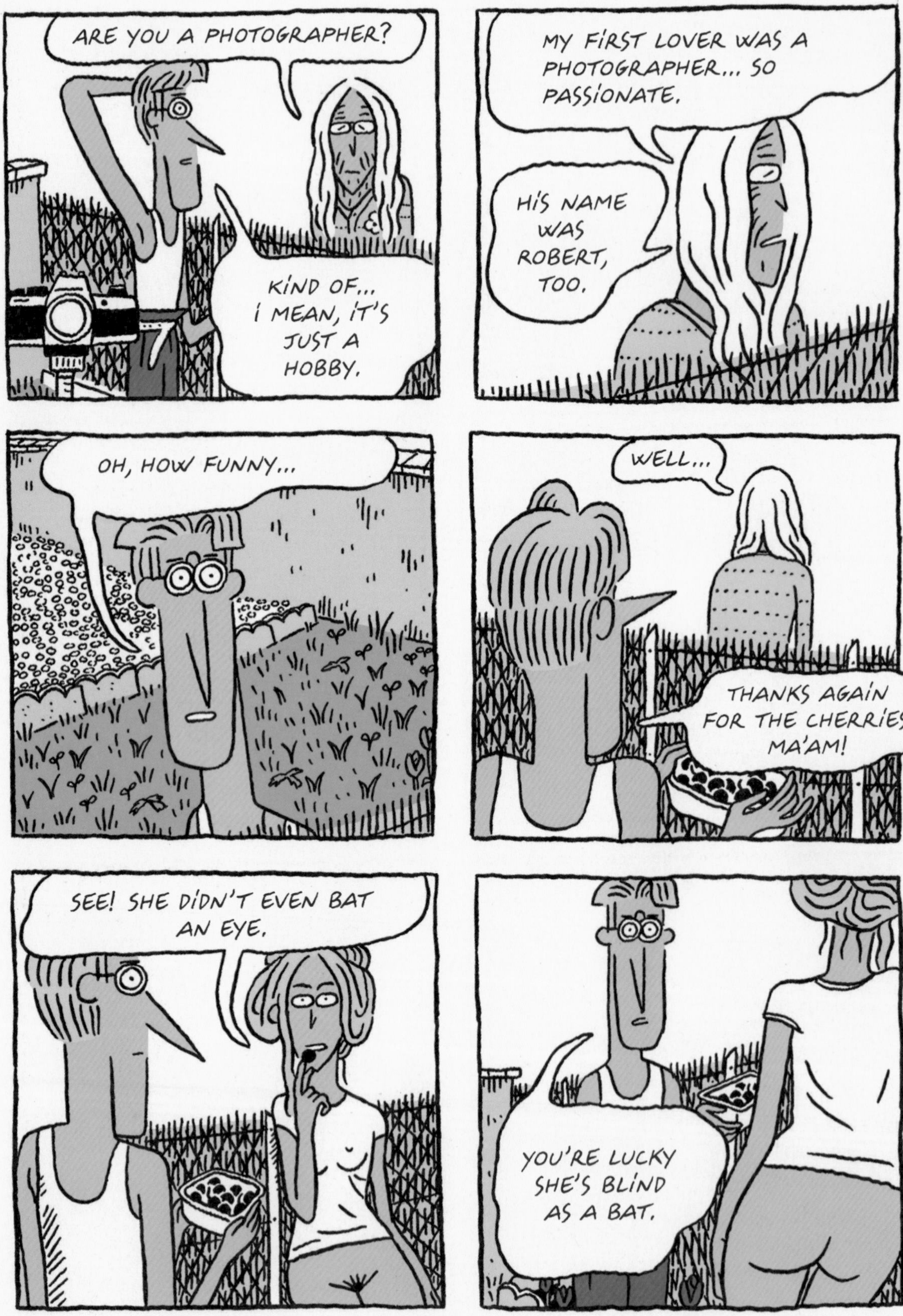
ARE YOU A PHOTOGRAPHER?
KIND OF... I MEAN, IT'S JUST A HOBBY.
MY FIRST LOVER WAS A PHOTOGRAPHER... SO PASSIONATE.
HIS NAME WAS ROBERT, TOO.
OH, HOW FUNNY...
WELL...
THANKS AGAIN FOR THE CHERRIES, MA'AM!
SEE! SHE DIDN'T EVEN BAT AN EYE.
YOU'RE LUCKY SHE'S BLIND AS A BAT.

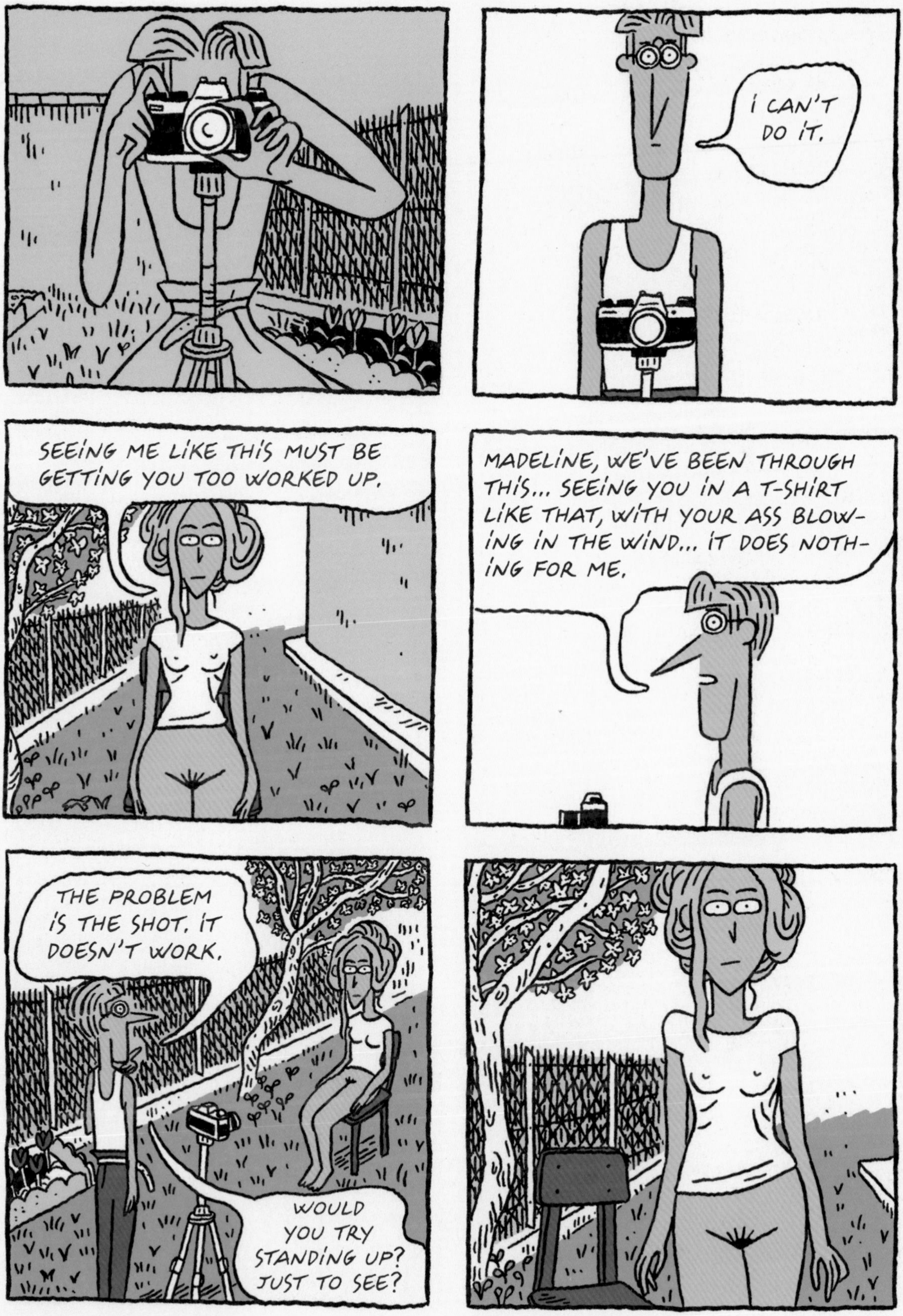
I CAN'T DO IT.
SEEING ME LIKE THIS MUST BE GETTING YOU TOO WORKED UP.
MADELINE, WE'VE BEEN THROUGH THIS... SEEING YOU IN A T-SHIRT LIKE THAT, WITH YOUR ASS BLOWING IN THE WIND... IT DOES NOTHING FOR ME.
THE PROBLEM IS THE SHOT. IT DOESN'T WORK.
WOULD YOU TRY STANDING UP? JUST TO SEE?
...

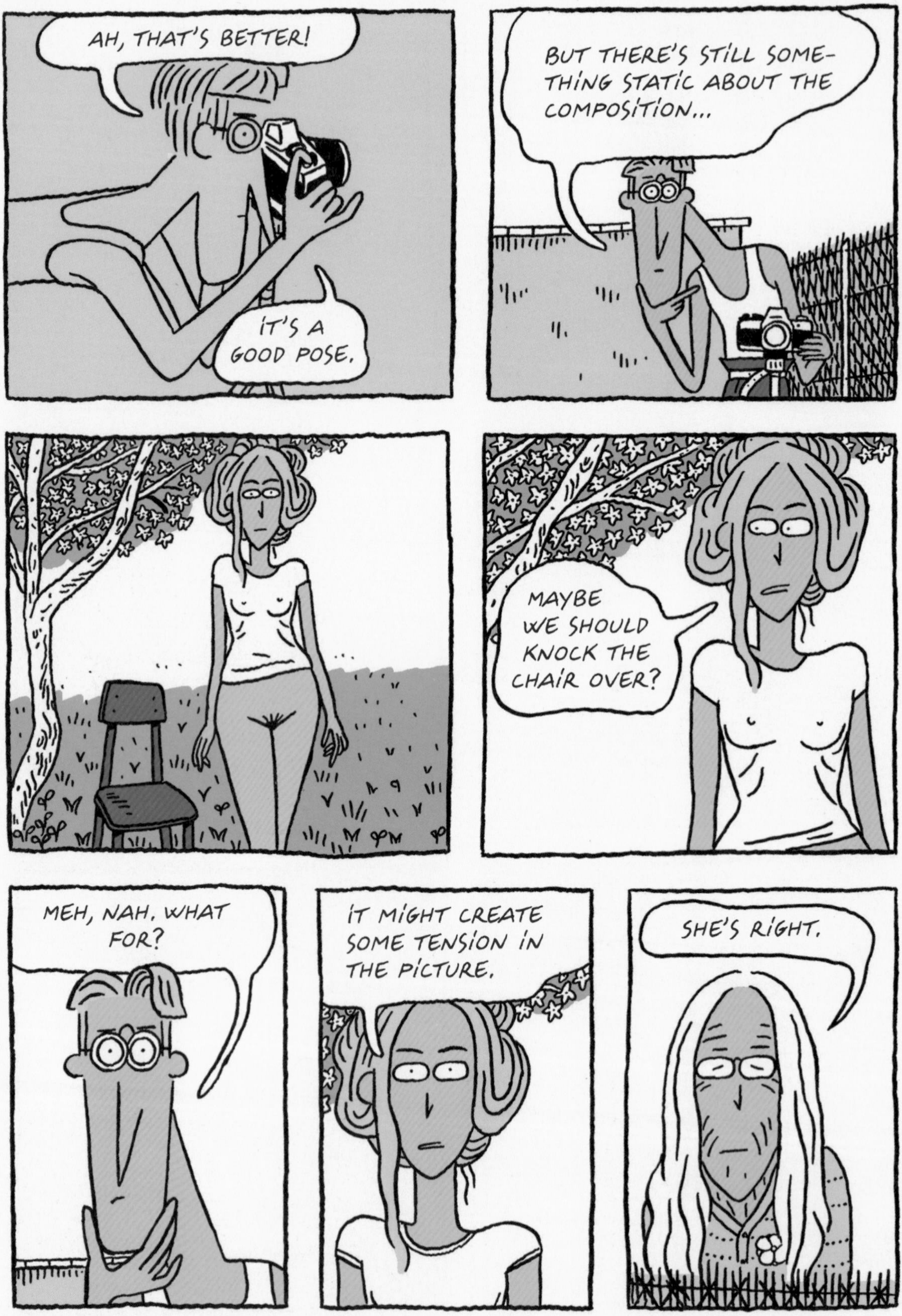
AH, THAT'S BETTER!
IT'S A GOOD POSE.
BUT THERE'S STILL SOME-THING STATIC ABOUT THE COMPOSITION...
MAYBE WE SHOULD KNOCK THE CHAIR OVER?
MEH, NAH. WHAT FOR?
IT MIGHT CREATE SOME TENSION IN THE PICTURE.
SHE'S RIGHT.

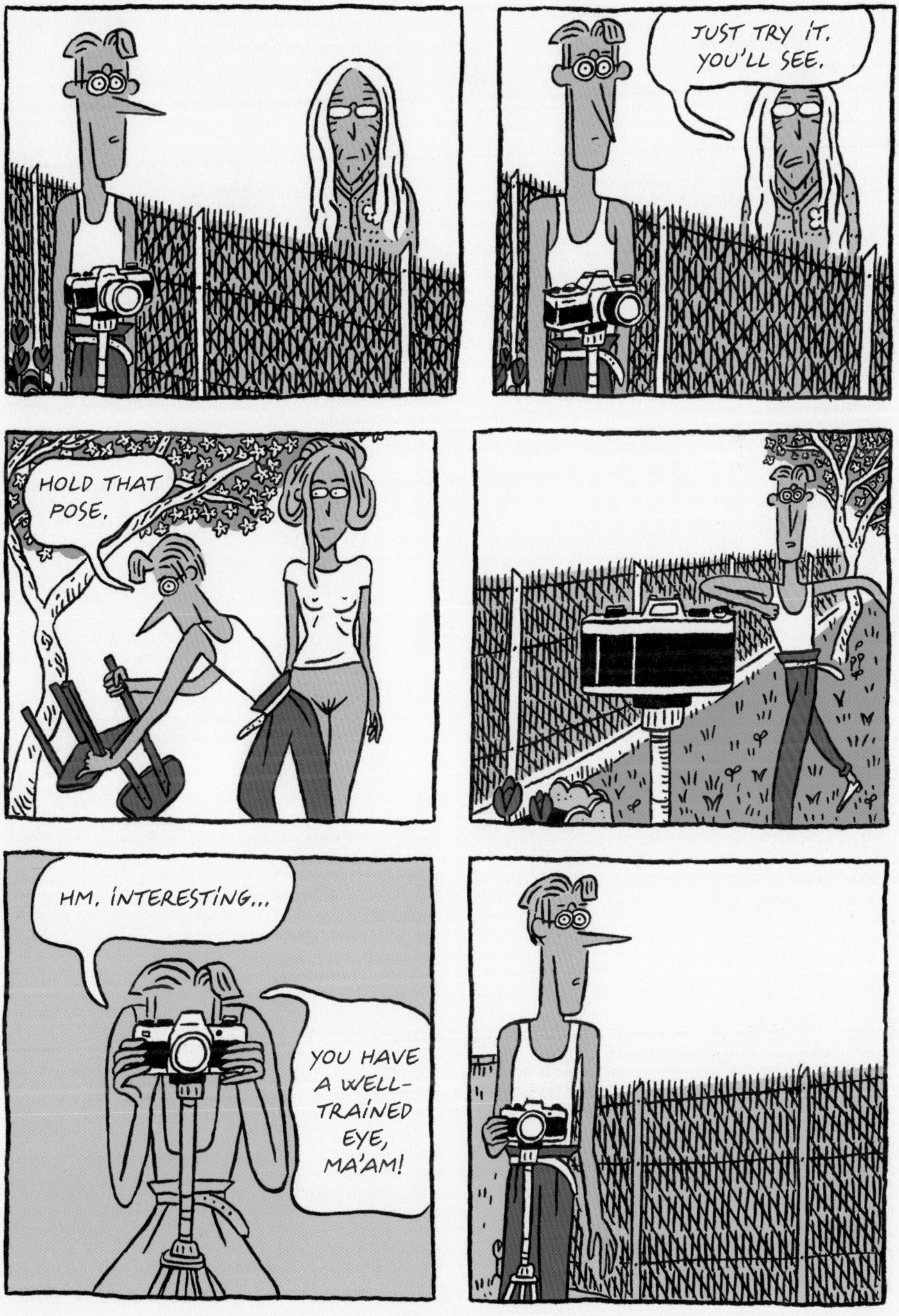

JUST TRY IT. YOU'LL SEE.
HOLD THAT POSE.
HM. INTERESTING...
YOU HAVE A WELL-TRAINED EYE, MA'AM!

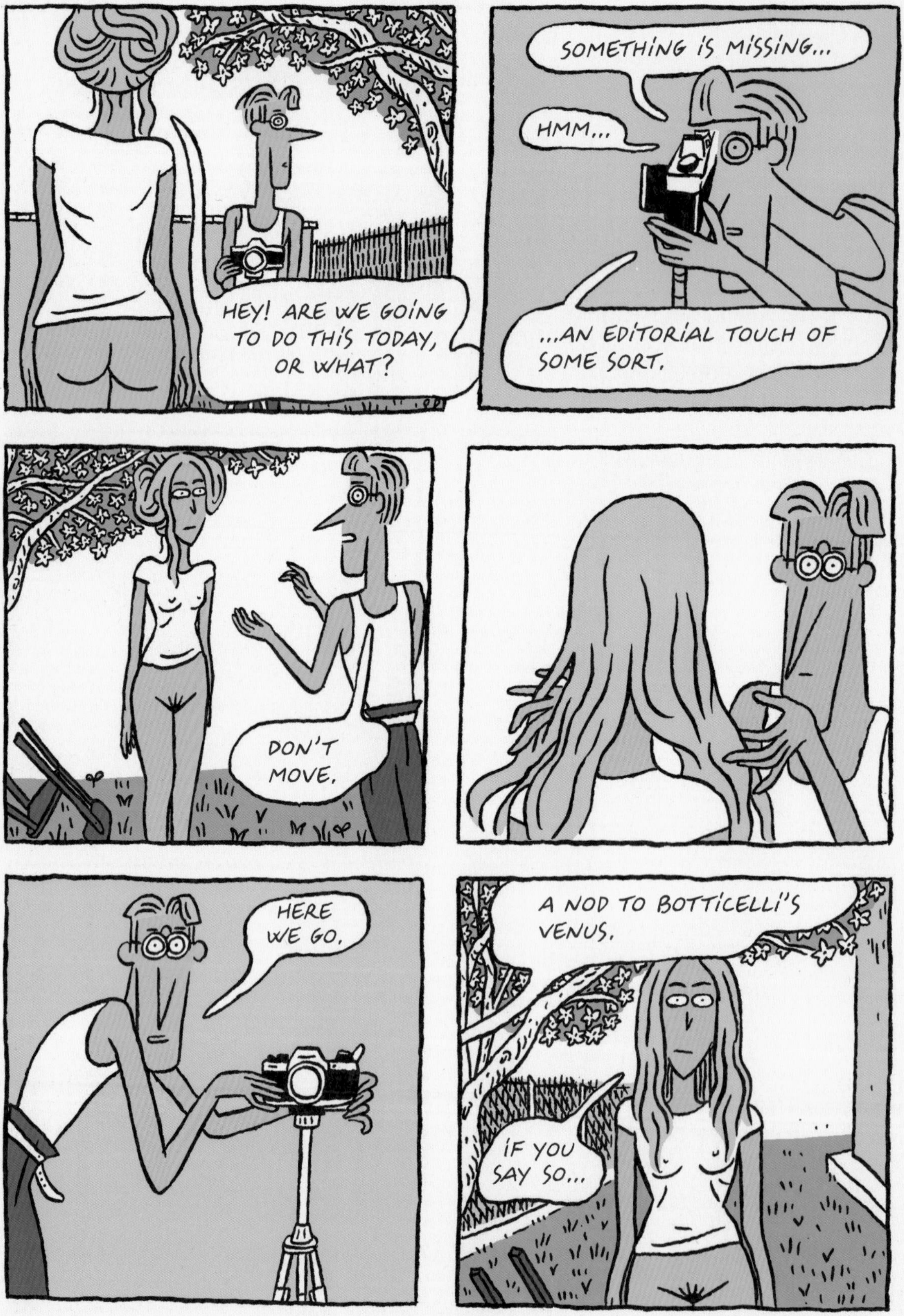
HEY! ARE WE GOING TO DO THIS TODAY, OR WHAT?
SOMETHING IS MISSING...
HMM...
...AN EDITORIAL TOUCH OF SOME SORT.
DON'T MOVE.
HERE WE GO.
A NOD TO BOTTICELLI'S VENUS.
IF YOU SAY SO...

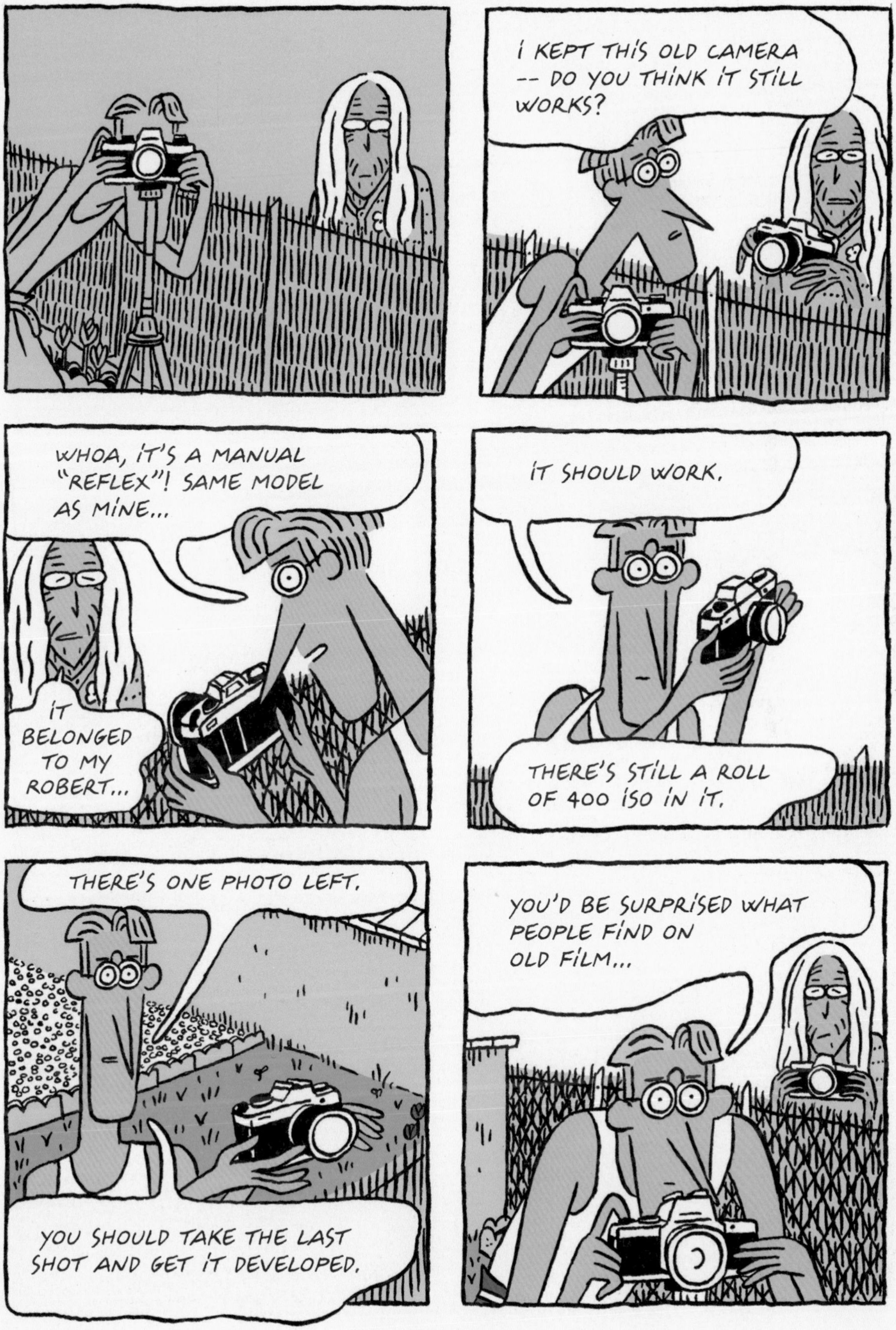
I KEPT THIS OLD CAMERA -- DO YOU THINK IT STILL WORKS?
WHOA, IT'S A MANUAL "REFLEX"! SAME MODEL AS MINE...
IT BELONGED TO MY ROBERT...
IT SHOULD WORK.
THERE'S STILL A ROLL OF 400 ISO IN IT.
THERE'S ONE PHOTO LEFT.
YOU SHOULD TAKE THE LAST SHOT AND GET IT DEVELOPED.
YOU'D BE SURPRISED WHAT PEOPLE FIND ON OLD FILM...

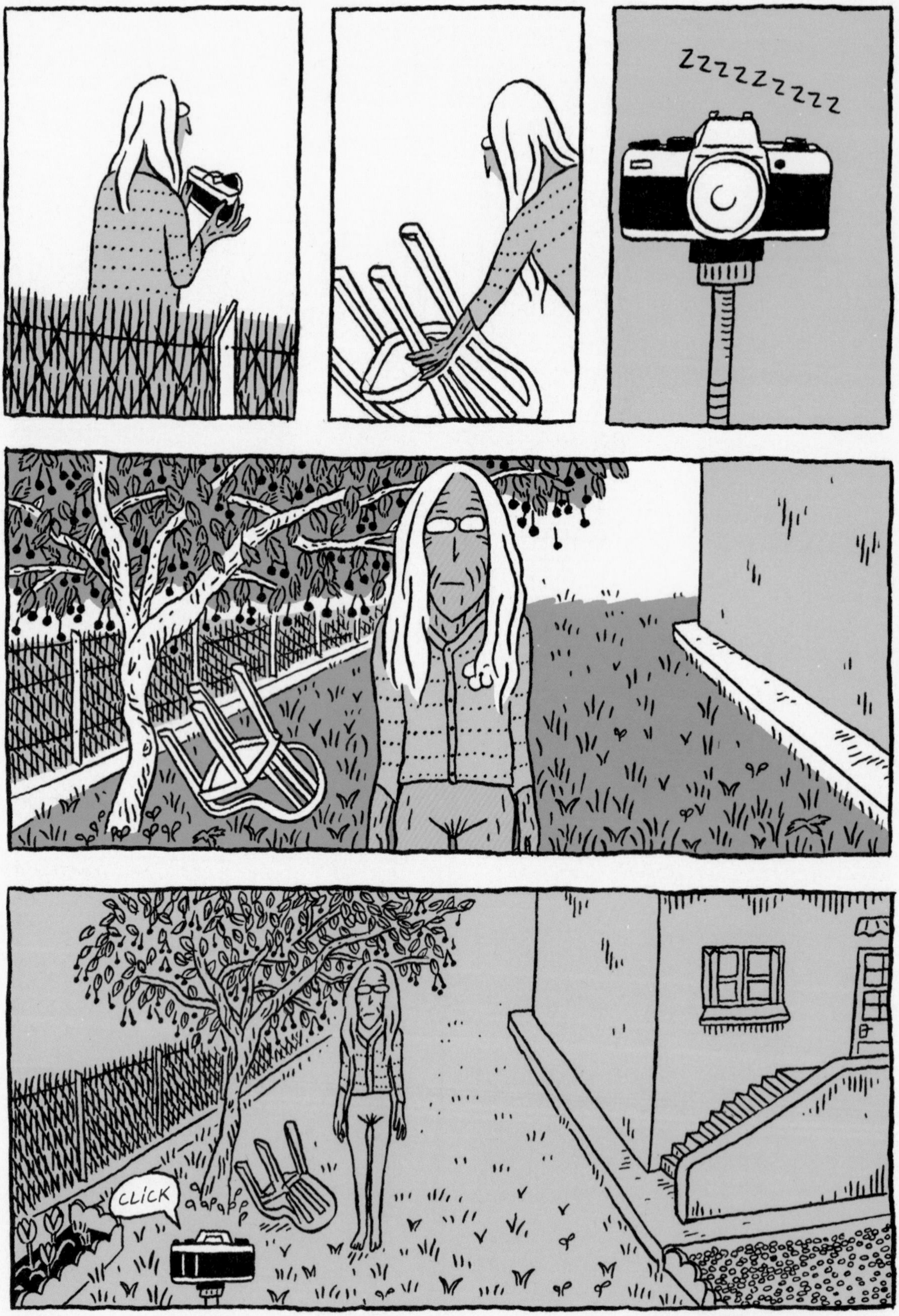
ZZZZZZZZZZ
CLICK

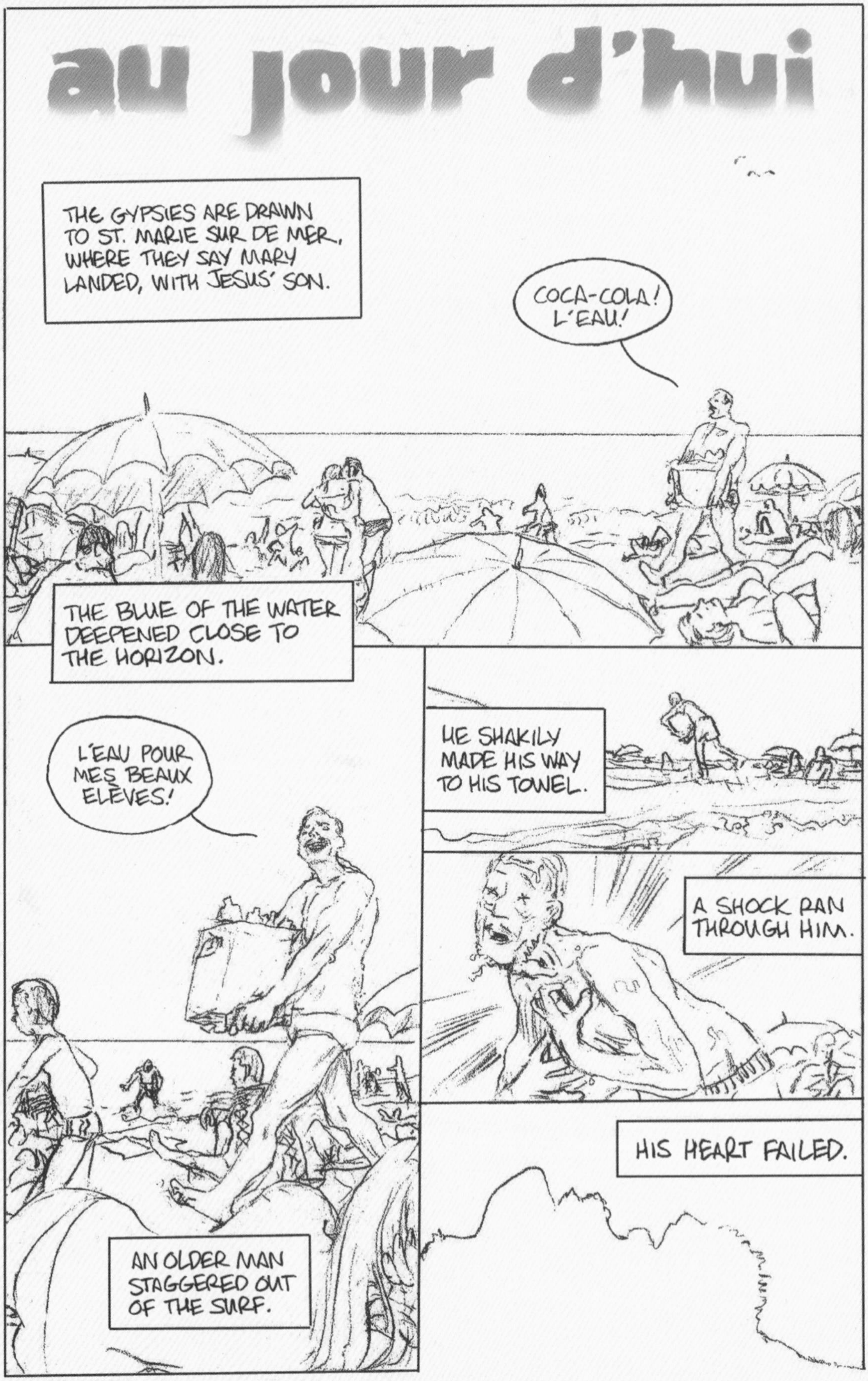
au jour d'hui
THE GYPSIES ARE DRAWN TO ST. MARIE SUR DE MER, WHERE THEY SAY MARY LANDED, WITH JESUS' SON.
COCA-COLA! L'EAU!
THE BLUE OF THE WATER DEEPENED CLOSE TO THE HORIZON.
L'EAU POUR MES BEAUX ELÈVES!
AN OLDER MAN STAGGERED OUT OF THE SURF.
HE SHAKILY MADE HIS WAY TO HIS TOWEL.
A SHOCK RAN THROUGH HIM.
HIS HEART FAILED.

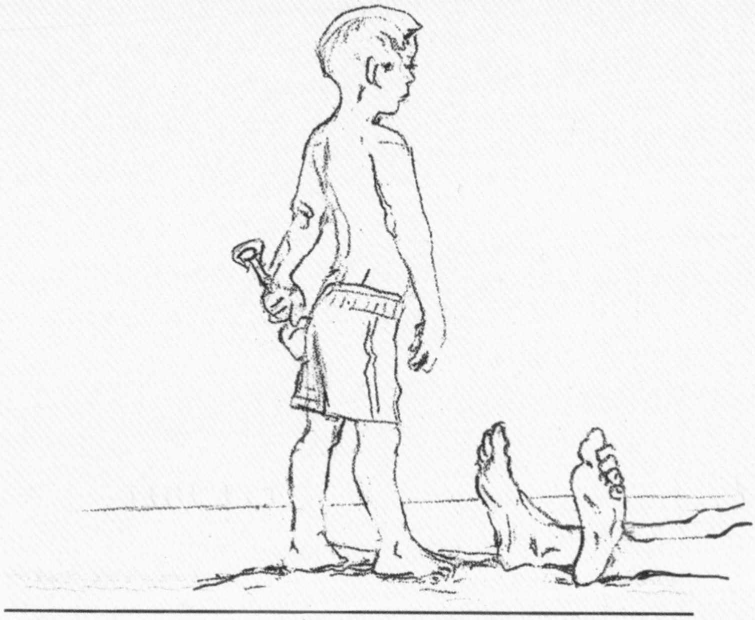

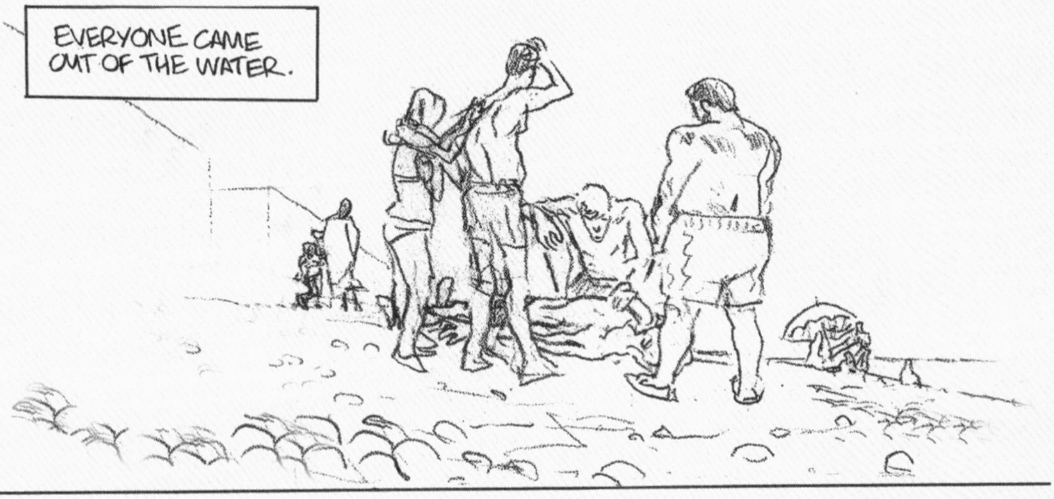
EVERYONE CAME OUT OF THE WATER.

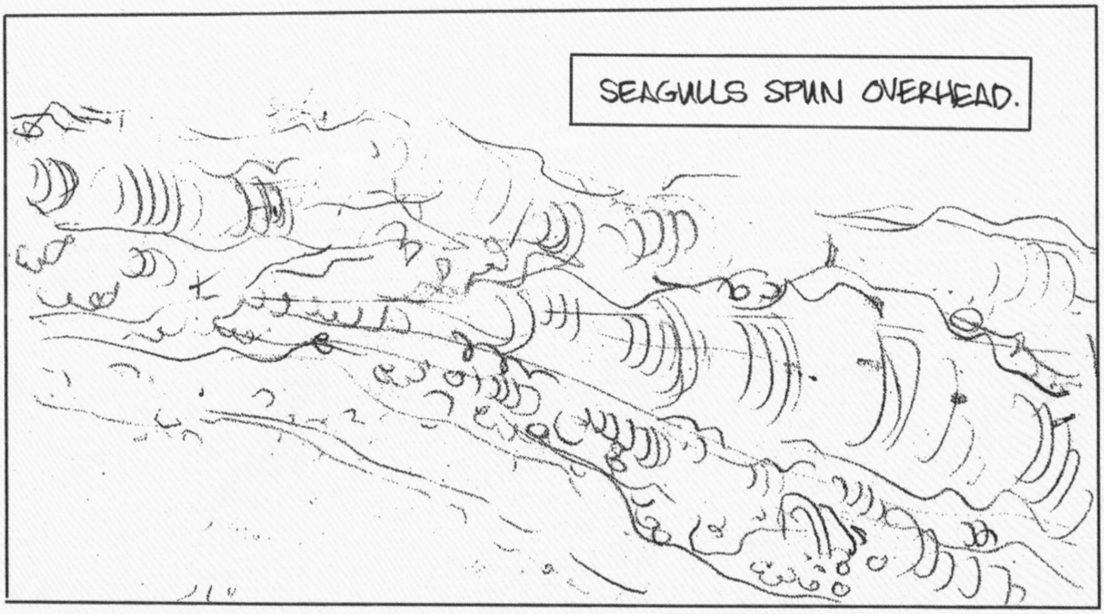
SEAGULLS SPUN OVERHEAD.

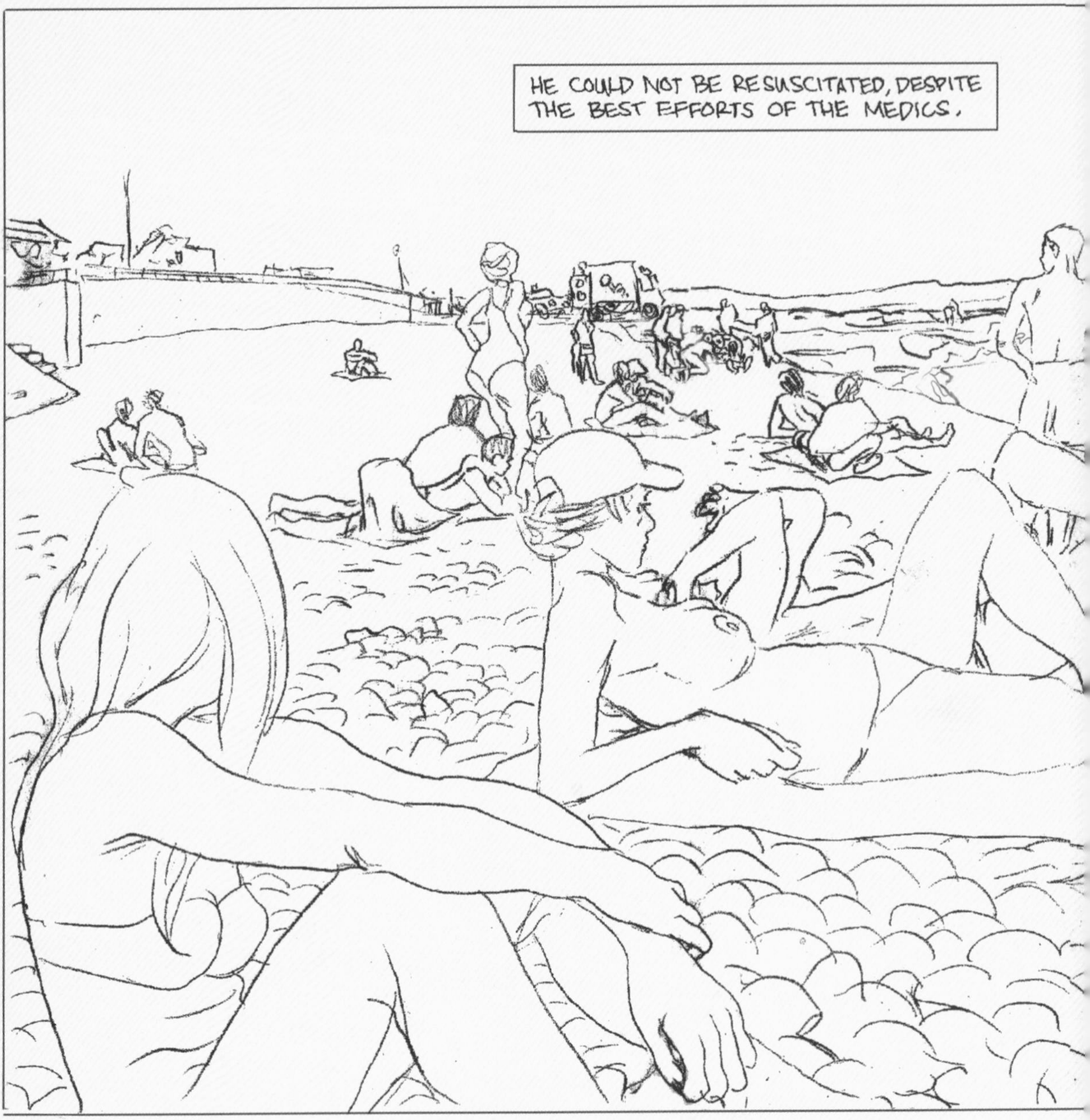
HE COULD NOT BE RESUSCITATED, DESPITE THE BEST EFFORTS OF THE MEDICS.

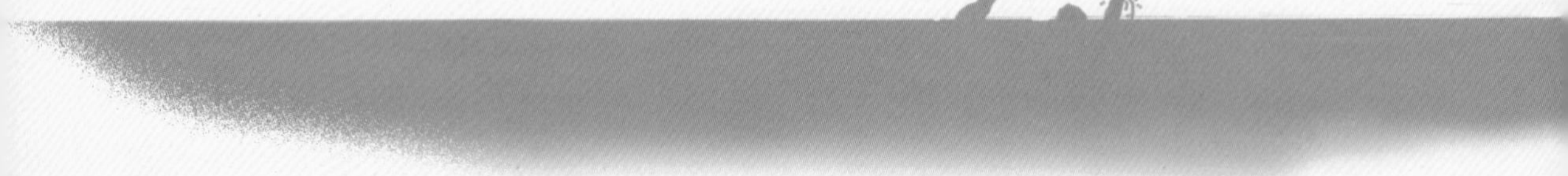

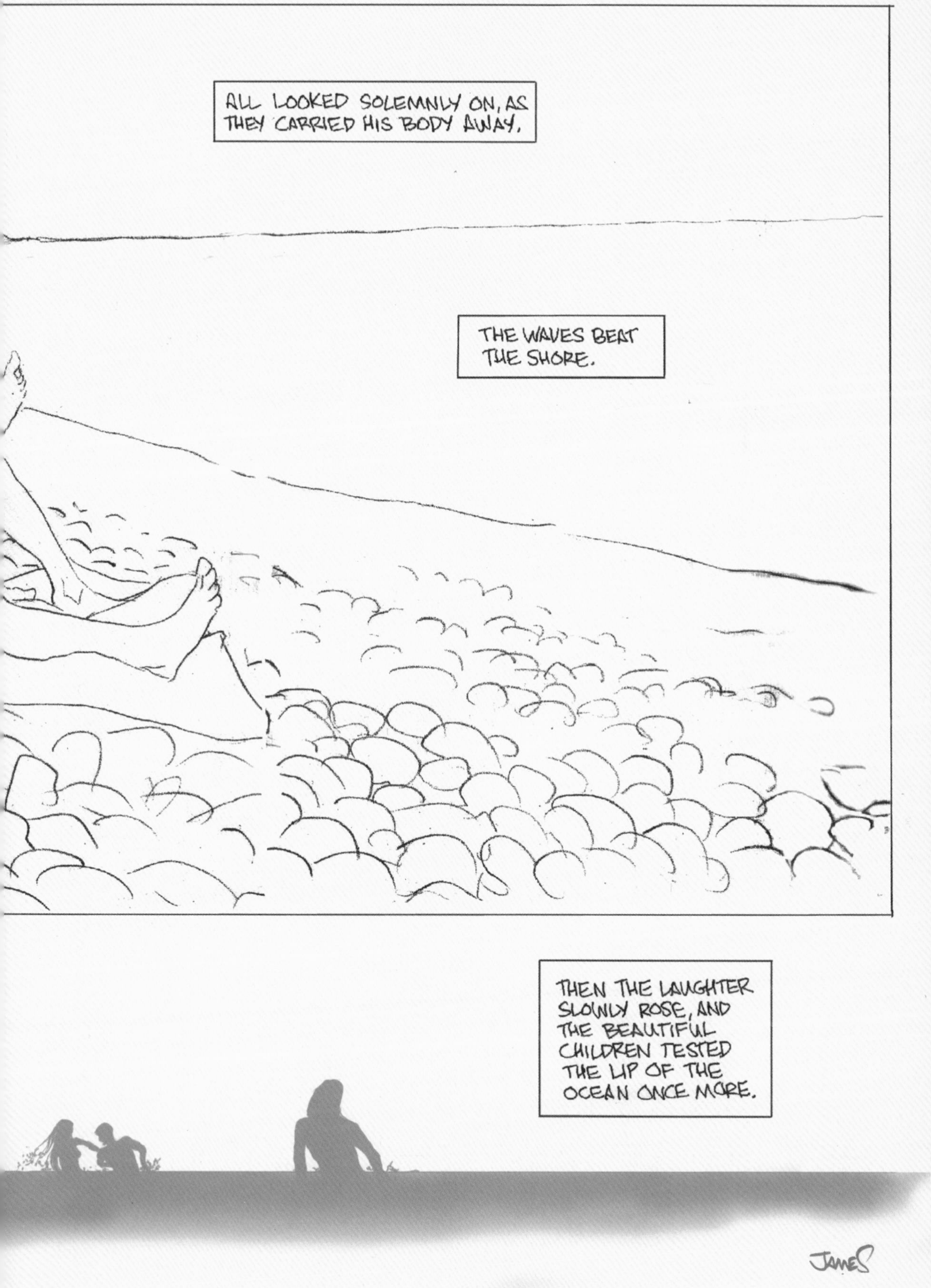
ALL LOOKED SOLEMNLY ON, AS THEY CARRIED HIS BODY AWAY.
THE WAVES BEAT THE SHORE.
THEN THE LAUGHTER SLOWLY ROSE, AND THE BEAUTIFUL CHILDREN TESTED THE LIP OF THE OCEAN ONCE MORE.
JAMES

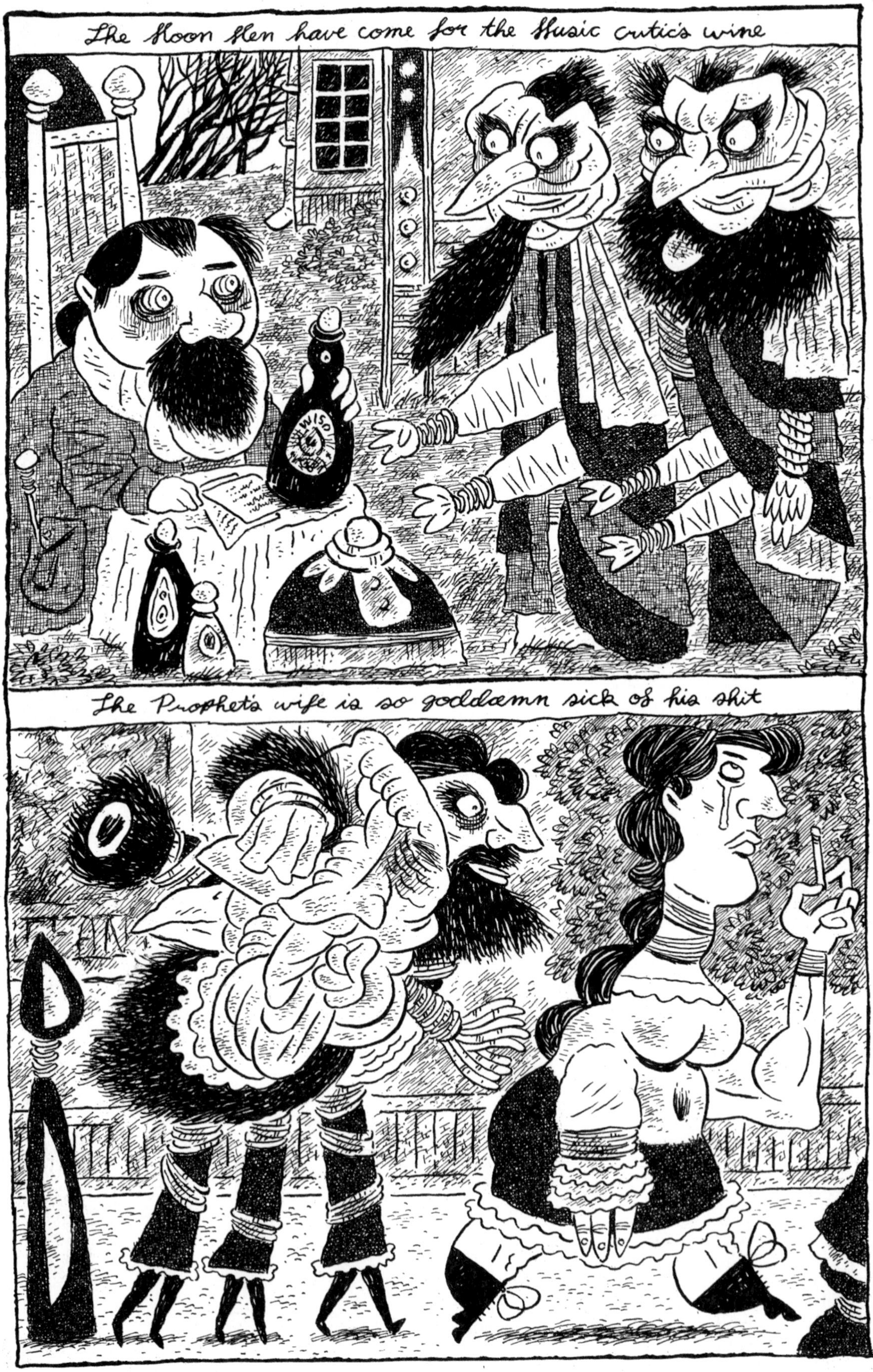
The Moon Men have come for the Music Critic's wine
The Prophet's wife is so goddamn sick of his shit

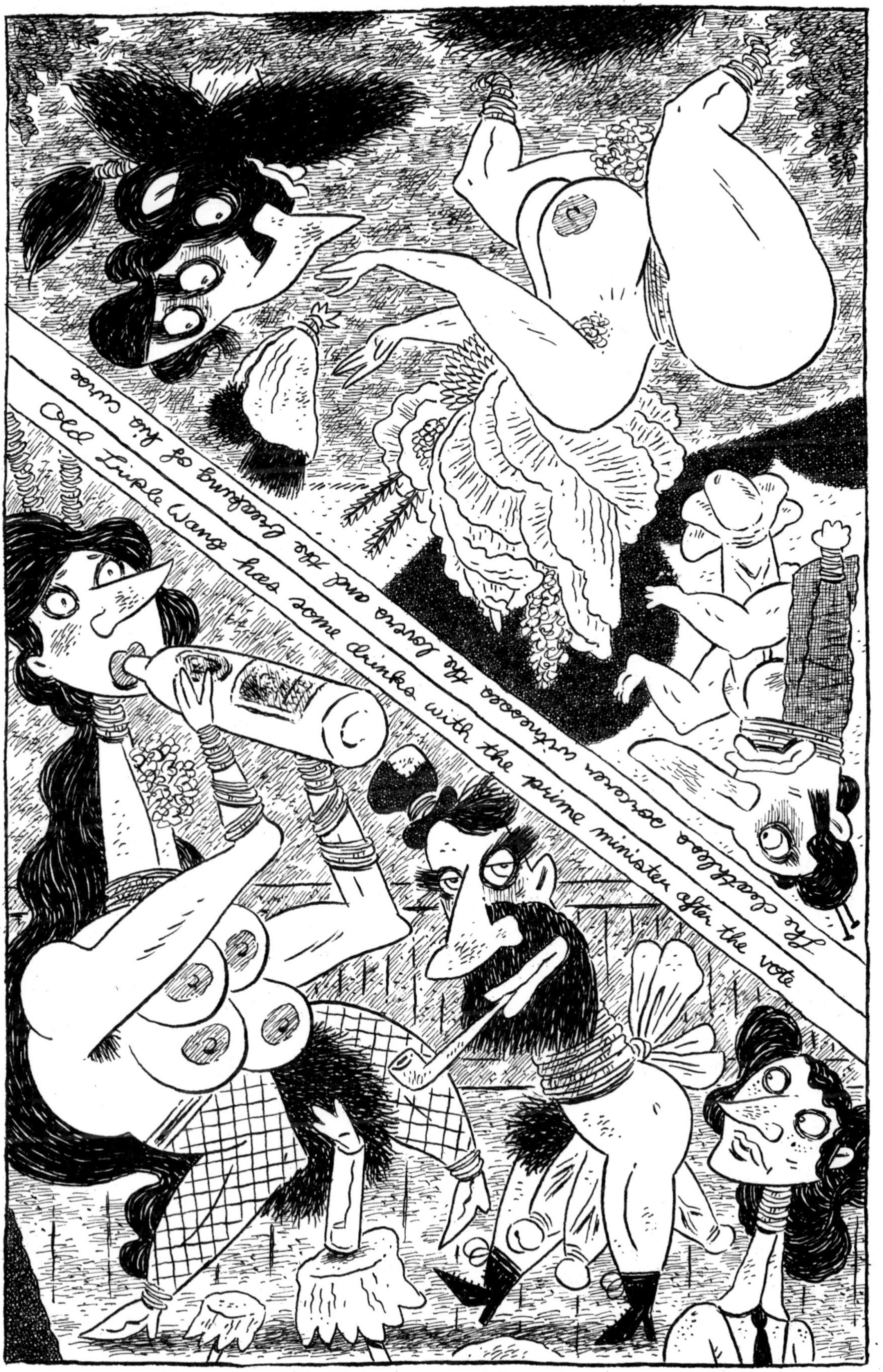
Old Triple Wang has some drinks with the prime minister after the vote
The deathless sorcerer witnesses the lovers and the breaking of his curse

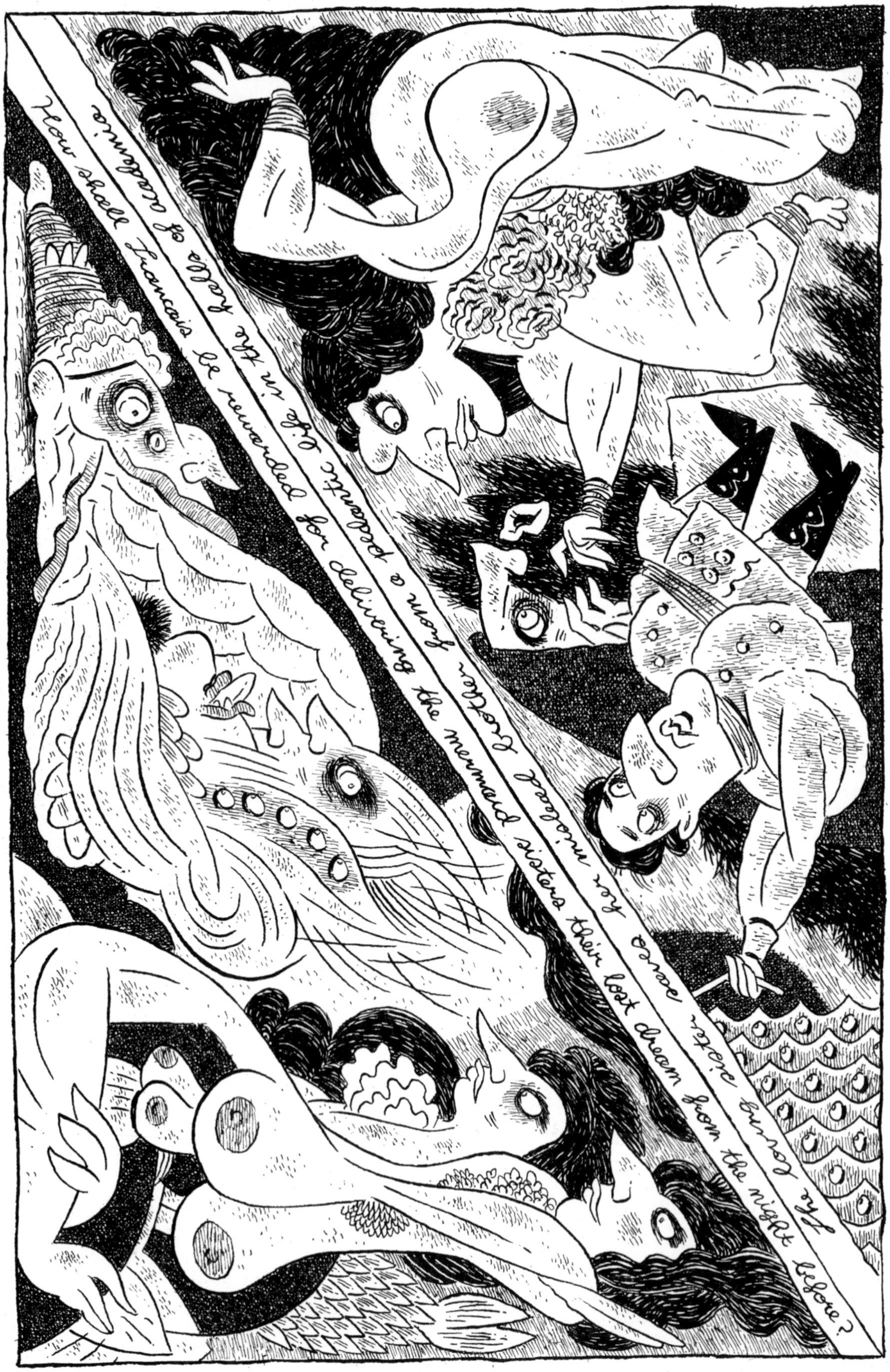
How shall Francois be rewarded for delivering the mermaid sisters their lost dream from the night before?
The loving sister saves her mislead brother from a pedantic life in the halls of academia

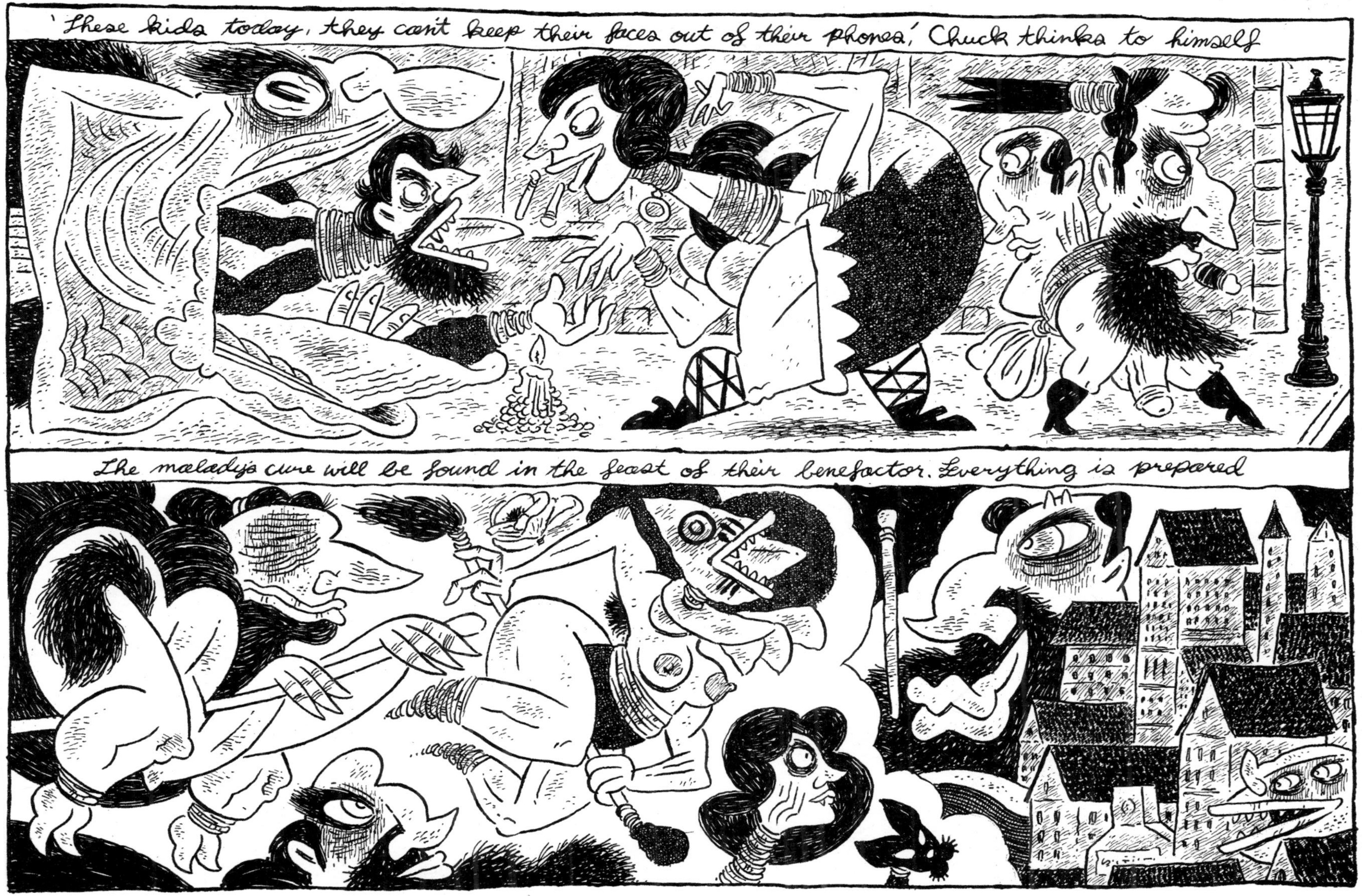
'These kids today, they can't keep their faces out of their phones,' Chuck thinks to himself
The mælady's cure will be found in the feast of their benefactor. Everything is prepared

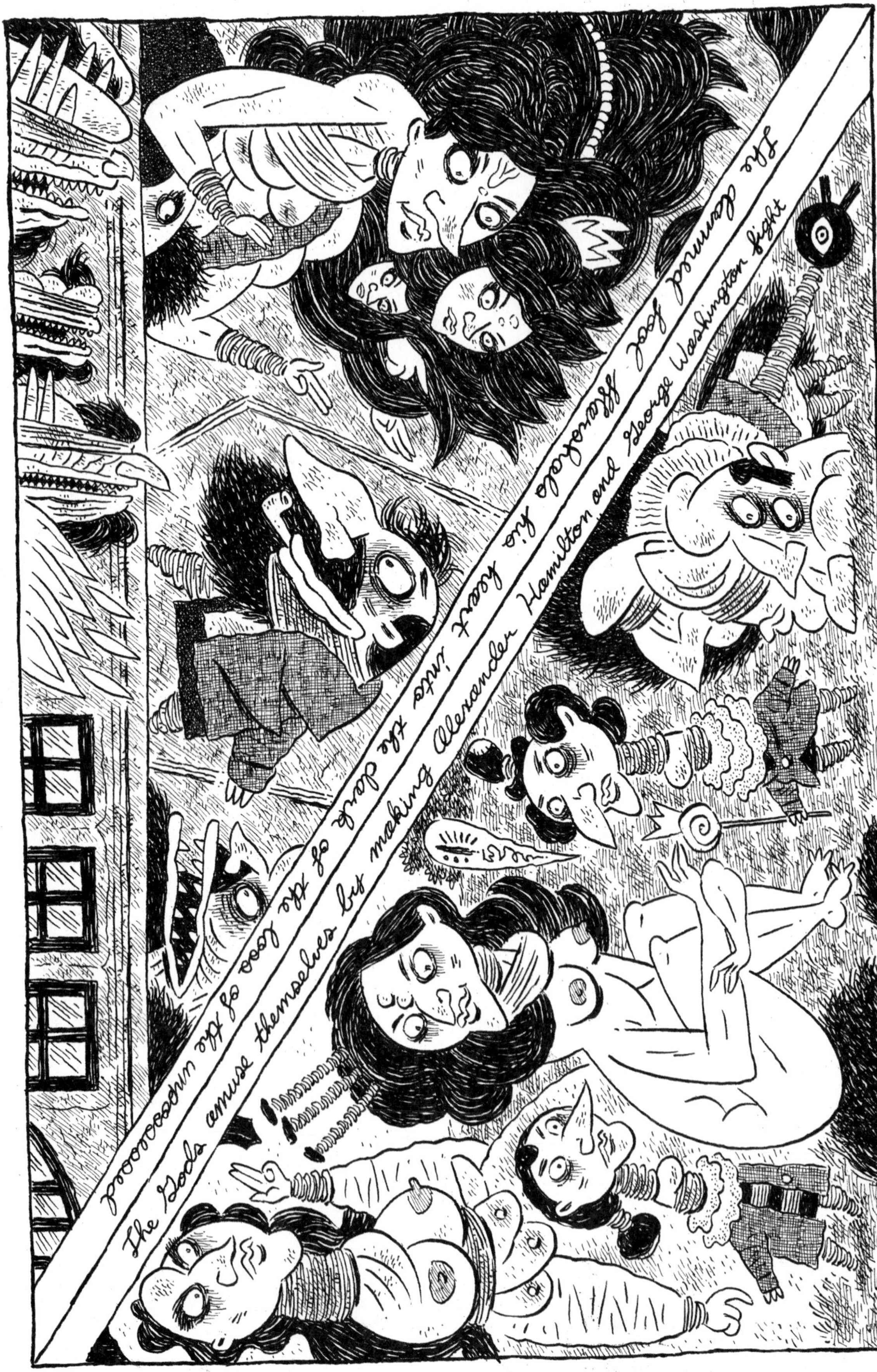
The Gods amuse themselves by making Alexander Hamilton and George Washington fight
The damned fool marshals his heart into the dark of the loss of the unpossessed

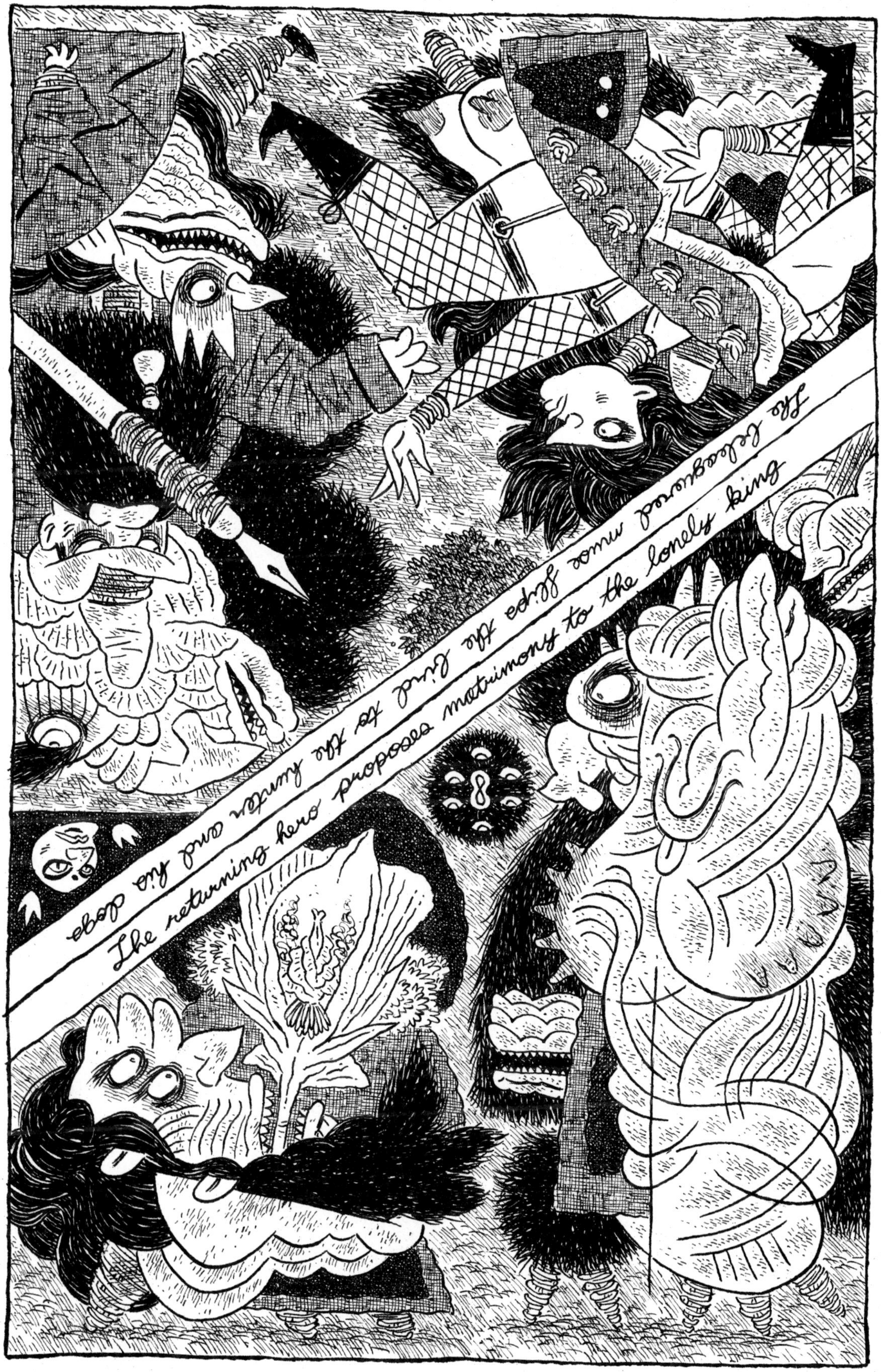
The beleaguered mum flips the bird to the hunter and his dogs
The returning hero proposes matrimony to the lonely king

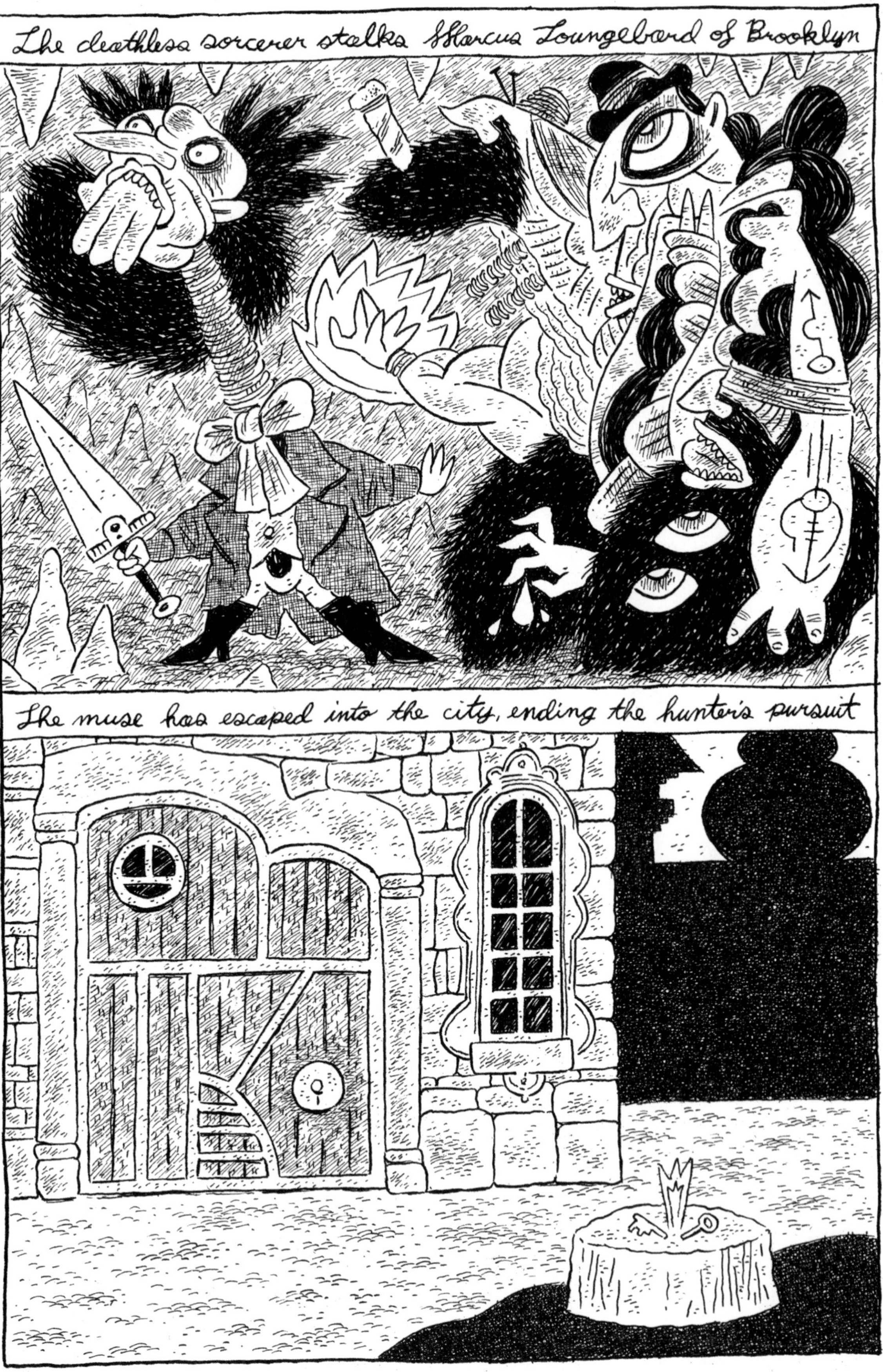
The deathless sorcerer stalks Marcus Loungebard of Brooklyn
The muse has escaped into the city, ending the hunter's pursuit

between
december
and march

kurt
ankeny

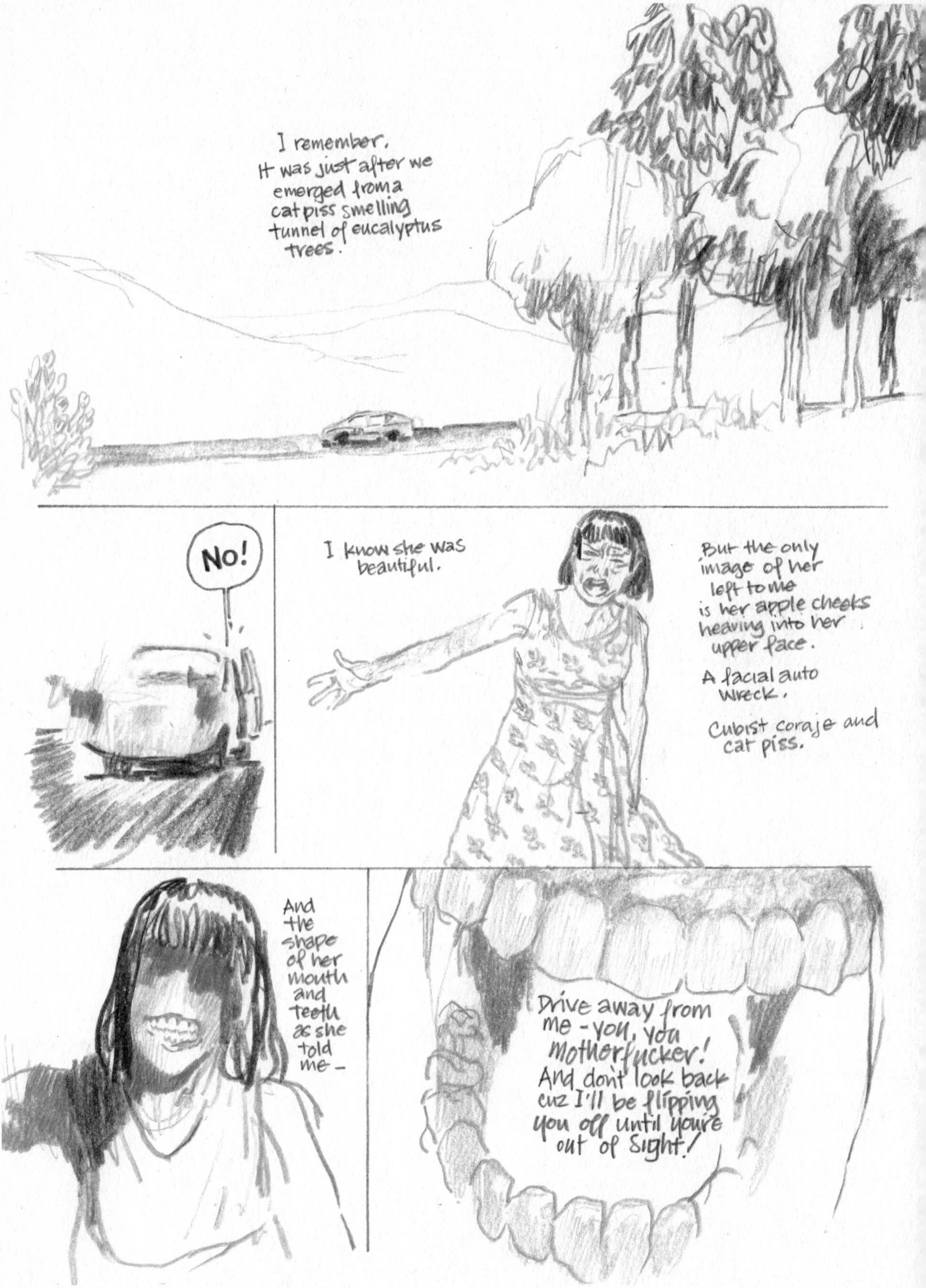
I remember. It was just after we emerged from a cat piss smelling tunnel of eucalyptus trees.
No!
I know she was beautiful.
But the only image of her left to me is her apple cheeks heaving into her upper face.
A facial auto wreck.
Cubist coraje and cat piss.
And the shape of her mouth and teeth as she told me -
Drive away from me - you, you Motherfucker! And don't look back cuz I'll be flipping you off until you're out of sight!

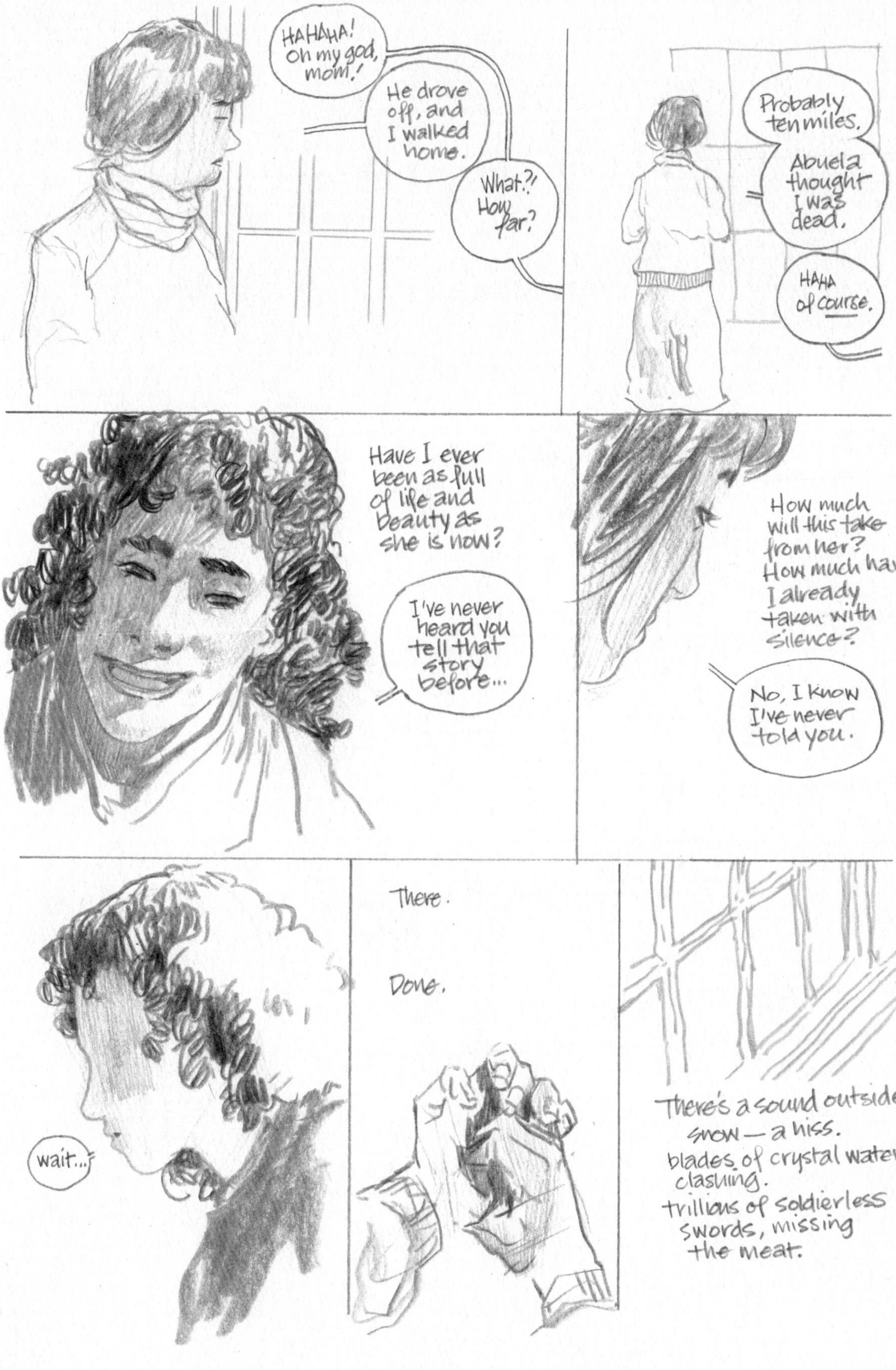
HAHAHA! Oh my god, mom!
He drove off, and I walked home.
What?! How far?
Probably ten miles.
Abuela thought I was dead.
HAHA of course.
Have I ever been as full of life and beauty as she is now?
I've never heard you tell that story before...
How much will this take from her? How much have I already taken with silence?
No, I know I've never told you.
wait...
There.
Done.
There's a sound outside. snow — a hiss. blades of crystal water clashing. trillions of soldierless swords, missing the meat.

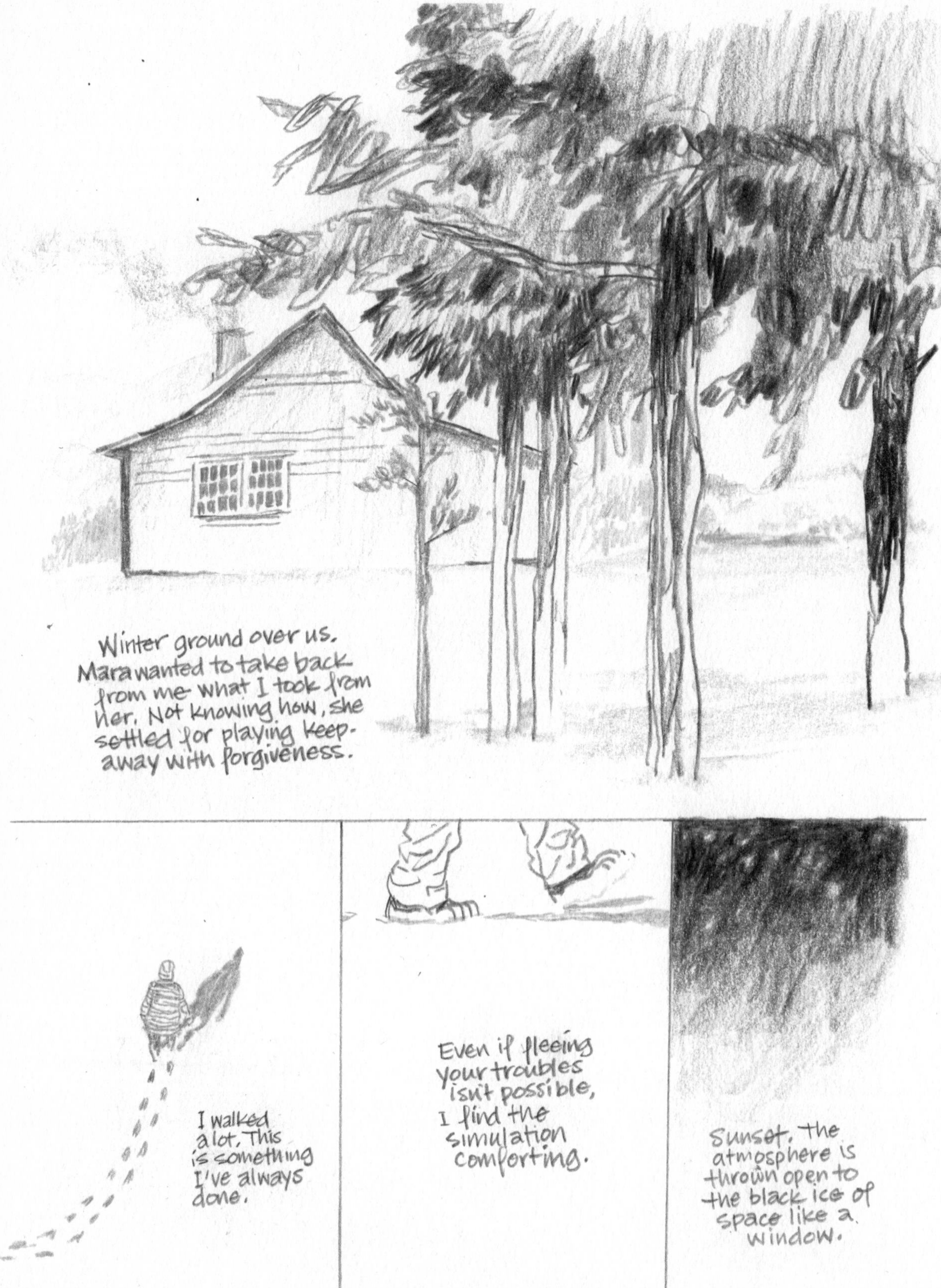
Winter ground over us. Mara wanted to take back from me what I took from her. Not knowing how, she settled for playing keep-away with forgiveness.
I walked a lot. This is something I've always done.
Even if fleeing your troubles isn't possible, I find the simulation comforting.
Sunset. the atmosphere is thrown open to the black ice of space like a window.

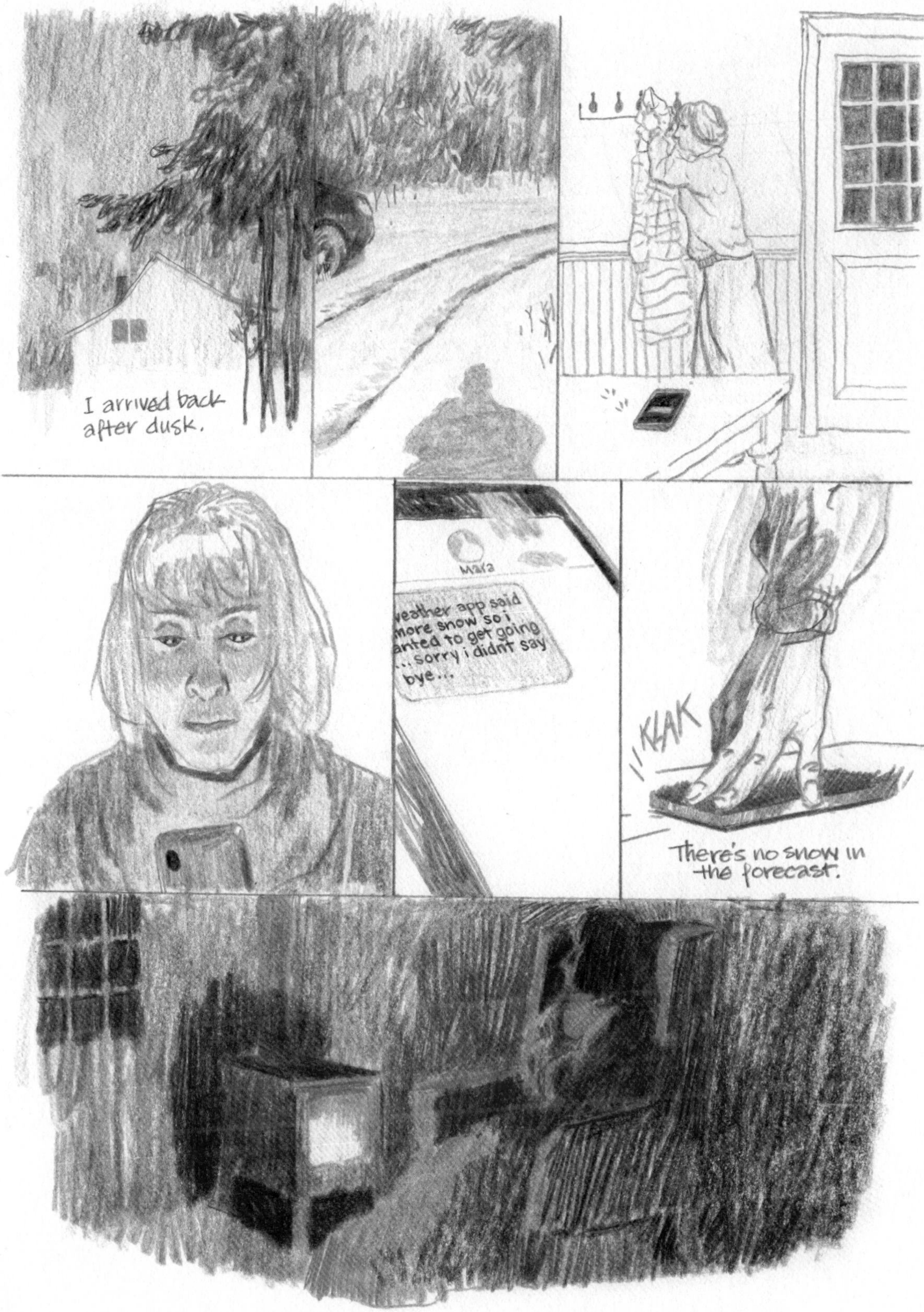

I arrived back after dusk.
Mara
veather app said more snow so i anted to get going ...sorry i didnt say bye...
KLAK
There's no snow in the forecast.

My mood festered in the snowblinding days that followed.

But the sky in the west got dark. Mara texted several times and I let them stay unread.

Then the storm let loose. Maybe Mara wasn't lying. No service in the area for a week, though.

College kids aren't the only ones who get to be petty.

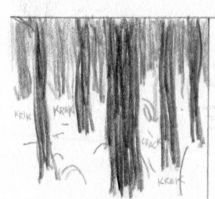

Cold clapped through the thicket out back.

Luckily, I always liked cutting kindling.

Reminds me of my mom.

Mom once heard that saying, 'Firewood warms you twice.'
'No,' she said.' It is violence. Violence warms you twice.'

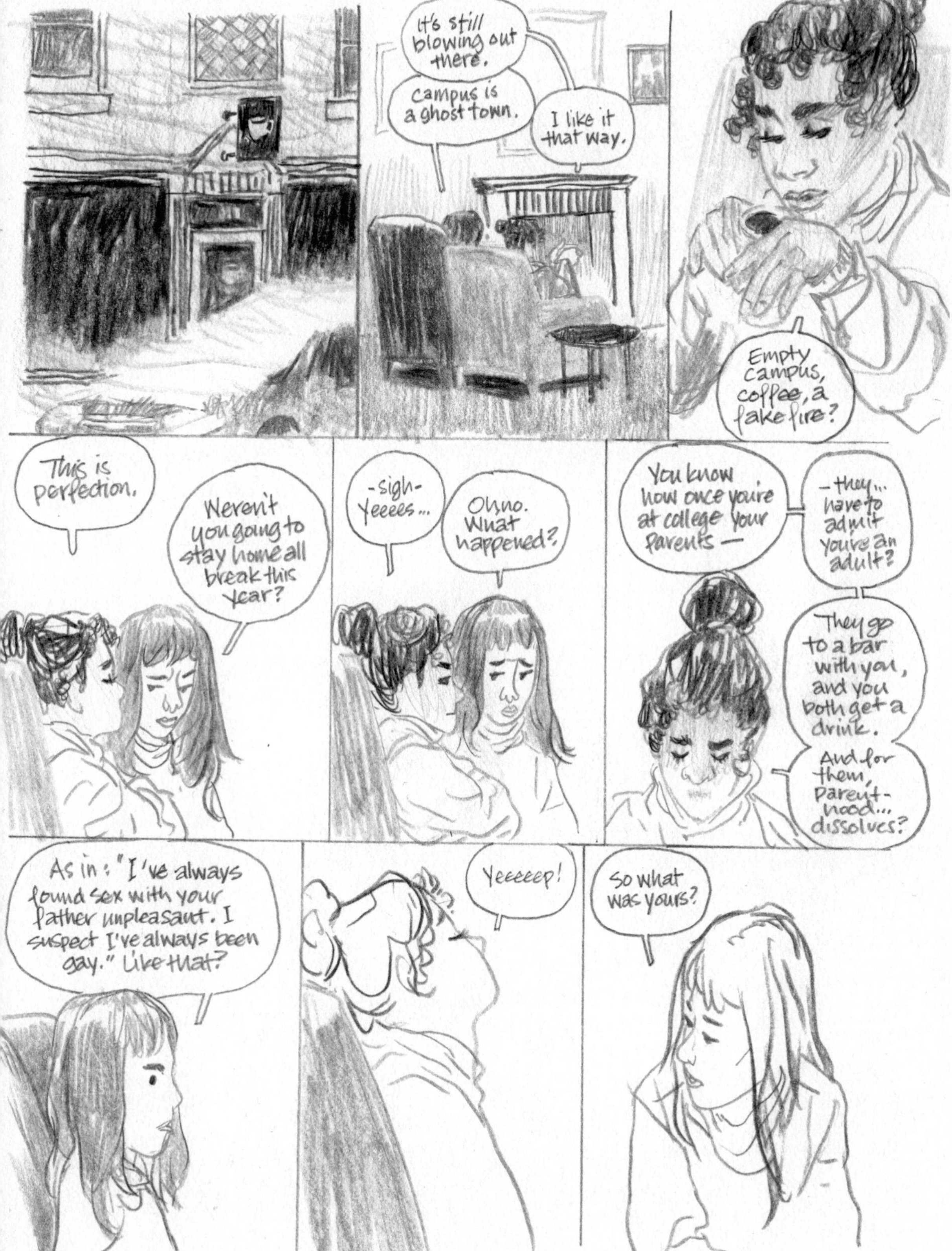
It's still blowing out there.
Campus is a ghost town.
I like it that way.
Empty campus, coffee, a fake fire?
This is perfection.
Weren't you going to stay home all break this year?
-sigh- Yeeees...
Oh no. What happened?
You know how once you're at college your parents —
— they... have to admit you're an adult?
They go to a bar with you, and you both get a drink.
And for them, parenthood... dissolves?
As in: "I've always found sex with your father unpleasant. I suspect I've always been gay." Like that?
Yeeeeep!
So what was yours?

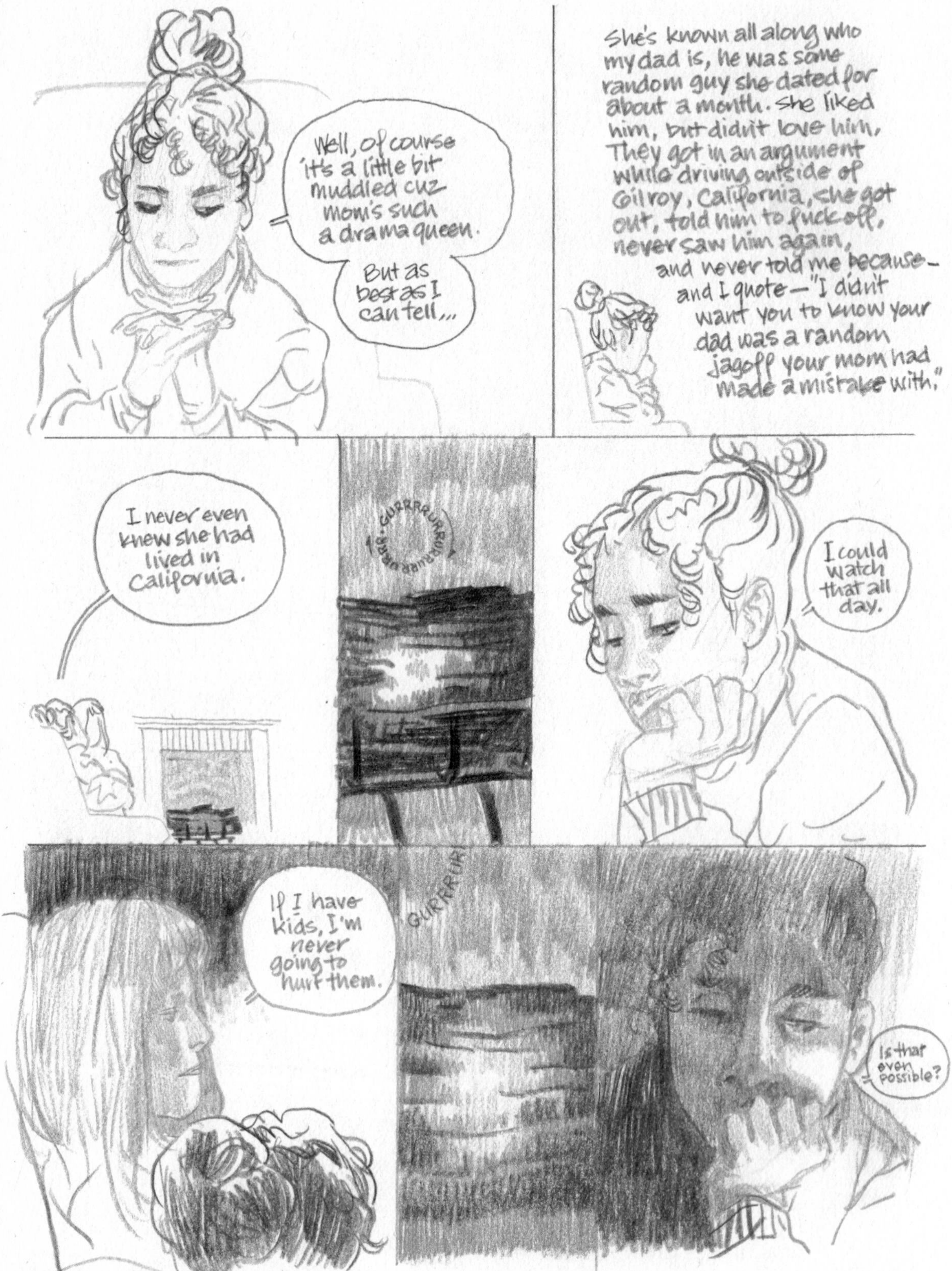
Well, of course it's a little bit muddled cuz mom's such a drama queen.
But as best as I can tell,...
She's known all along who my dad is, he was some random guy she dated for about a month. She liked him, but didn't love him. They got in an argument while driving outside of Gilroy, California, she got out, told him to fuck off, never saw him again, and never told me because— and I quote— "I didn't want you to know your dad was a random jagoff your mom had made a mistake with."
I never even knew she had lived in California.
GURRRRURRURRURURR-URRR
I could watch that all day.
If I have kids, I'm never going to hurt them.
GURRRUR!
Is that even possible?

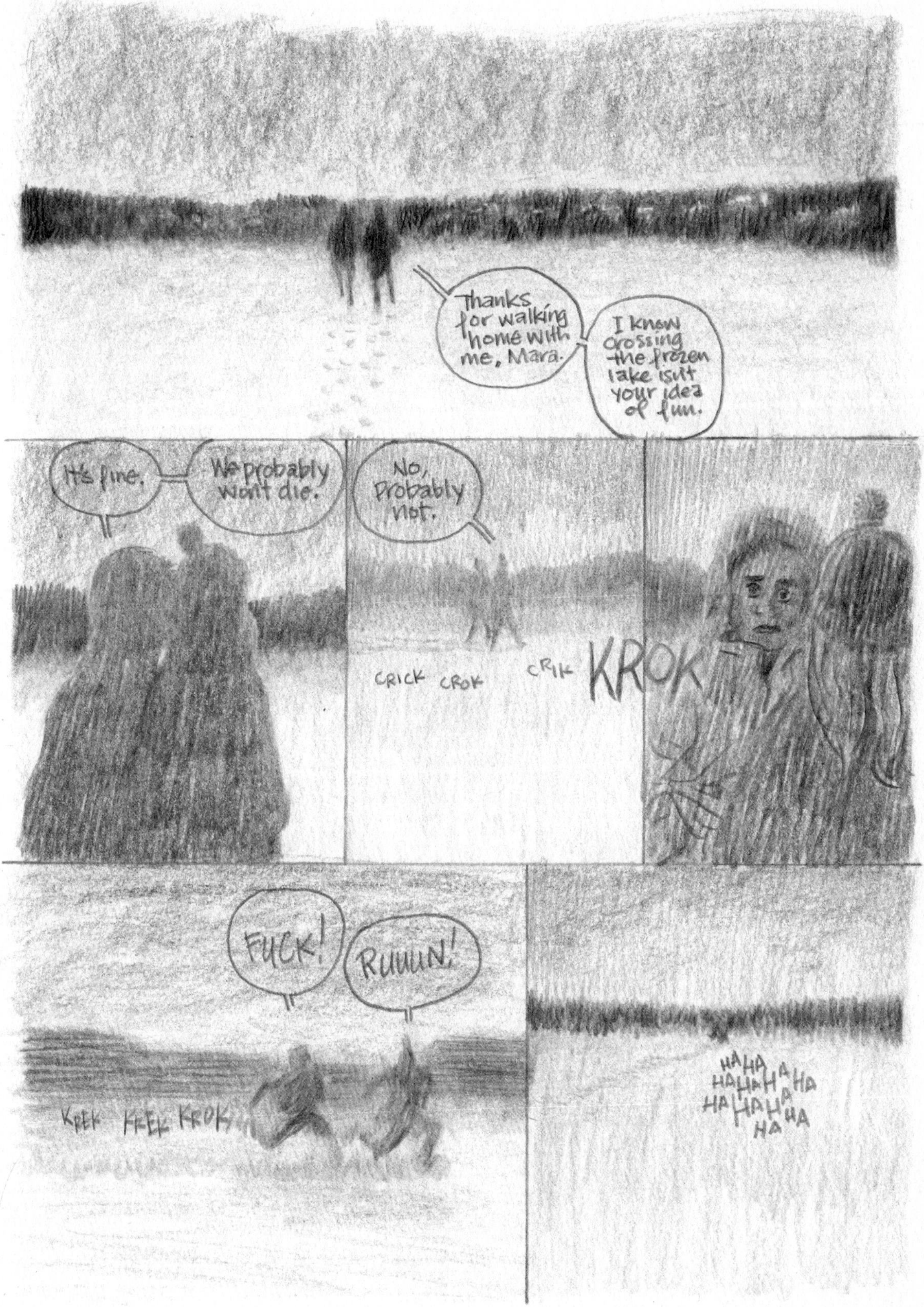
Thanks for walking home with me, Mara.
I know crossing the frozen lake isn't your idea of fun.
It's fine.
We probably won't die.
No, Probably not.
CRICK CROK CRIK
KROK
FUCK!
RUUUN!
KREK KREK KROK
HA HA HA HA HA HA HA HA HA HA HA HA

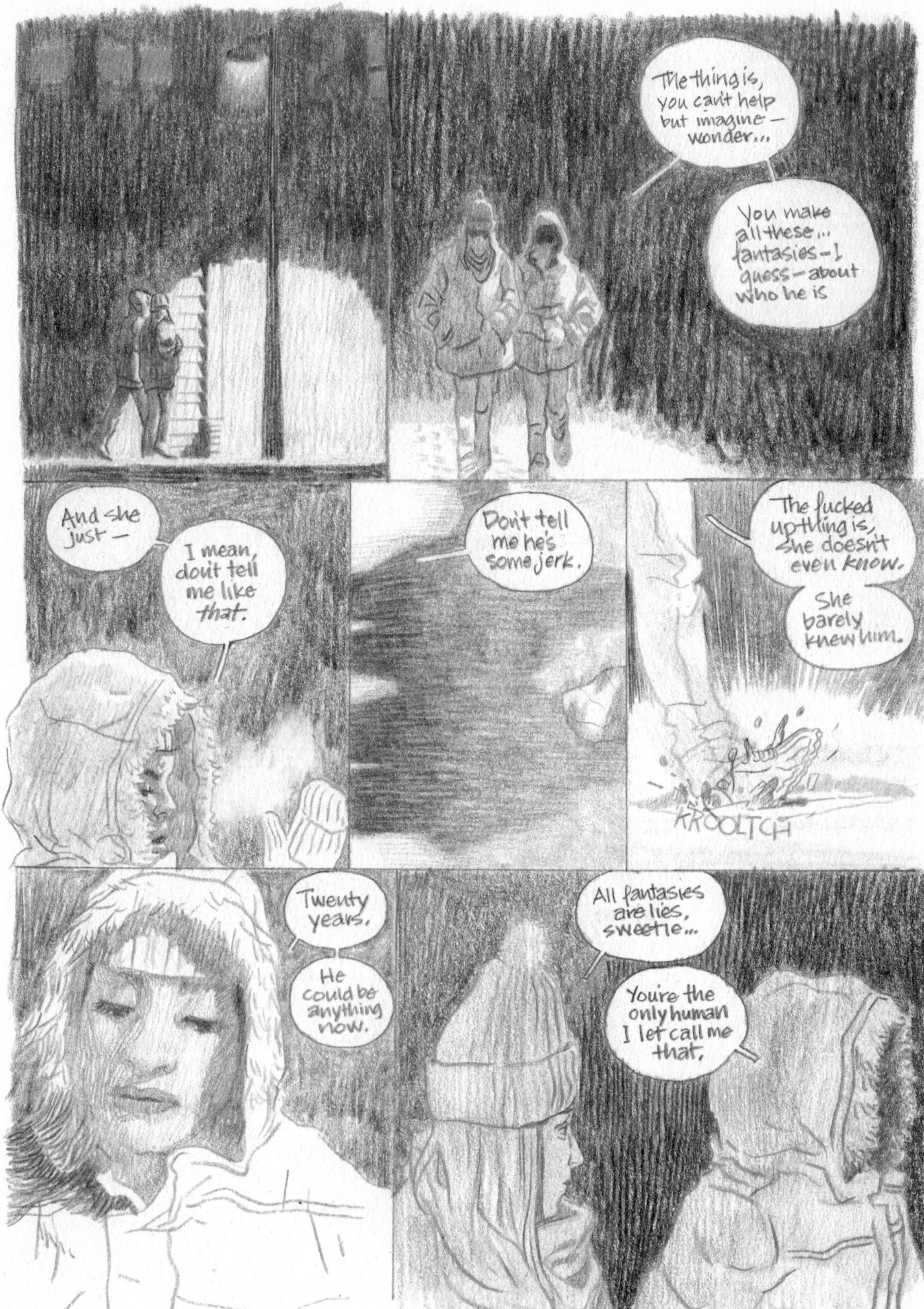
The thing is, you can't help but imagine — wonder...
You make all these... fantasies — I guess — about who he is
And she just —
I mean, don't tell me like that.
Don't tell me he's some jerk.
The fucked up thing is, she doesn't even know.
She barely knew him.
KROOLTCH
Twenty years.
He could be anything now.
All fantasies are lies, sweetie...
You're the only human I let call me that.

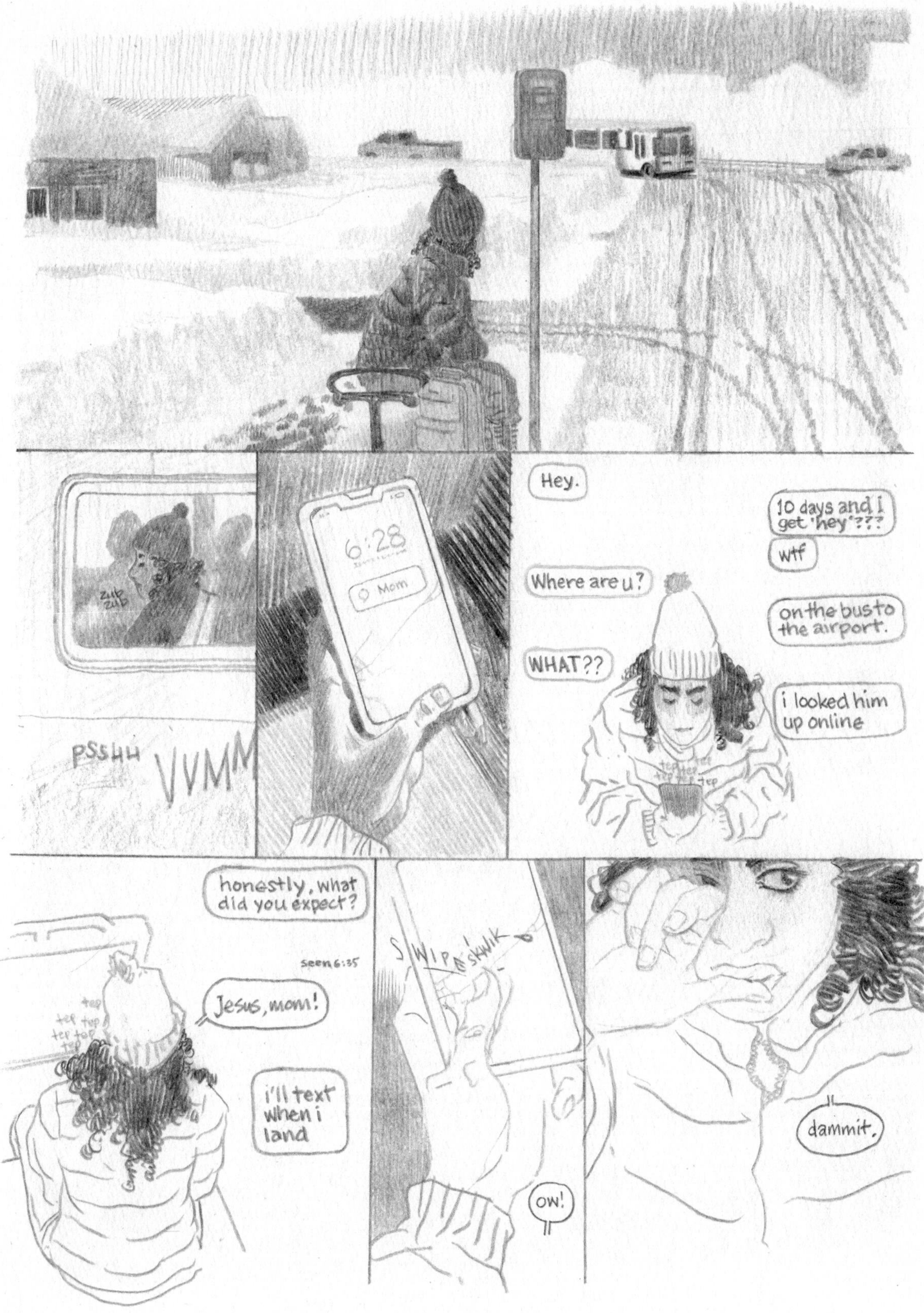
zub zub
PSSHH
VVMM
6:28
Mom
Hey.
10 days and i get 'hey'???
wtf
Where are u?
on the bus to the airport.
WHAT??
i looked him up online
tep tep tep tep tep
honestly, what did you expect?
seen 6:35
tep tep tep tep tep tep
Jesus, mom!
i'll text when i land
SWIPE
skwik
OW!
dammit.

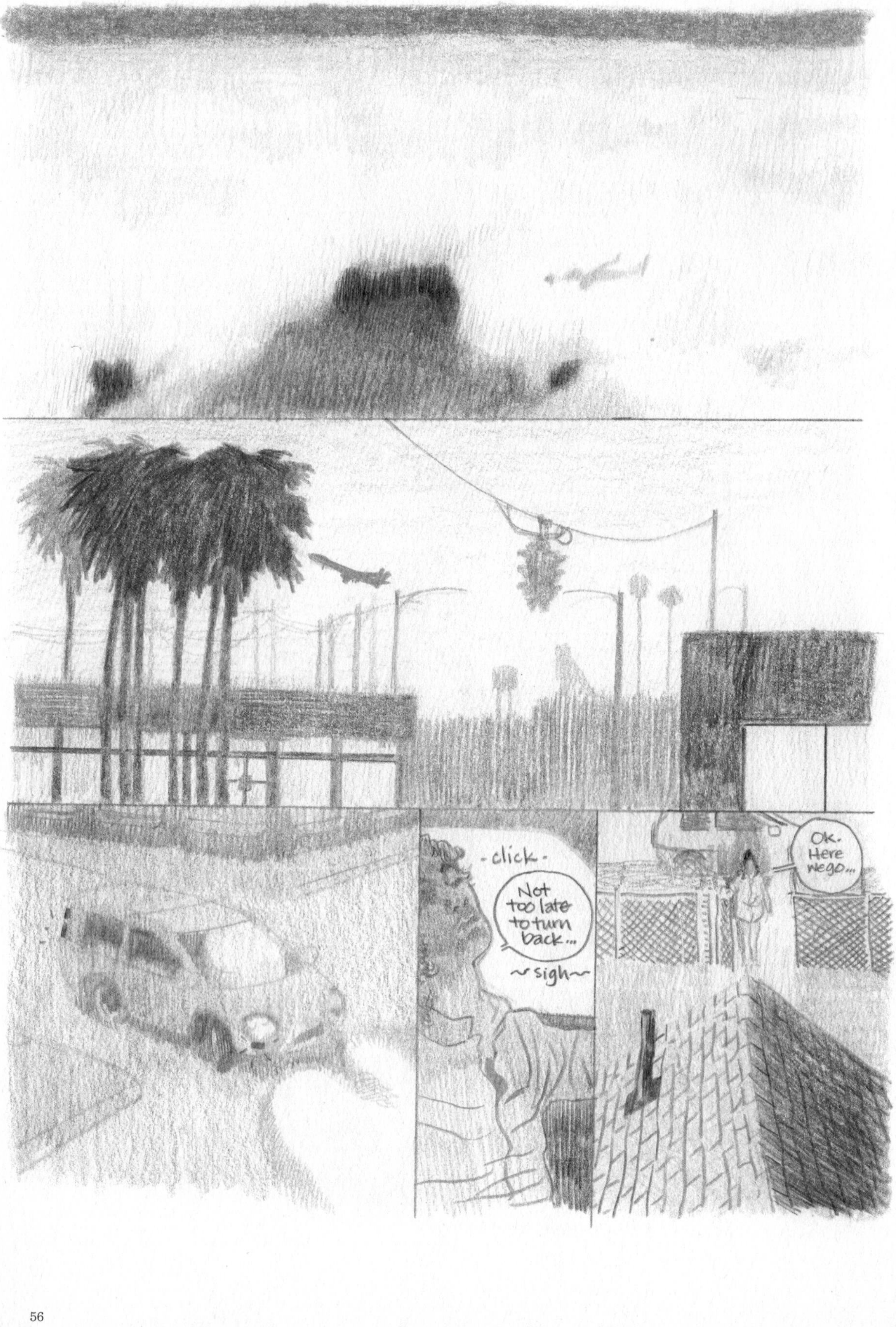
-click-
Not too late to turn back...
~sigh~
OK. Here we go...

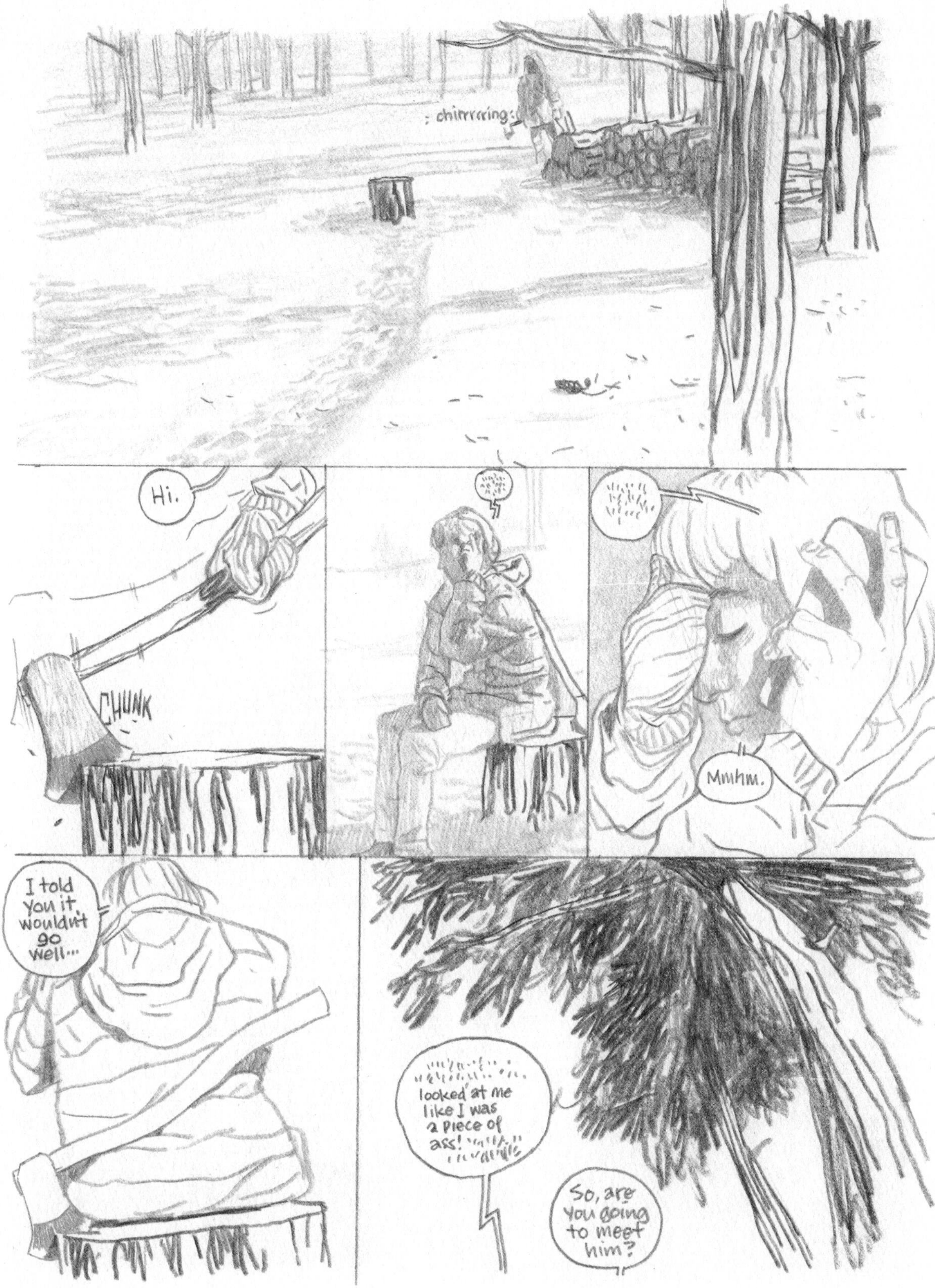
: chirrrrring :
Hi.
CHUNK
Mmhm.
I told you it wouldn't go well...
looked at me like I was a piece of ass!
So, are you going to meet him?

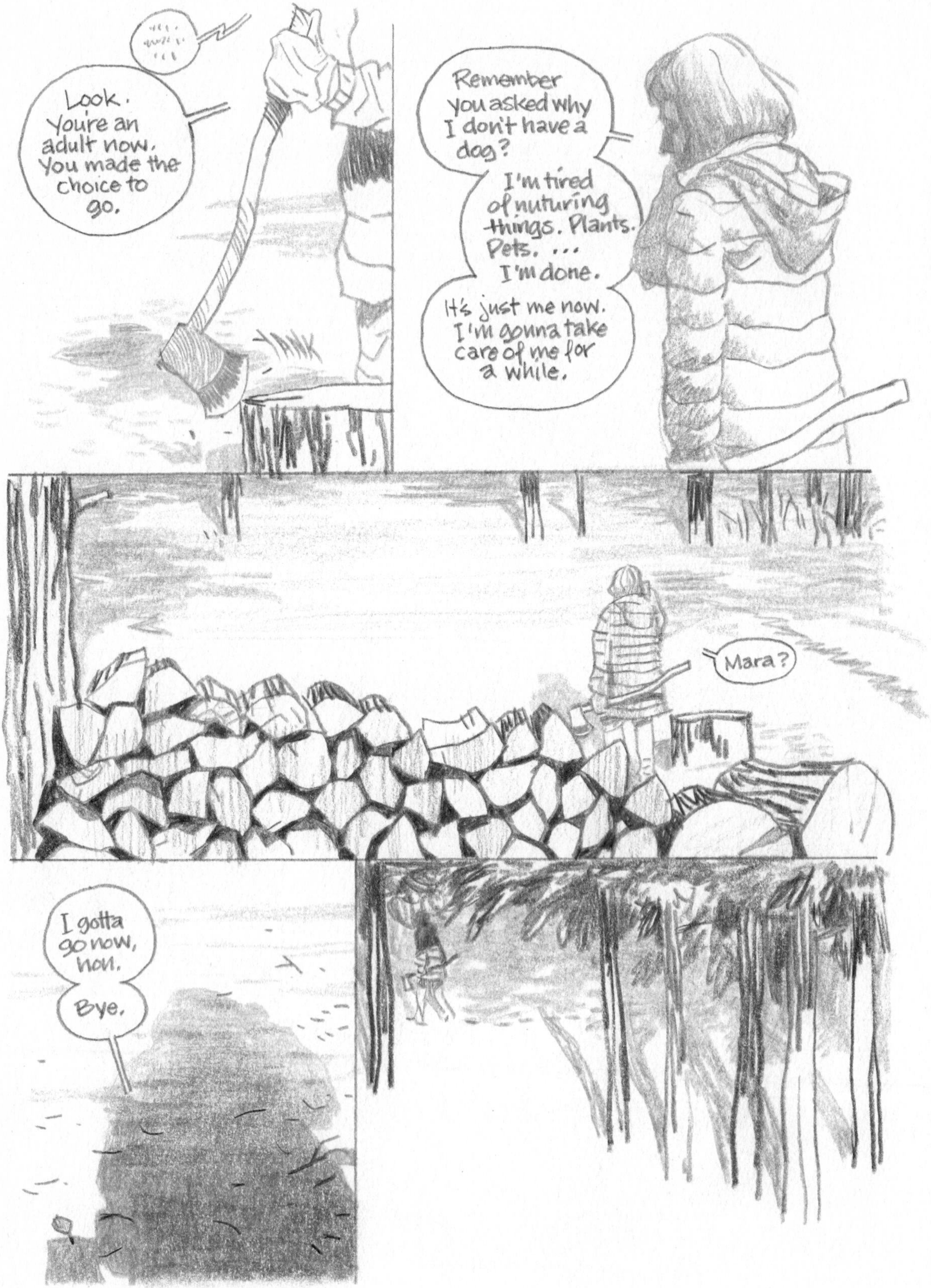
Look. You're an adult now. You made the choice to go.
Remember you asked why I don't have a dog?
I'm tired of nuturing things. Plants. Pets. ... I'm done.
It's just me now. I'm gonna take care of me for a while.
Mara?
I gotta go now, hon.
Bye.

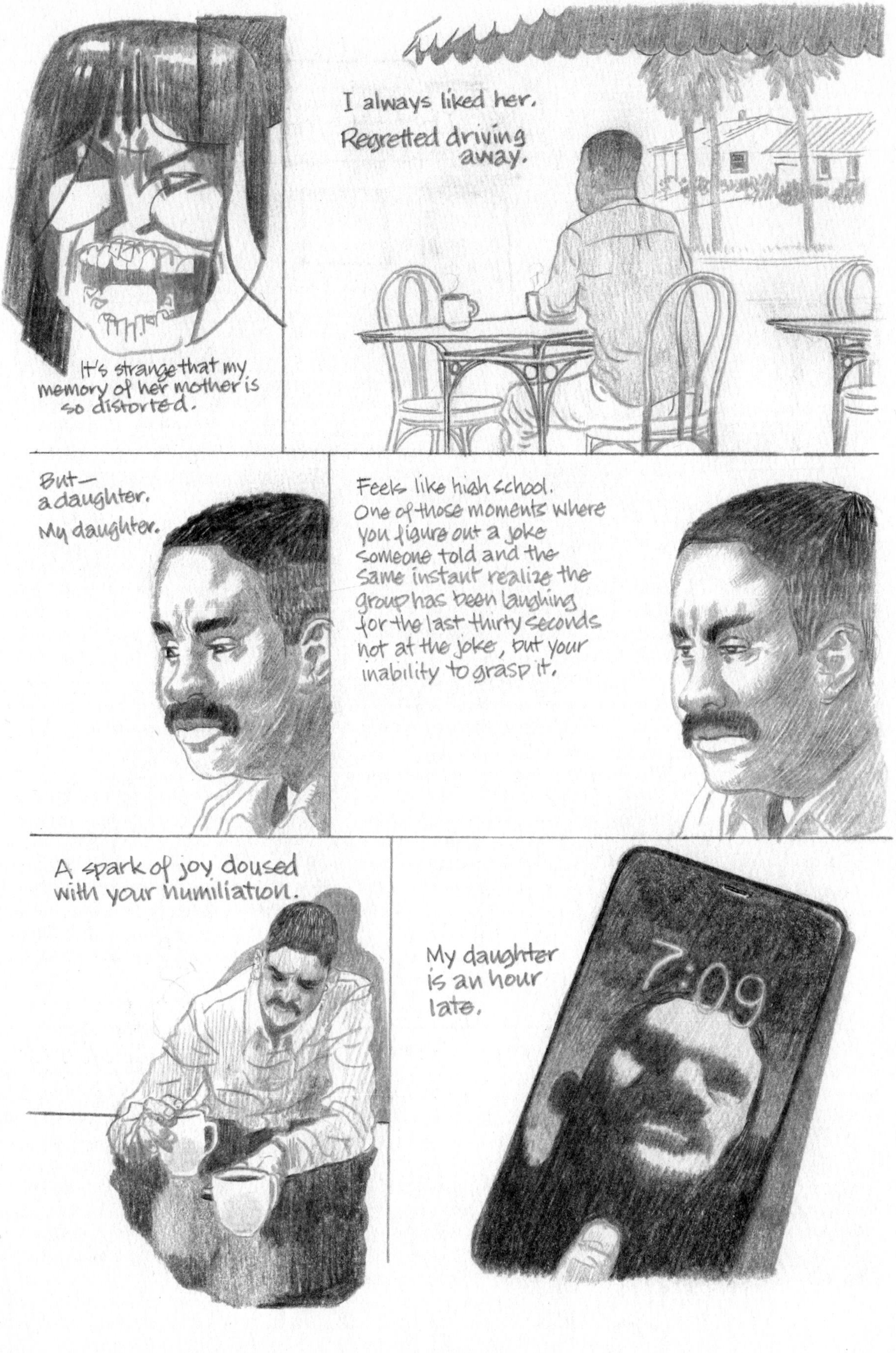
It's strange that my memory of her mother is so distorted.
I always liked her.
Regretted driving away.
But— a daughter.
My daughter.
Feels like high school. One of those moments where you figure out a joke someone told and the same instant realize the group has been laughing for the last thirty seconds not at the joke, but your inability to grasp it.
A spark of joy doused with your humiliation.
My daughter is an hour late.
7:09

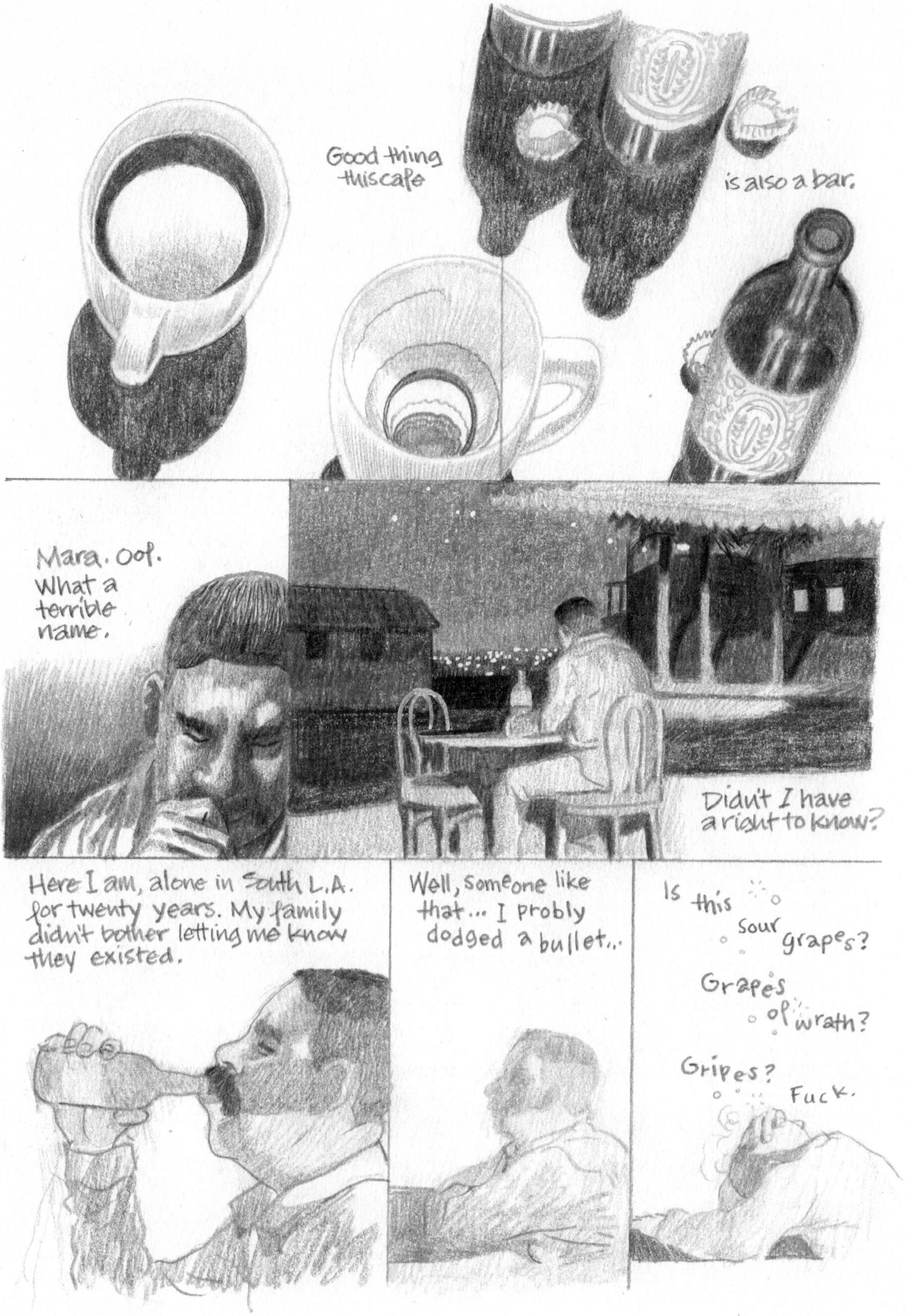
Good thing this cafe
is also a bar.
Mara. Oof. What a terrible name.
Didn't I have a right to know?
Here I am, alone in South L.A. for twenty years. My family didn't bother letting me know they existed.
Well, someone like that... I probly dodged a bullet...
Is this sour grapes?
Grapes of wrath?
Gripes?
Fuck.

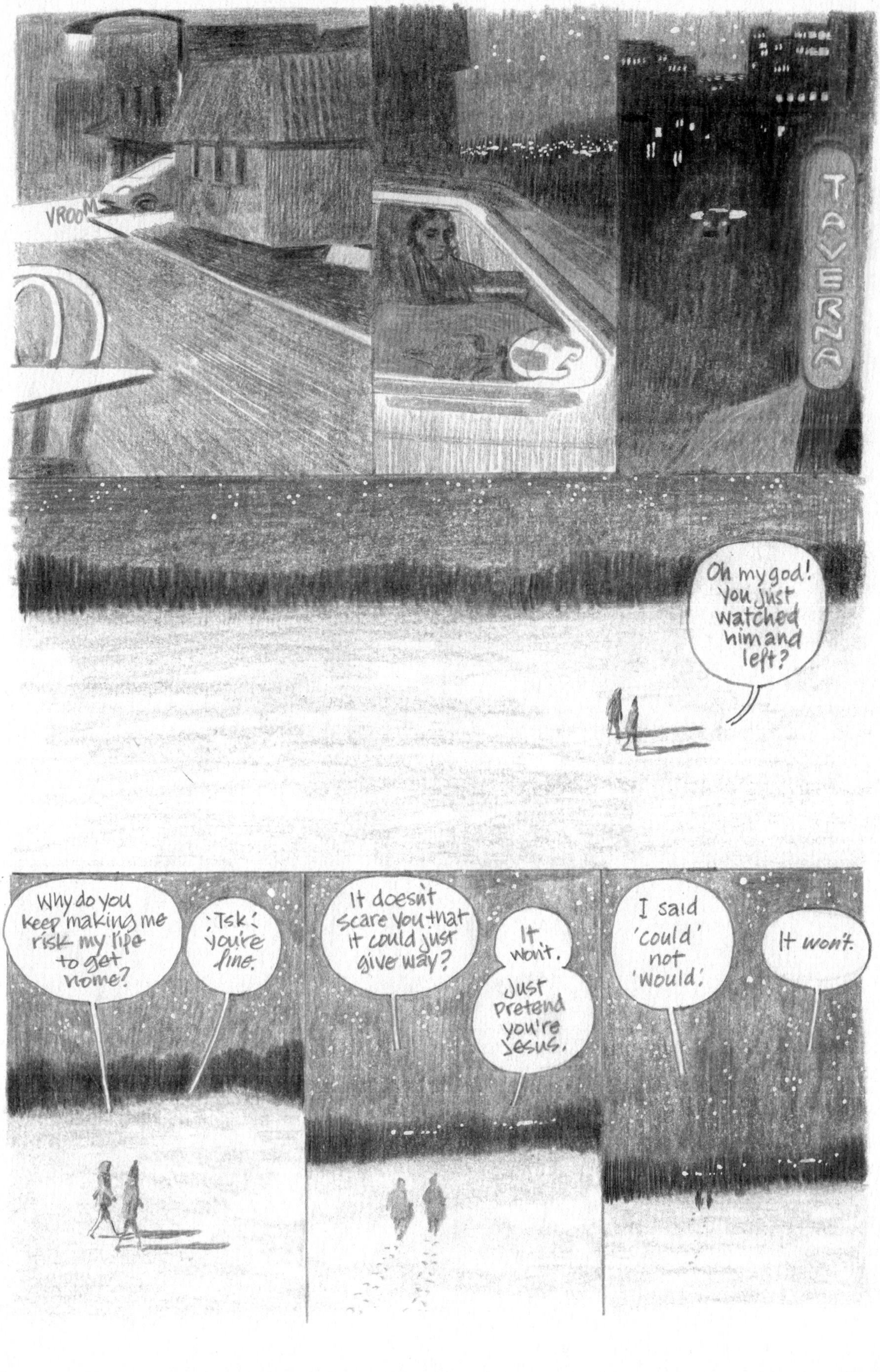
VROOM
TAVERNA
Oh my god! You just watched him and left?
Why do you keep making me risk my life to get home?
:Tsk: you're fine.
It doesn't scare you that it could just give way?
It won't.
Just pretend you're Jesus.
I said 'could' not 'would.'
It won't.

KREK
We're at its mercy out here.
...
Mara. You just... watched him and left?
I can't wait for spring.
I'm tired of pretending to be Jesus.
2018

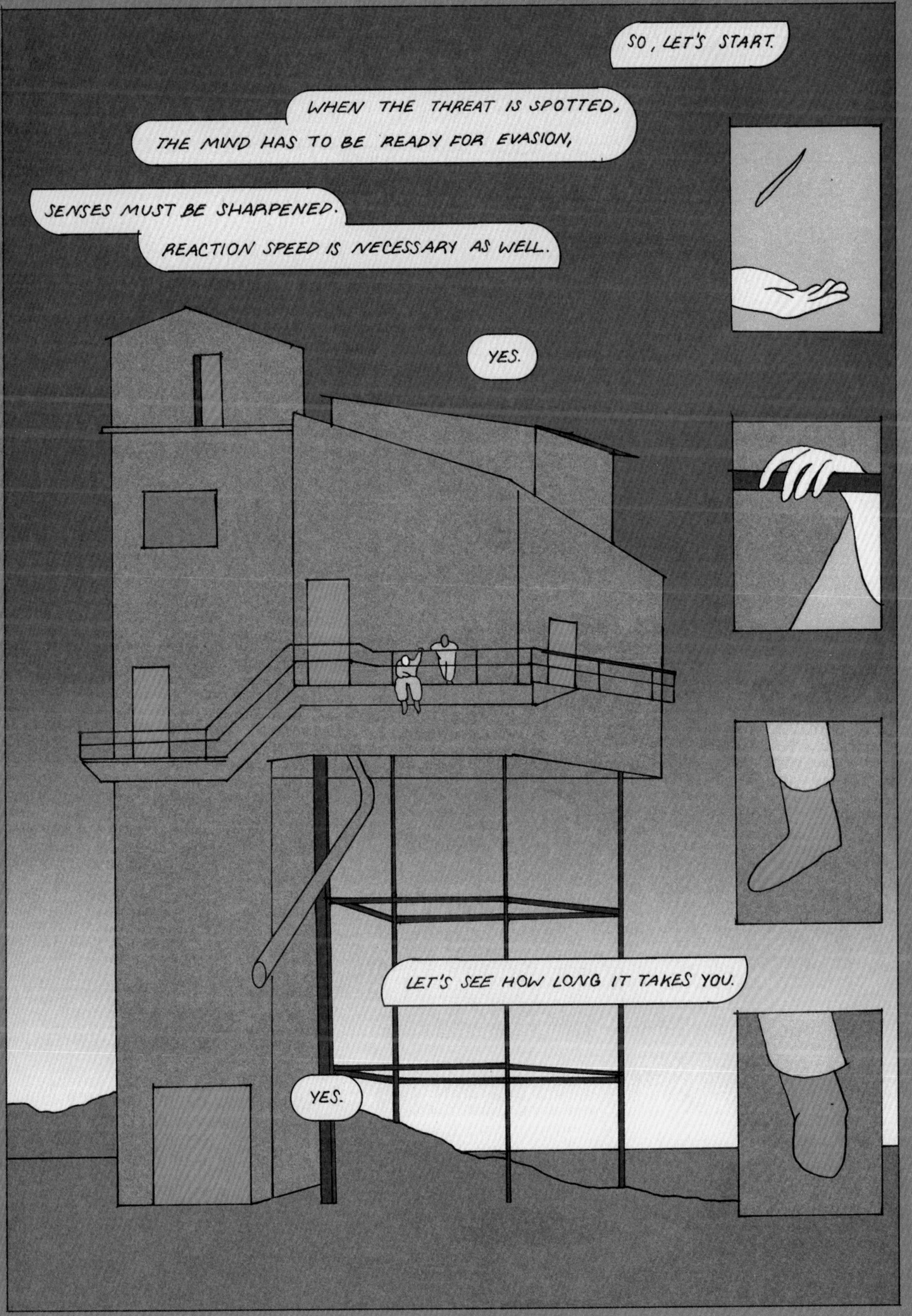
SO, LET'S START.
WHEN THE THREAT IS SPOTTED, THE MIND HAS TO BE READY FOR EVASION,
SENSES MUST BE SHARPENED.
REACTION SPEED IS NECESSARY AS WELL.
YES.
LET'S SEE HOW LONG IT TAKES YOU.
YES.

IT'S NOT RIGHT TO START ANY SOONER.
NO.
AS SOON AS YOU HAVE A PRESENTIMENT, YOU MAY START. WHEN IT HITS YOU, YOUR EVASION HAS TO BE -
HOW DID YOU PUT IT?
FIRM.
FIRM, THAT'S IT.
SHOULD I CLOSE THEM?
YES.

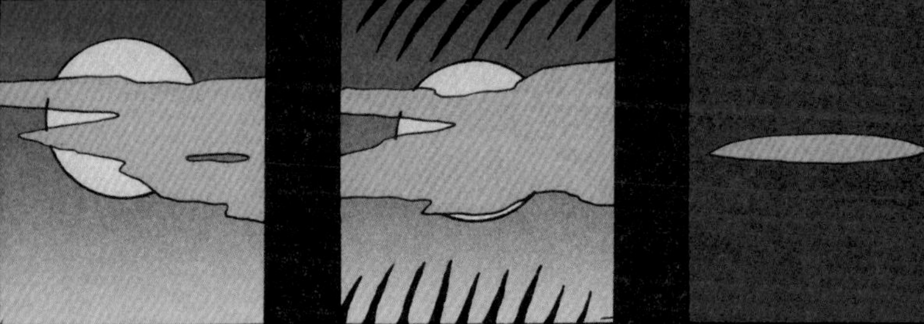

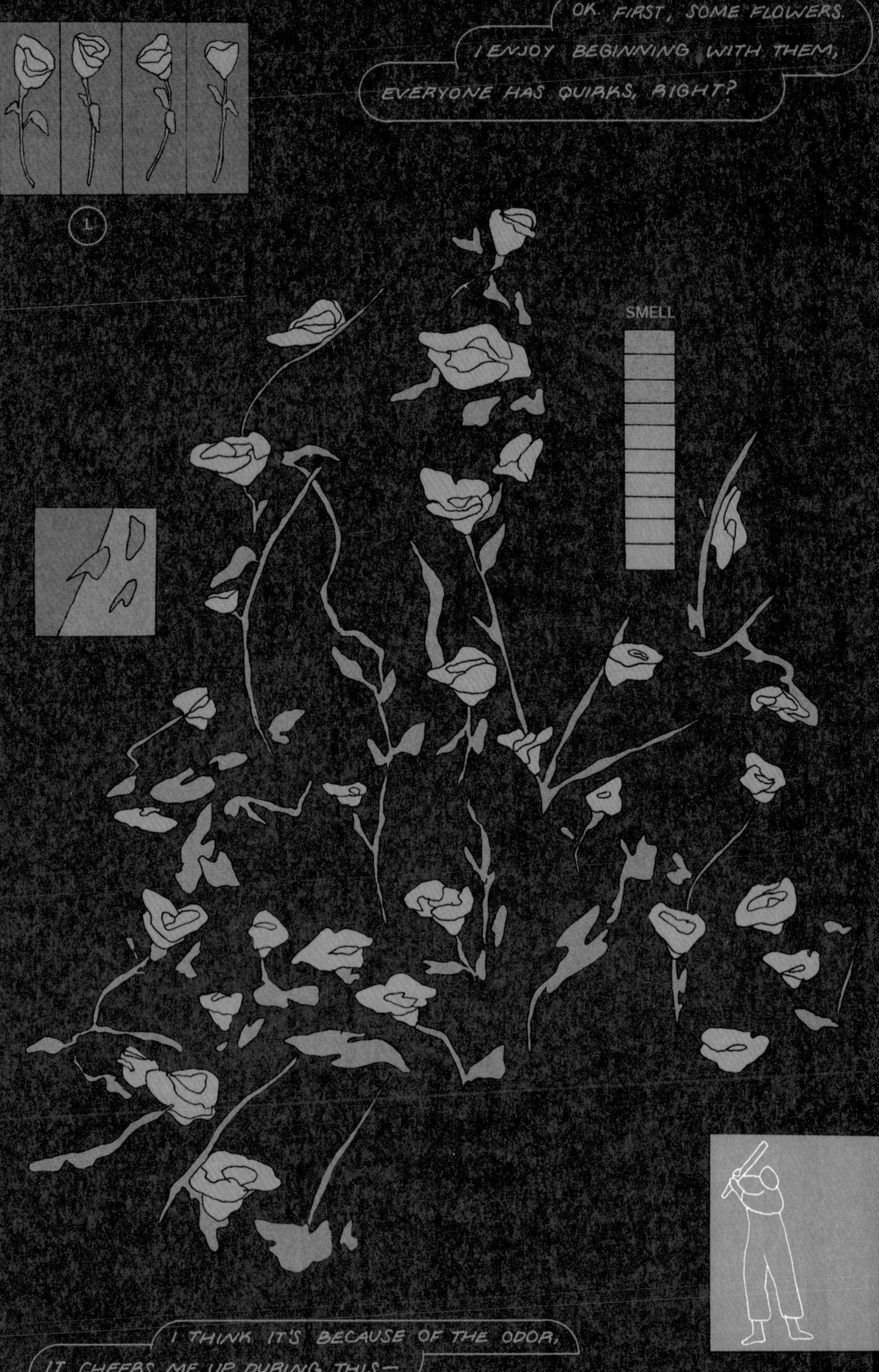
OK. FIRST, SOME FLOWERS.
I ENJOY BEGINNING WITH THEM,
EVERYONE HAS QUIRKS, RIGHT?
1.
SMELL
I THINK IT'S BECAUSE OF THE ODOR,
IT CHEERS ME UP DURING THIS—

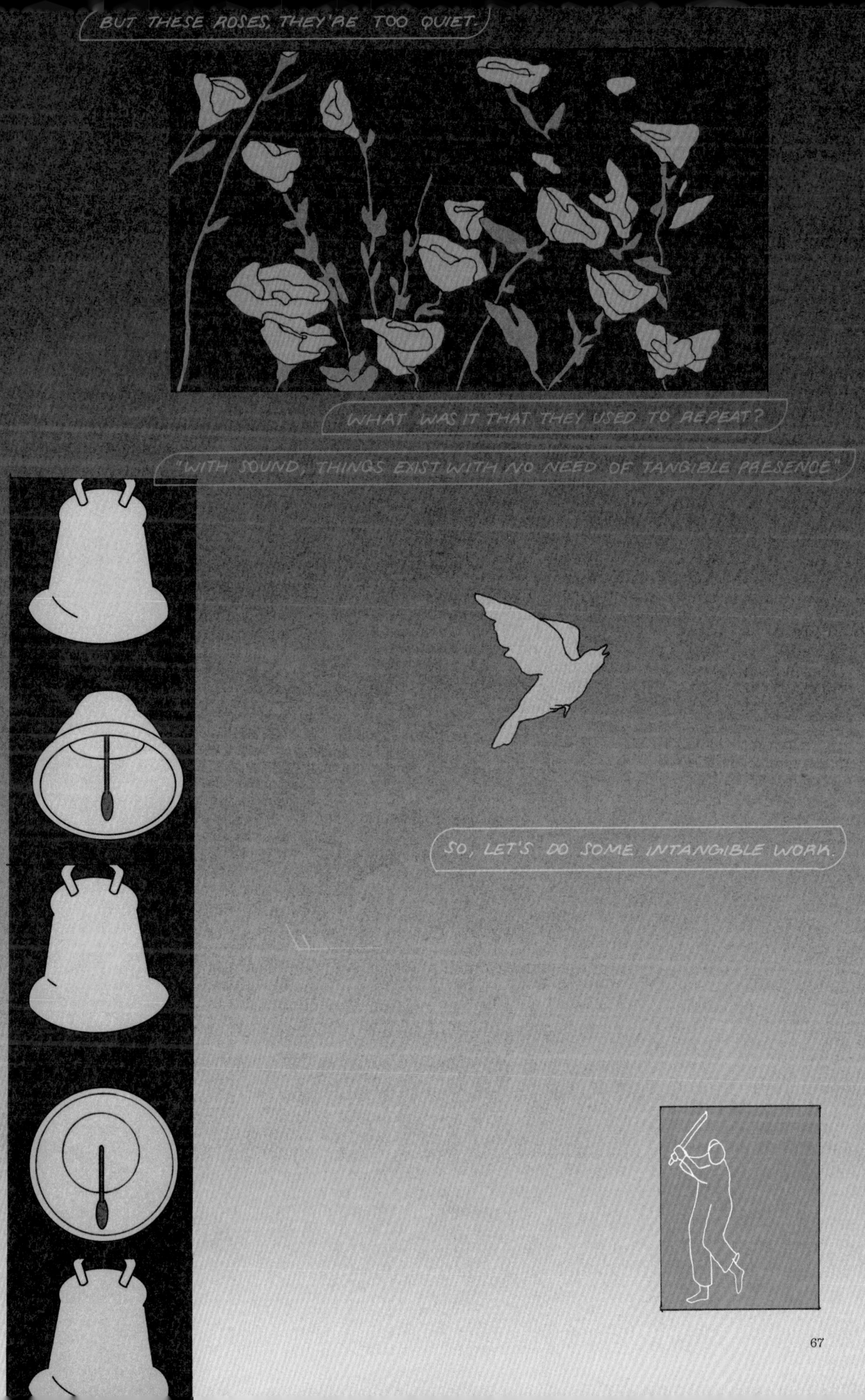
BUT THESE ROSES, THEY'RE TOO QUIET.
WHAT WAS IT THAT THEY USED TO REPEAT?
"WITH SOUND, THINGS EXIST WITH NO NEED OF TANGIBLE PRESENCE"
SO, LET'S DO SOME INTANGIBLE WORK.

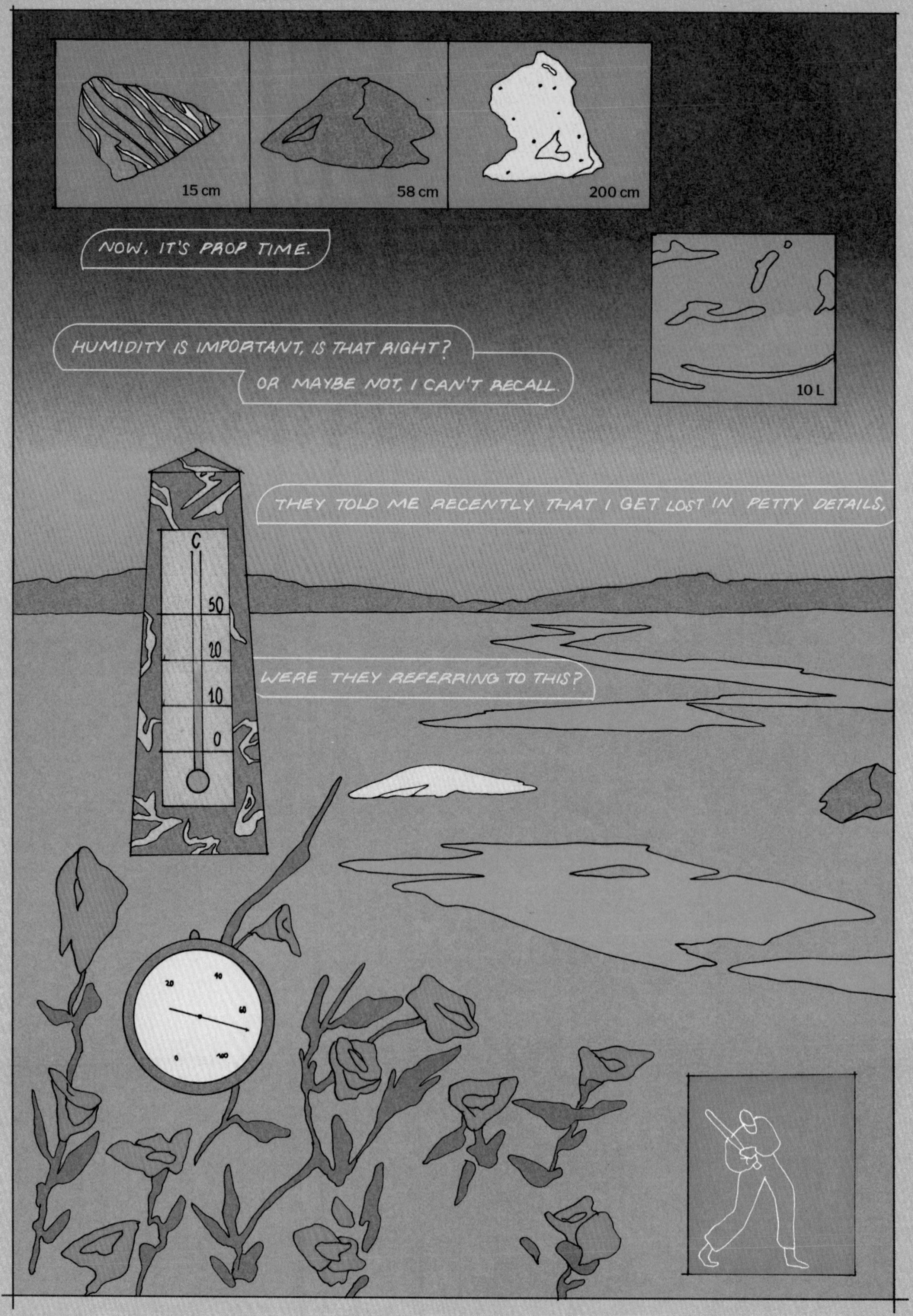
15 cm
58 cm
200 cm
NOW, IT'S PROP TIME.
10 L
HUMIDITY IS IMPORTANT, IS THAT RIGHT?
OR MAYBE NOT, I CAN'T RECALL.
THEY TOLD ME RECENTLY THAT I GET LOST IN PETTY DETAILS,
C
50
20
10
0
WERE THEY REFERRING TO THIS?

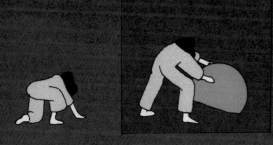

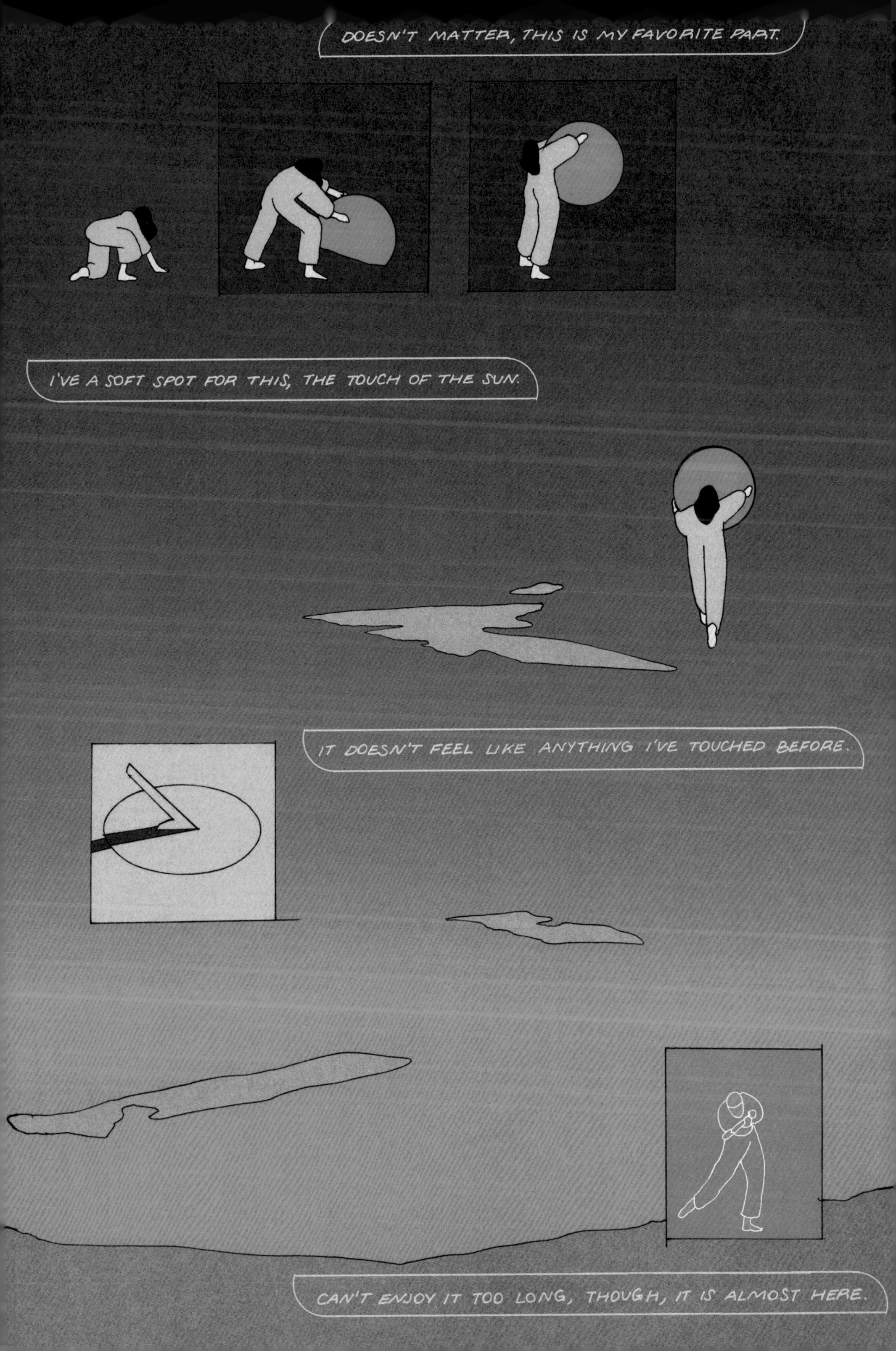

DOESN'T MATTER, THIS IS MY FAVORITE PART.

I'VE A SOFT SPOT FOR THIS, THE TOUCH OF THE SUN.

IT DOESN'T FEEL LIKE ANYTHING I'VE TOUCHED BEFORE.

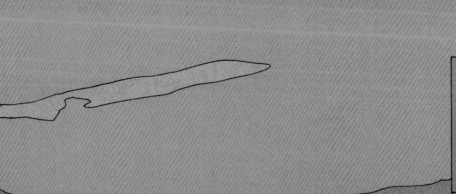

CAN'T ENJOY IT TOO LONG, THOUGH, IT IS ALMOST HERE.

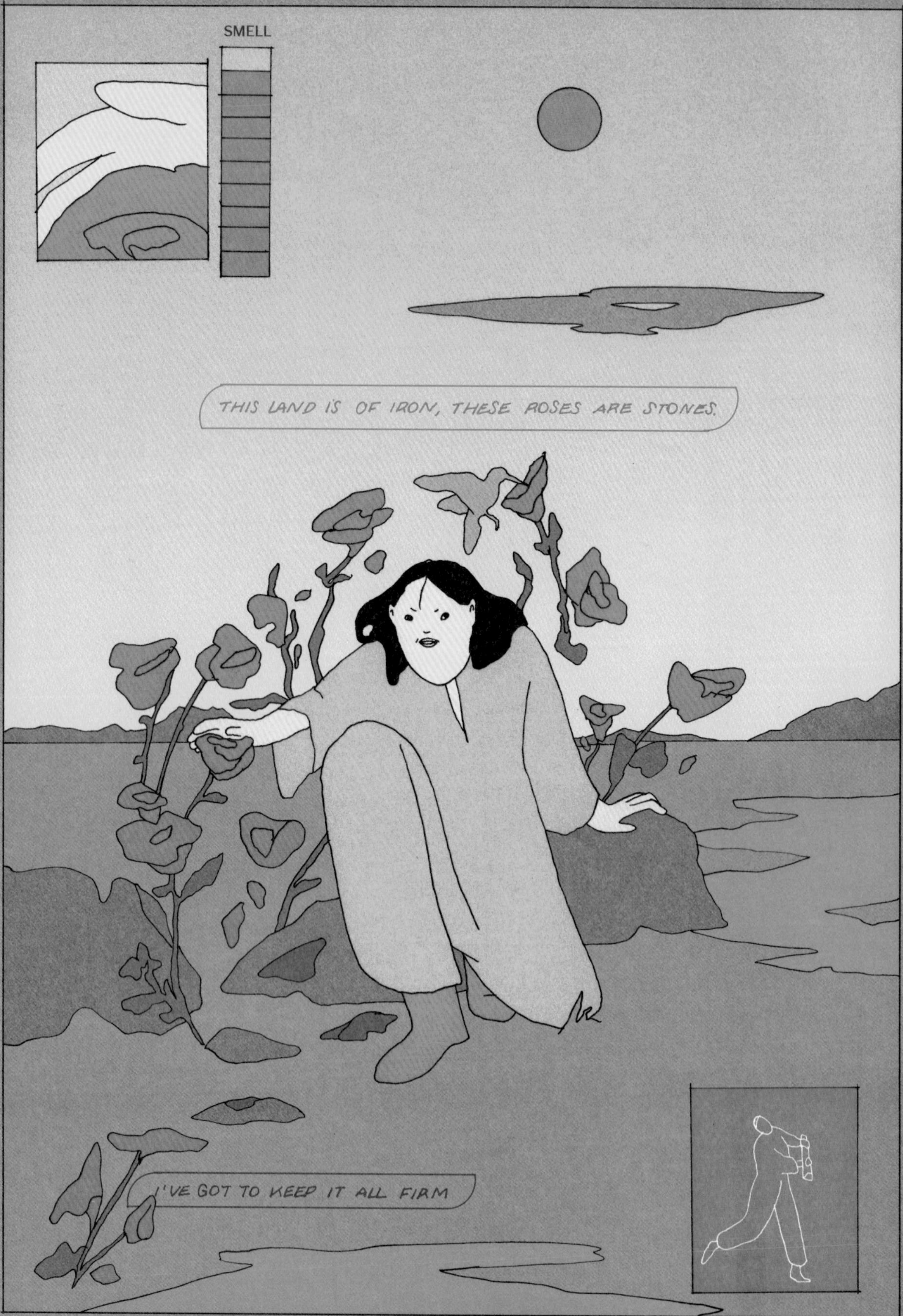
SMELL
THIS LAND IS OF IRON, THESE ROSES ARE STONES.
I'VE GOT TO KEEP IT ALL FIRM

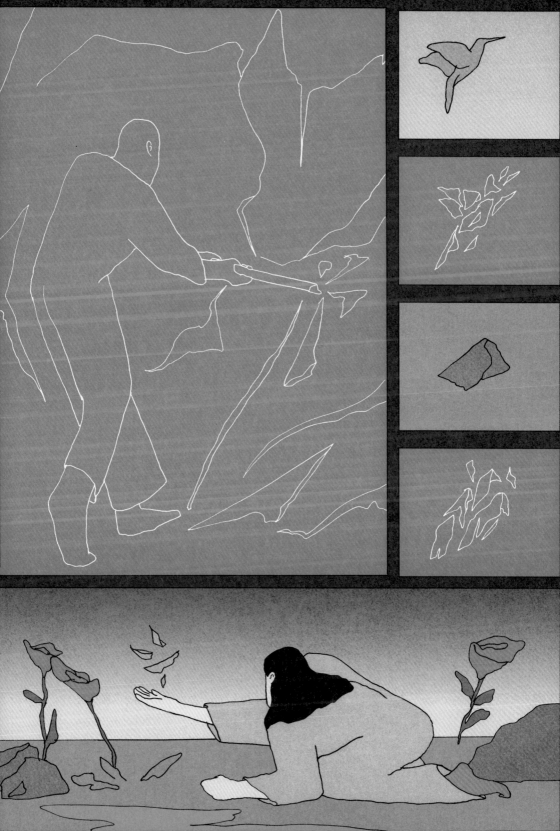

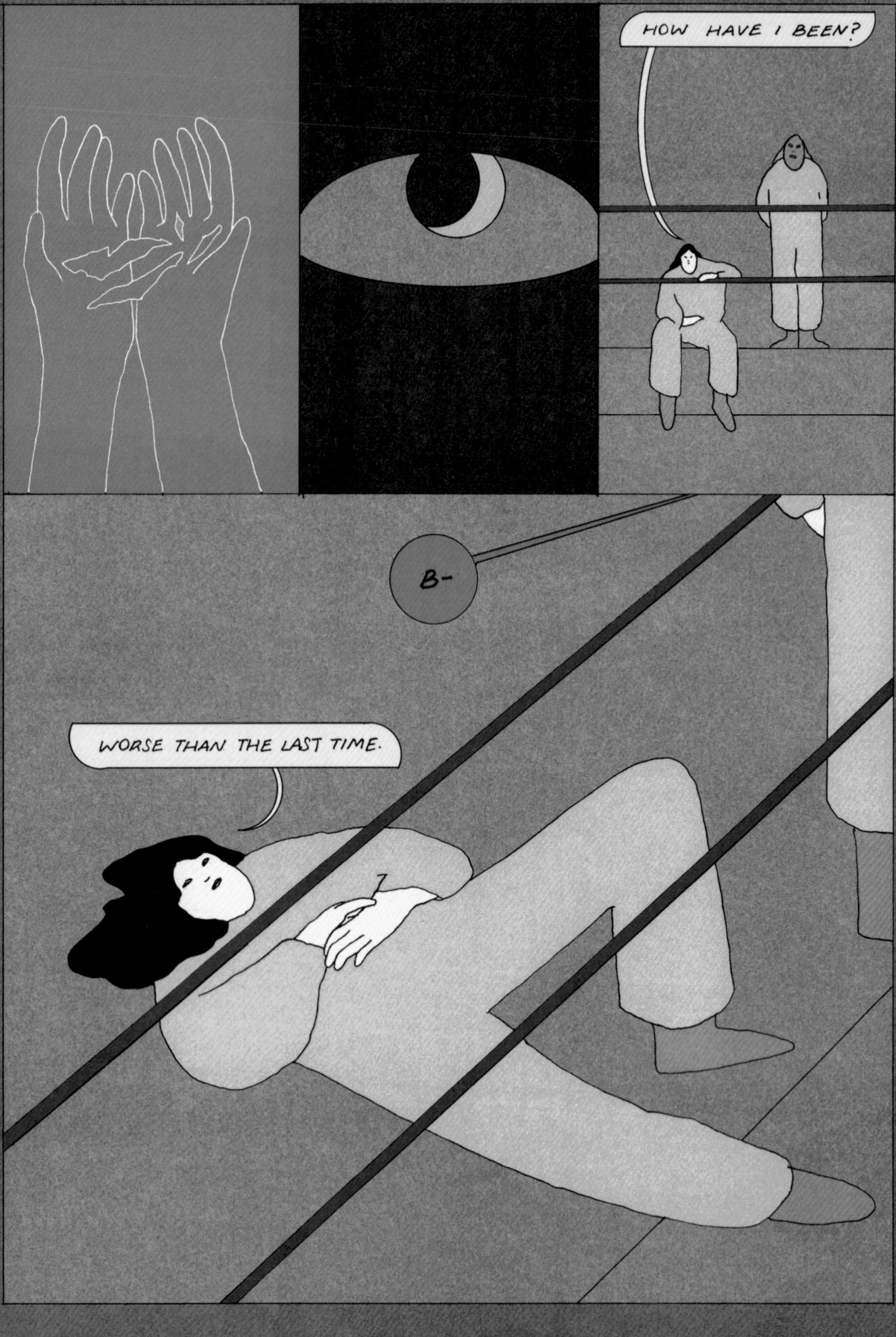
HOW HAVE I BEEN?
B-
WORSE THAN THE LAST TIME.

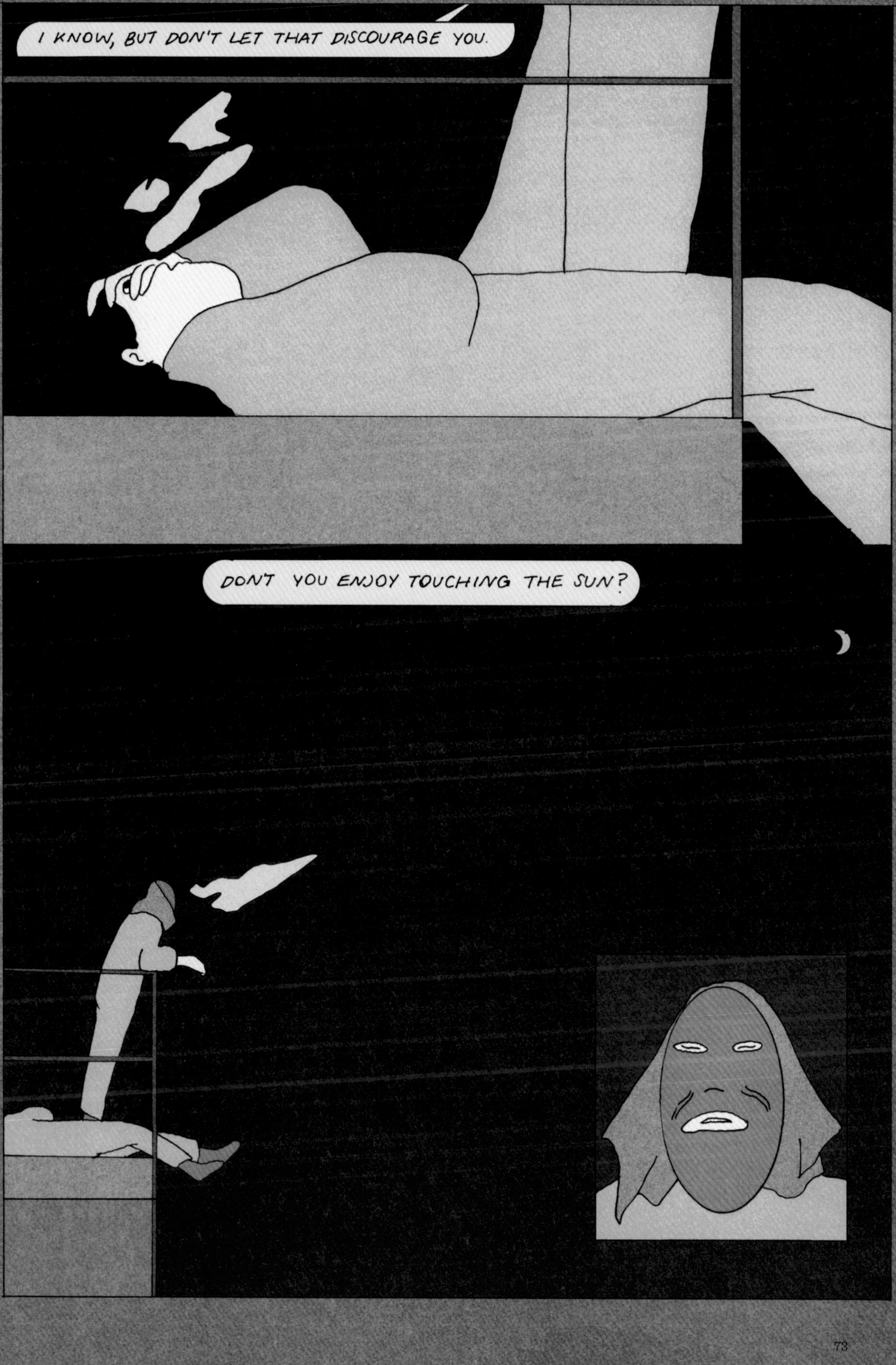
I KNOW, BUT DON'T LET THAT DISCOURAGE YOU.
DON'T YOU ENJOY TOUCHING THE SUN?

PRIMA MATERIA
THE BLOCK SCREAMS
IN PAIN
UNDER THE MASTER'S HAND
KINSHIP
"SON, YOU MUST-"
"INDEED, I WILL"
TEMPTATION...
BETRAYAL!
BROTHERHOOD AMONG THE HARLEQUINS

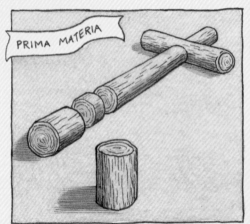

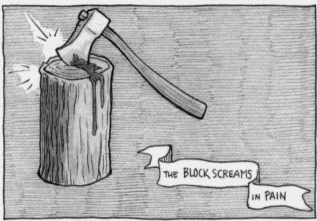

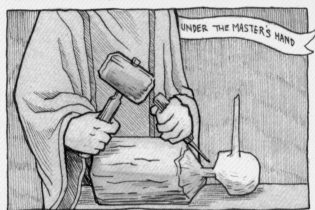

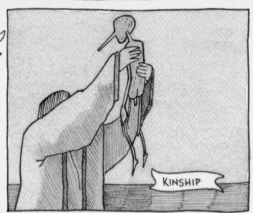

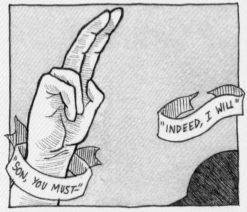

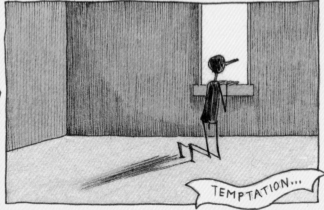

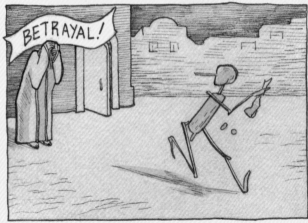

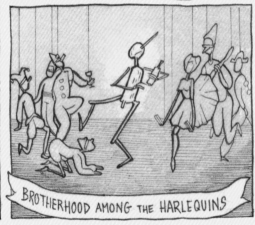

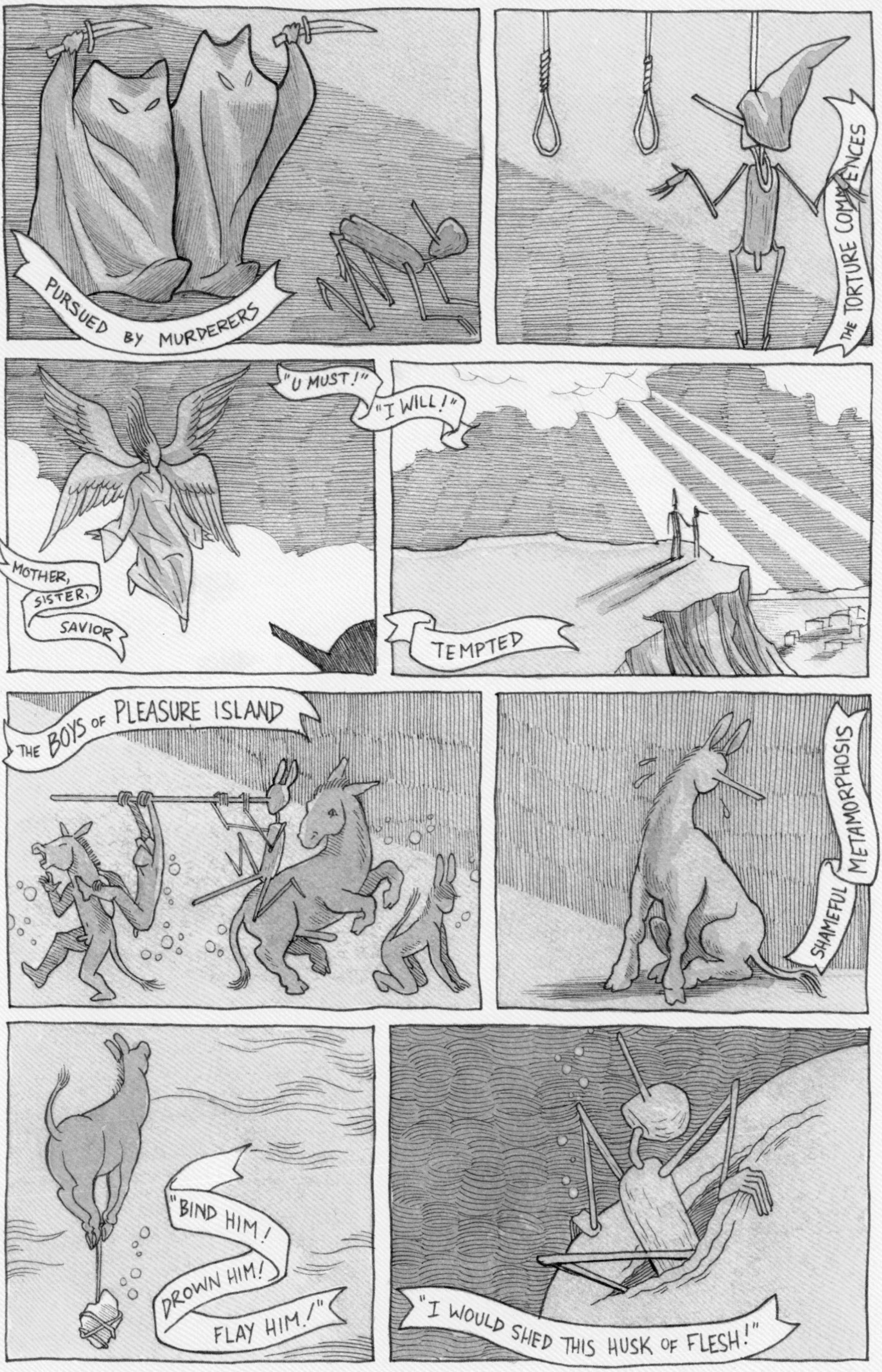
PURSUED BY MURDERERS
THE TORTURE COMMENCES
"U MUST!"
"I WILL!"
MOTHER, SISTER, SAVIOR
TEMPTED
THE BOYS OF PLEASURE ISLAND
SHAMEFUL METAMORPHOSIS
"BIND HIM! DROWN HIM! FLAY HIM!"
"I WOULD SHED THIS HUSK OF FLESH!"

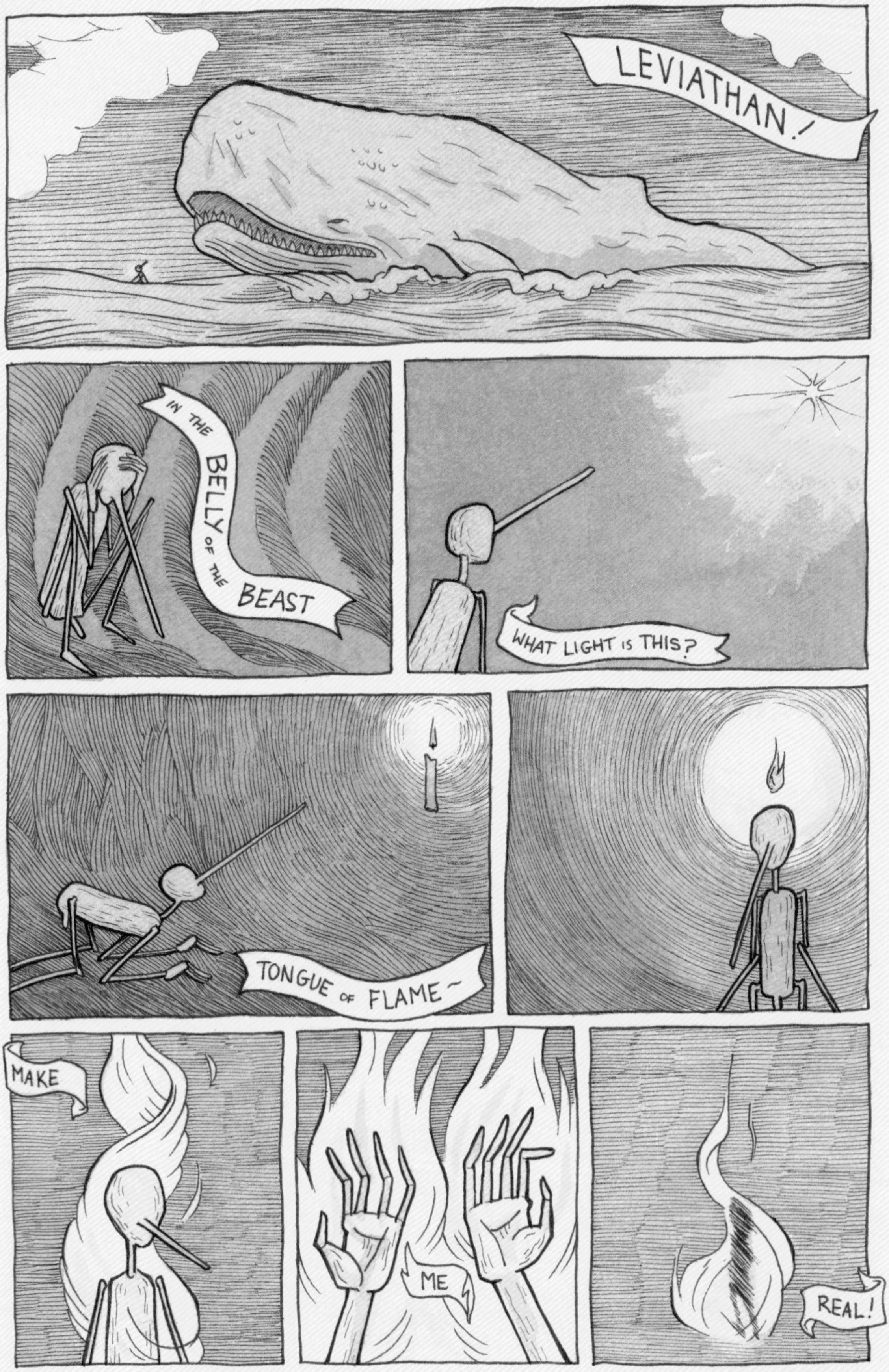
LEVIATHAN!
IN THE BELLY OF THE BEAST
WHAT LIGHT IS THIS?
TONGUE OF FLAME~
MAKE
ME
REAL!

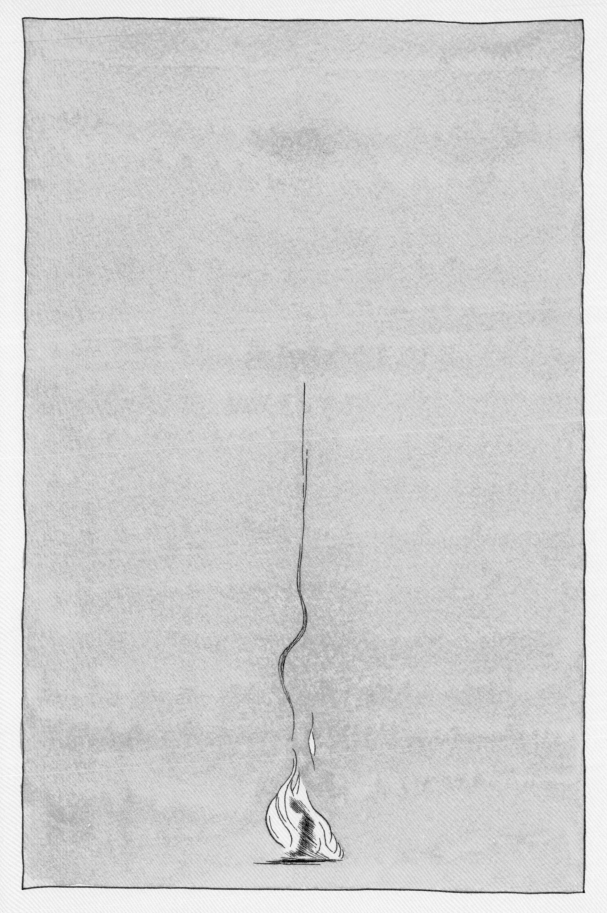

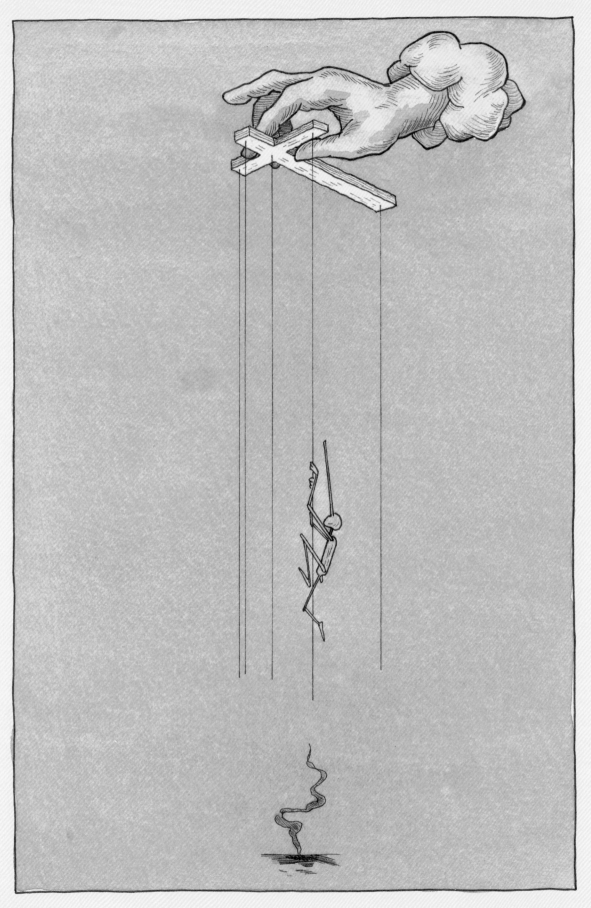

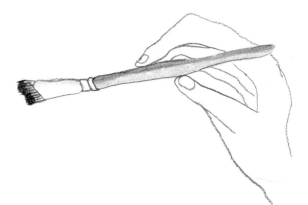

# The Boy who wanted to laugh

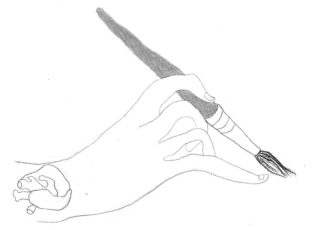

I tell you:

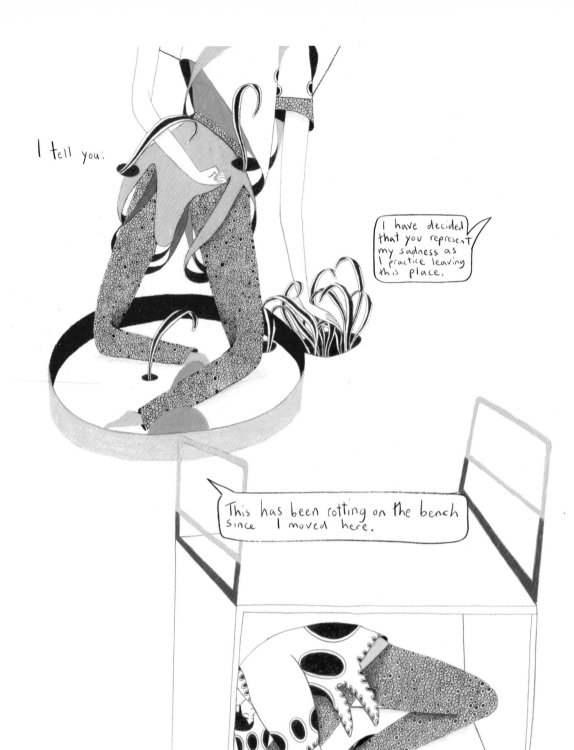

I have decided that you represent my sadness as I practice leaving this place.

This has been rotting on the bench since I moved here.

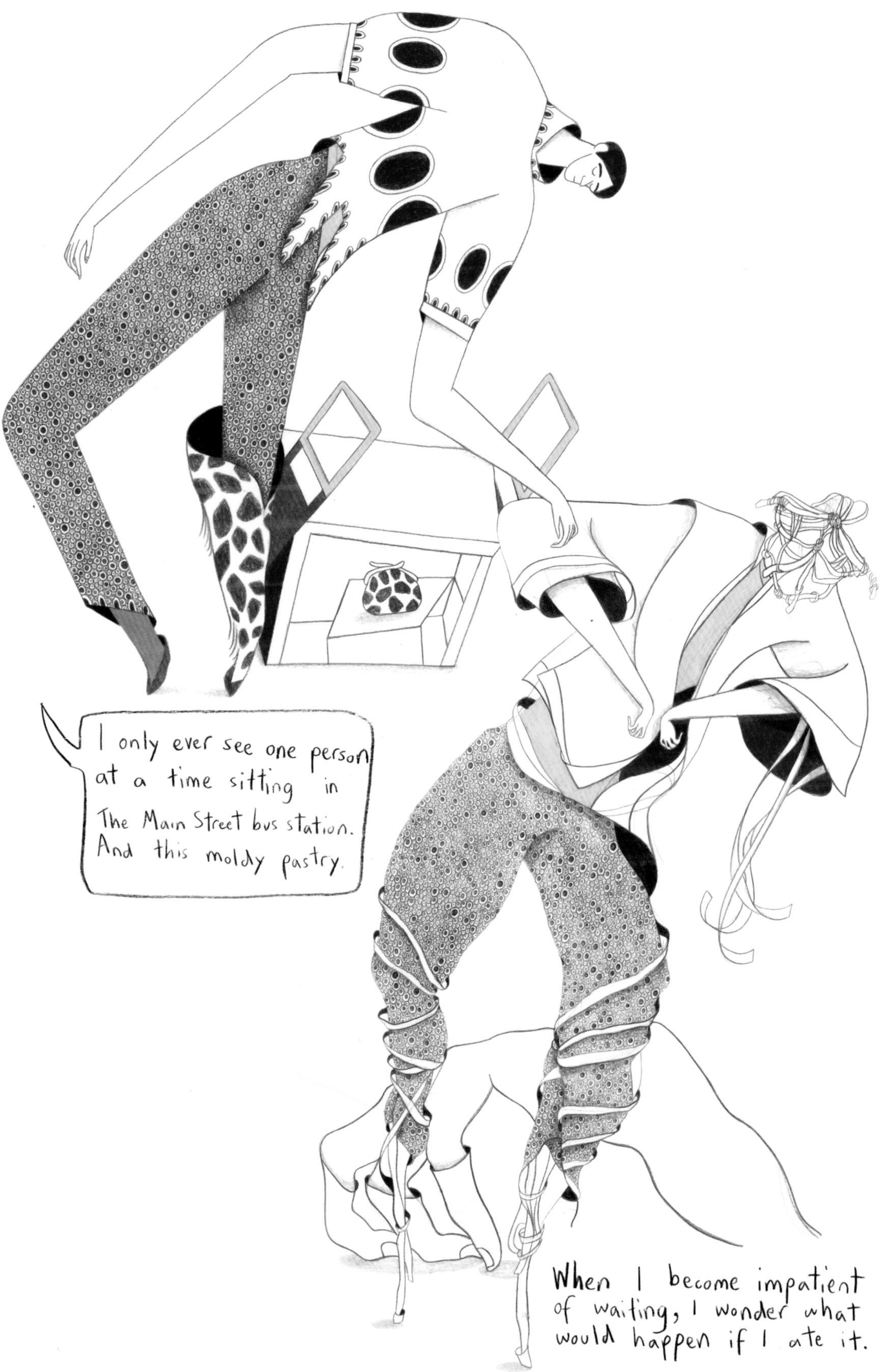
I only ever see one person at a time sitting in The Main Street bus station. And this moldy pastry.
When I become impatient of waiting, I wonder what would happen if I ate it.

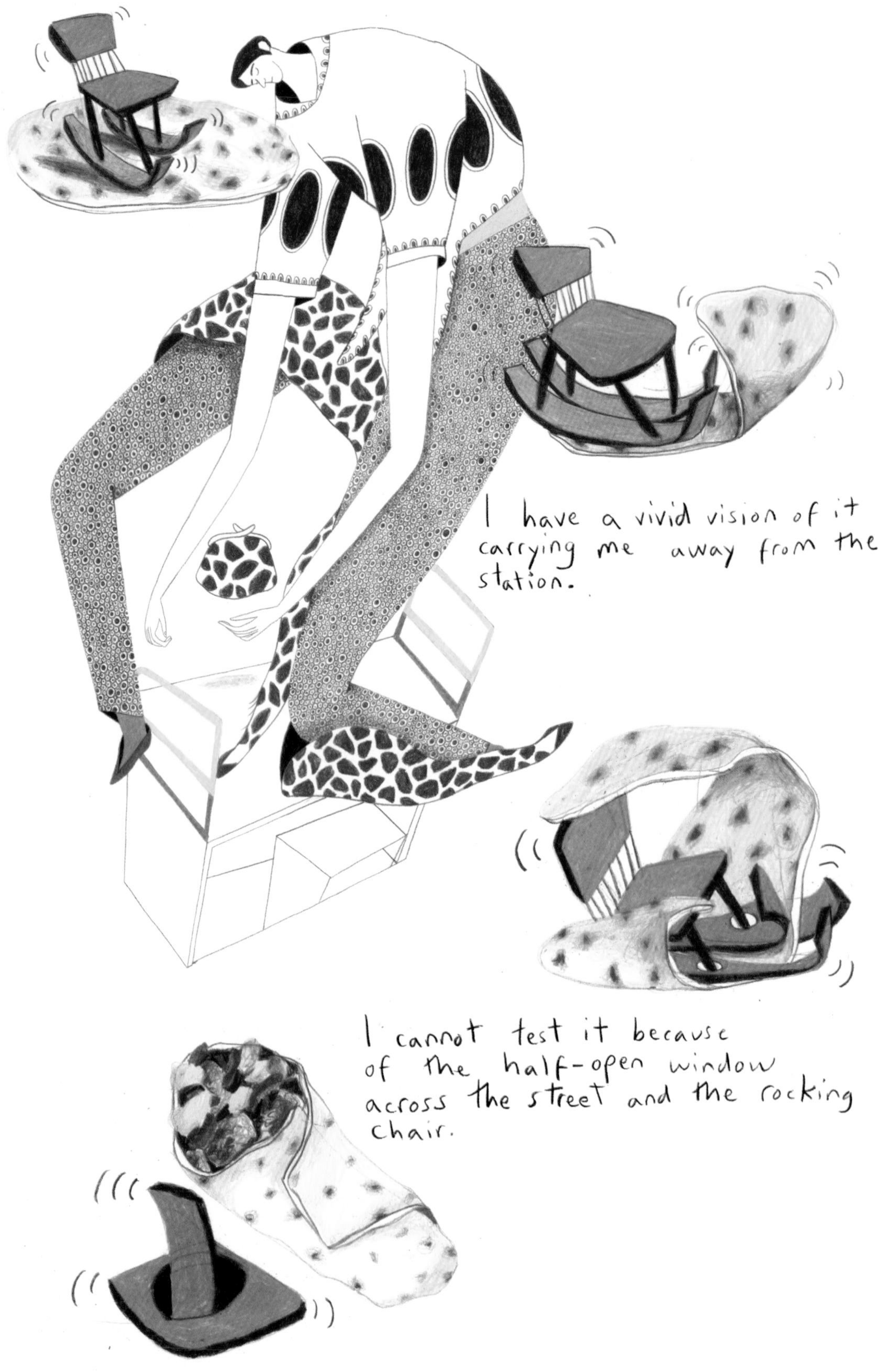
I have a vivid vision of it carrying me away from the station.
I cannot test it because of the half-open window across the street and the rocking chair.

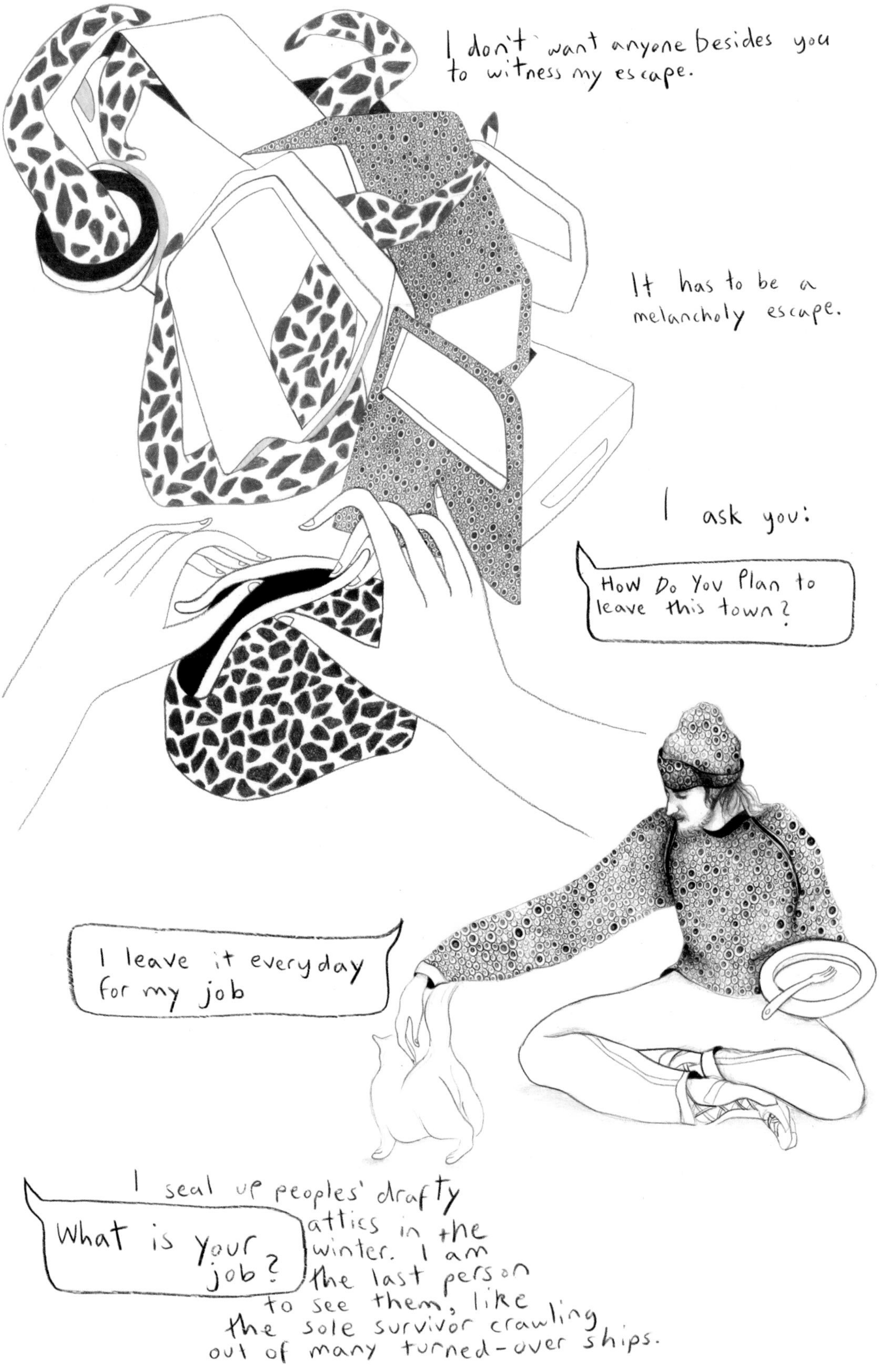
I don't want anyone besides you to witness my escape.
It has to be a melancholy escape.
I ask you:
How Do You Plan to leave this town?
I leave it everyday for my job
What is your job?
I seal up peoples' drafty attics in the winter. I am the last person to see them, like the sole survivor crawling out of many turned-over ships.

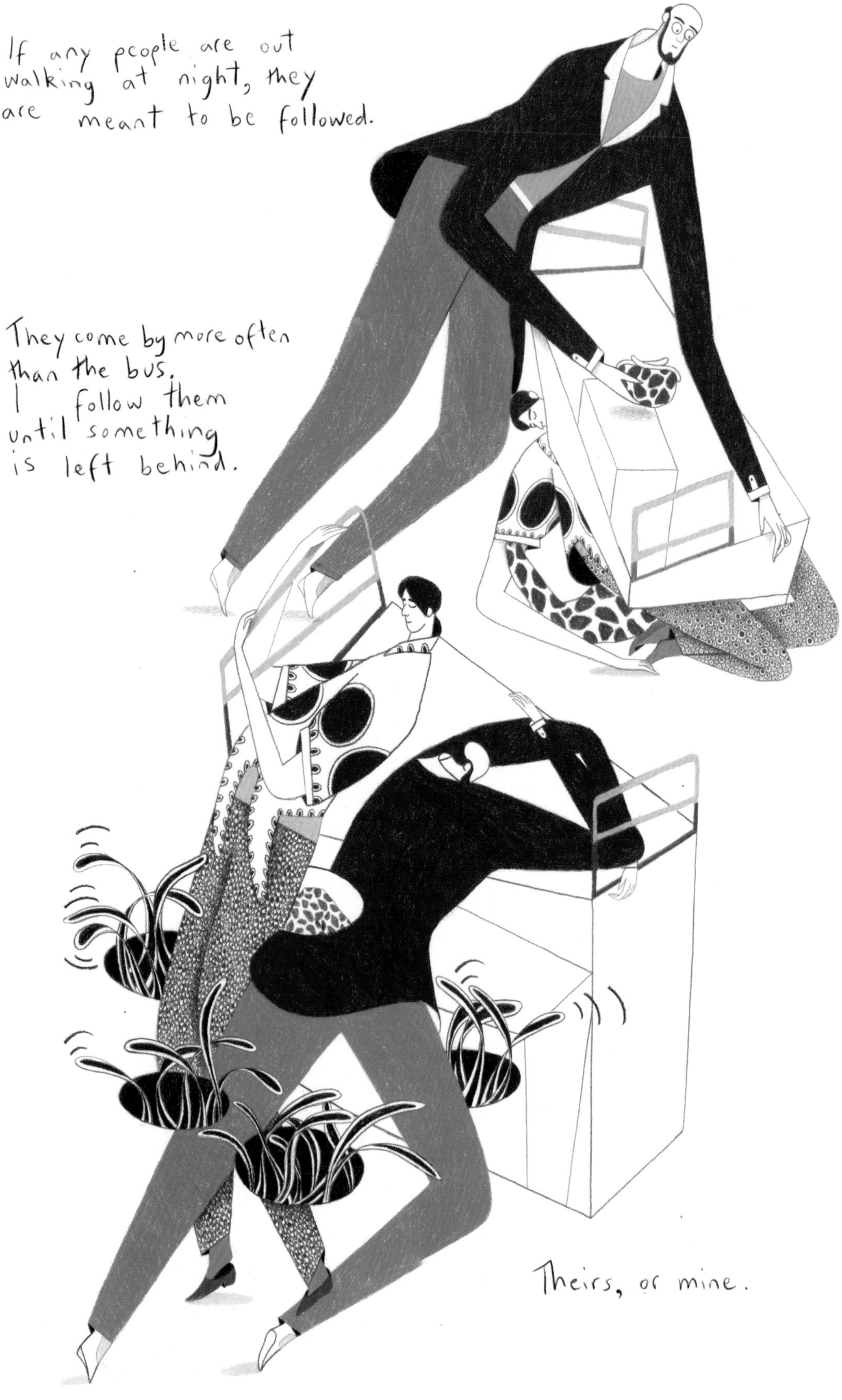
If any people are out walking at night, they are meant to be followed.
They come by more often than the bus. I follow them until something is left behind.
Theirs, or mine.

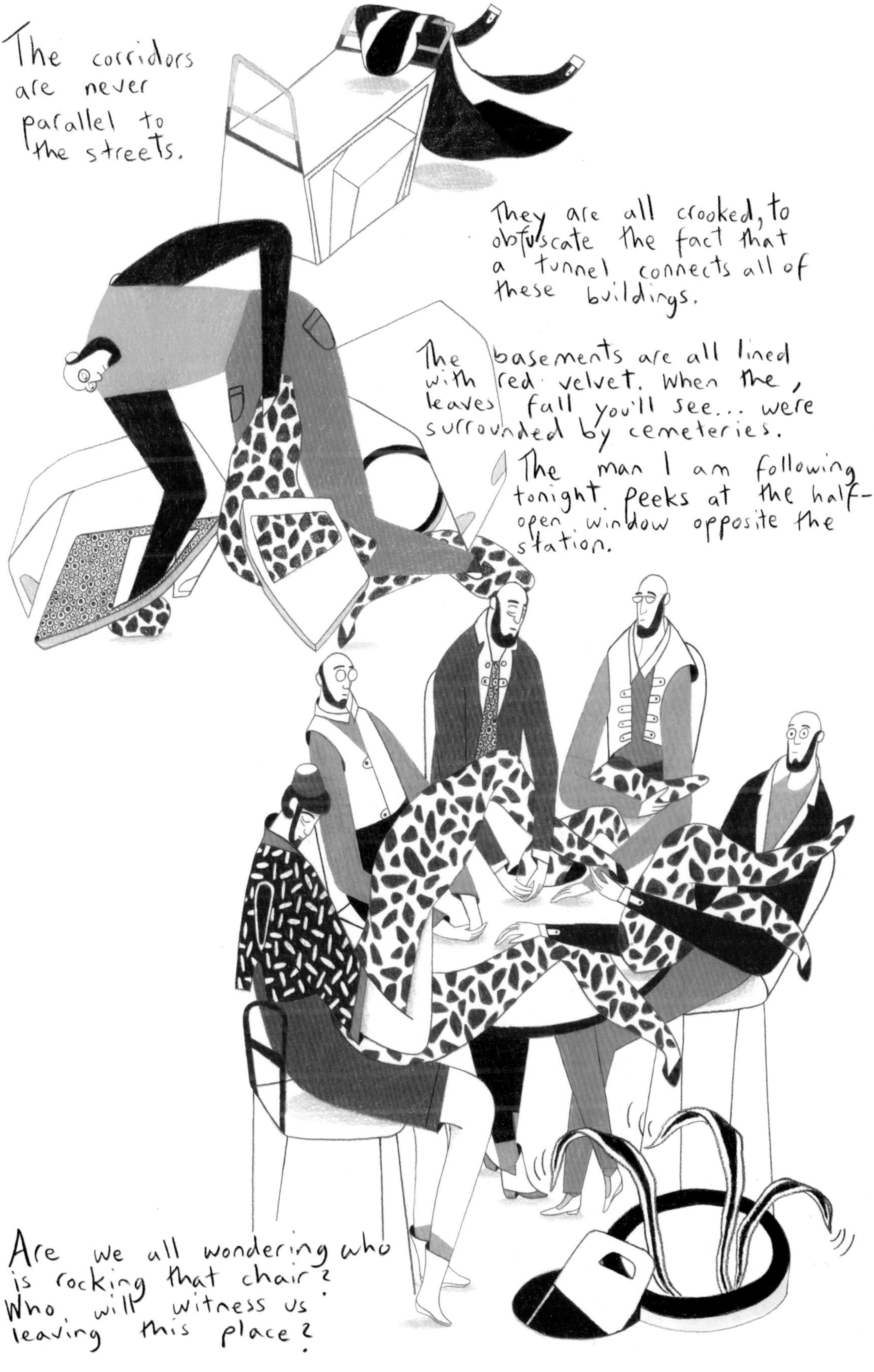
The corridors are never parallel to the streets.
They are all crooked, to obfuscate the fact that a tunnel connects all of these buildings.
The basements are all lined with red velvet. When the leaves fall you'll see... we're surrounded by cemeteries.
The man I am following tonight peeks at the half-open window opposite the station.
Are we all wondering who is rocking that chair? Who will witness us leaving this place?

The following night,
I am sitting in the communal
kitchen of the hostel reading
a twenty-year-old National
Geographic.

No one
is walking outside.

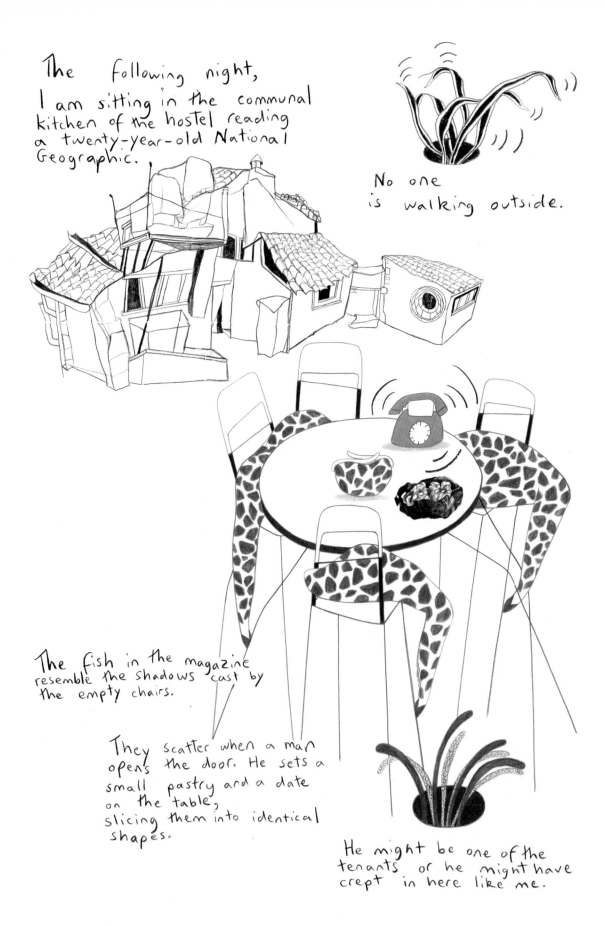

The fish in the magazine
resemble the shadows cast by
the empty chairs.

They scatter when a man
opens the door. He sets a
small pastry and a date
on the table,
slicing them into identical
shapes.

He might be one of the
tenants or he might have
crept in here like me.

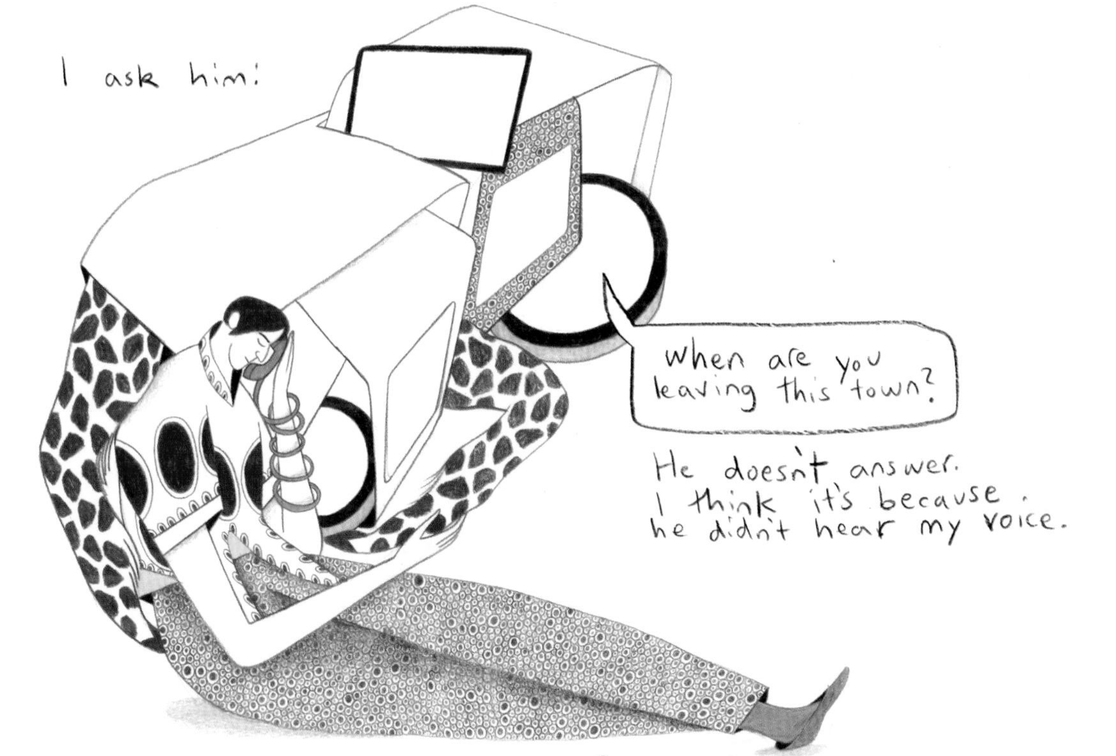
I ask him:
When are you leaving this town?
He doesn't answer. I think it's because he didn't hear my voice.

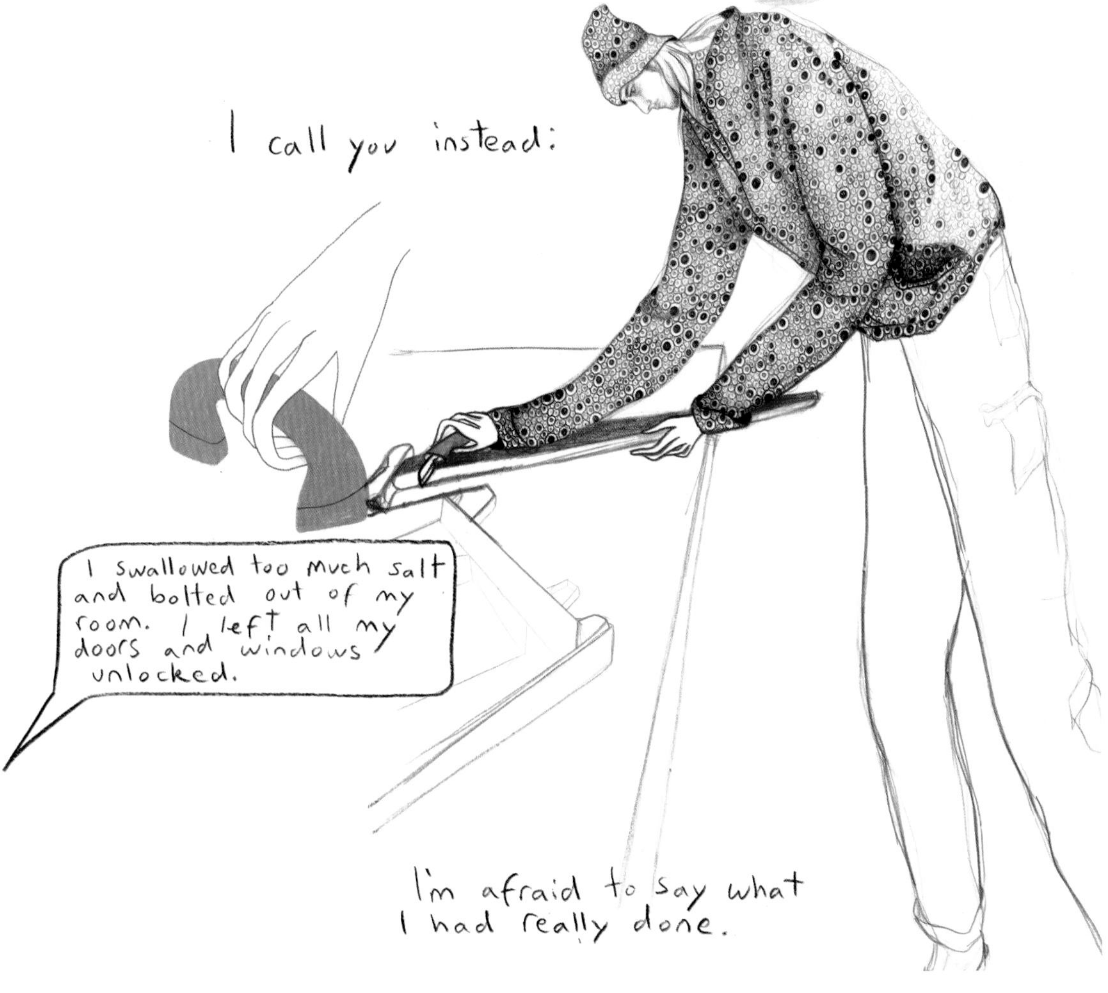
I call you instead:
I swallowed too much salt and bolted out of my room. I left all my doors and windows unlocked.
I'm afraid to say what I had really done.

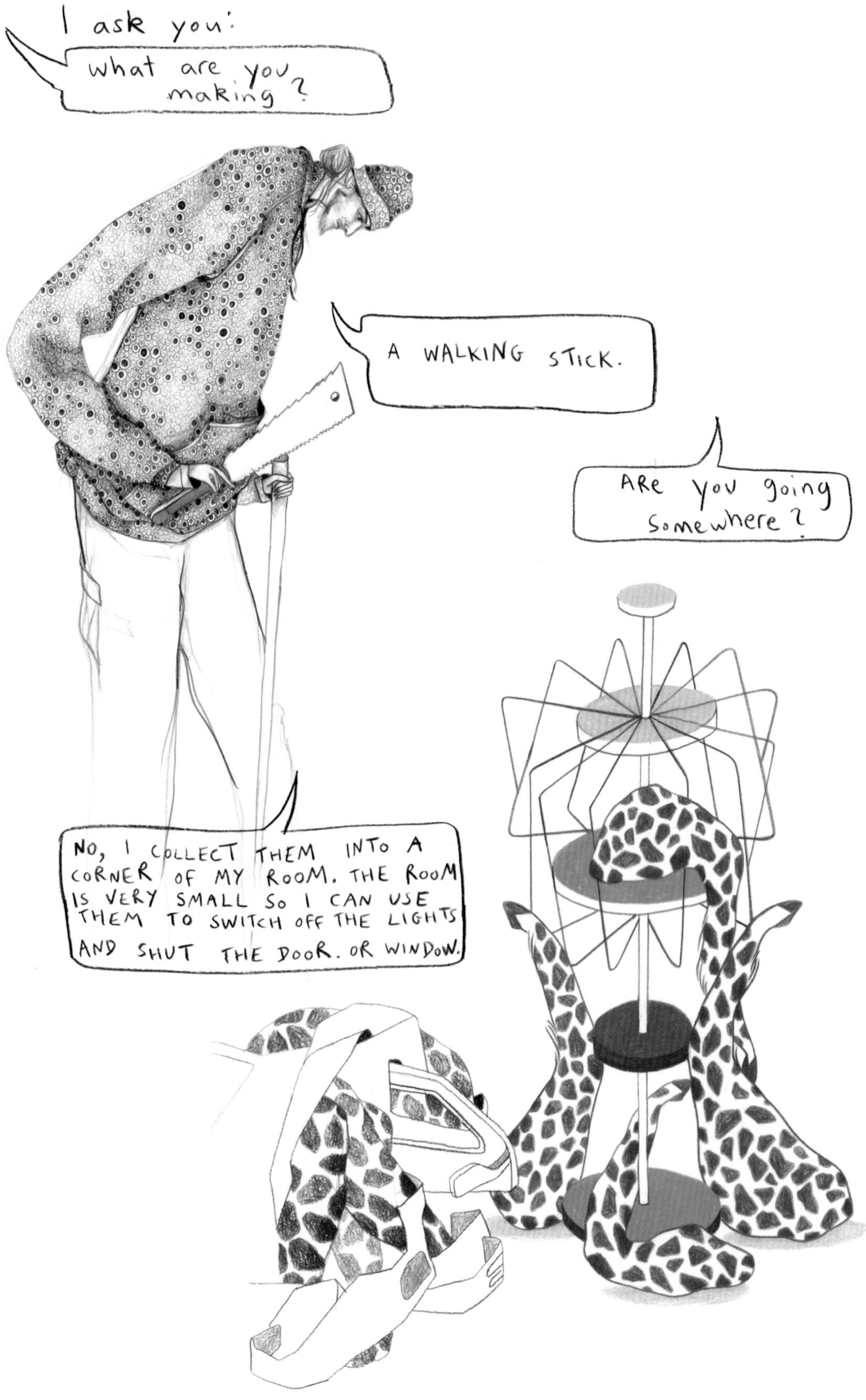
I ask you:
what are you making?
A WALKING STICK.
ARE you going somewhere?
NO, I COLLECT THEM INTO A CORNER OF MY ROOM. THE ROOM IS VERY SMALL SO I CAN USE THEM TO SWITCH OFF THE LIGHTS AND SHUT THE DOOR. OR WINDOW.

On Saturday we drive to a
location 45 minutes away.
I'm standing on a ramp midway
through construction.

The house is full of
sleep and surrounded by
a forest full of snow.

Two horses are required
to appear for balance.

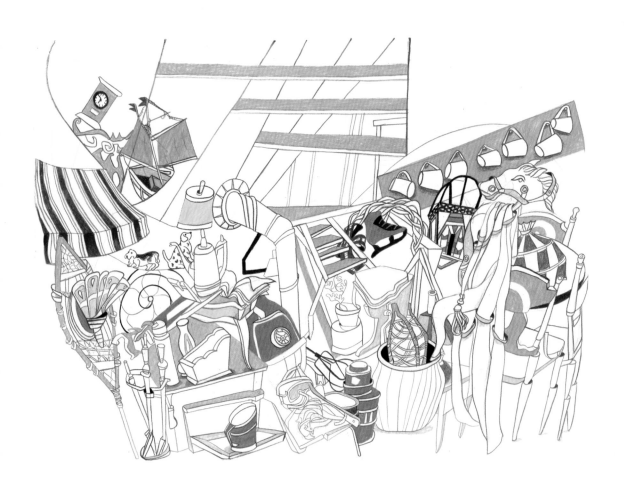

And they do.

We fill the basement with
firewood. I enjoy the
weight of the wheelbarrow.
It is unmeasurable between the
two of us walking.

We seal off the attic forever.
I make a list of what was
left in there.

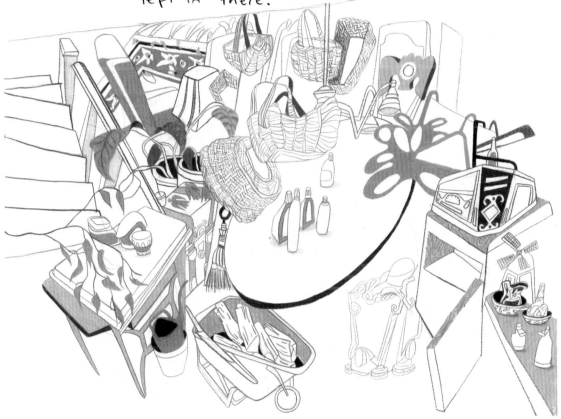

Baskets.

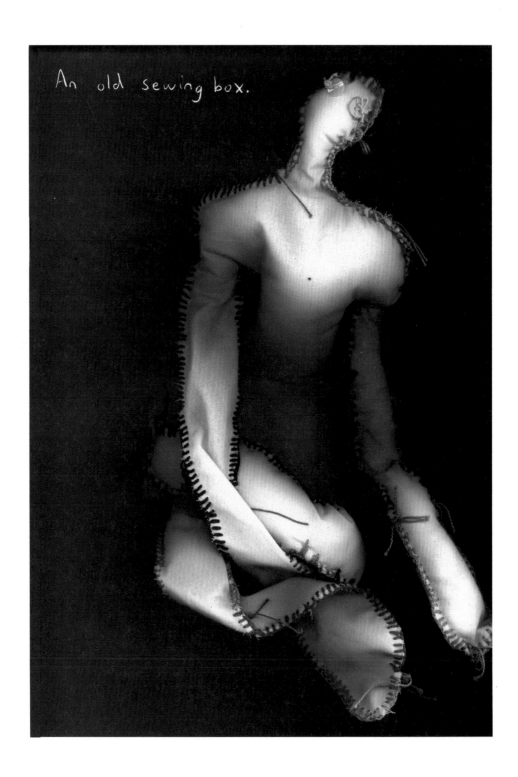

An old sewing box.

You drop me off at The Main Street bus stop and I remember more things that were sealed off in there.

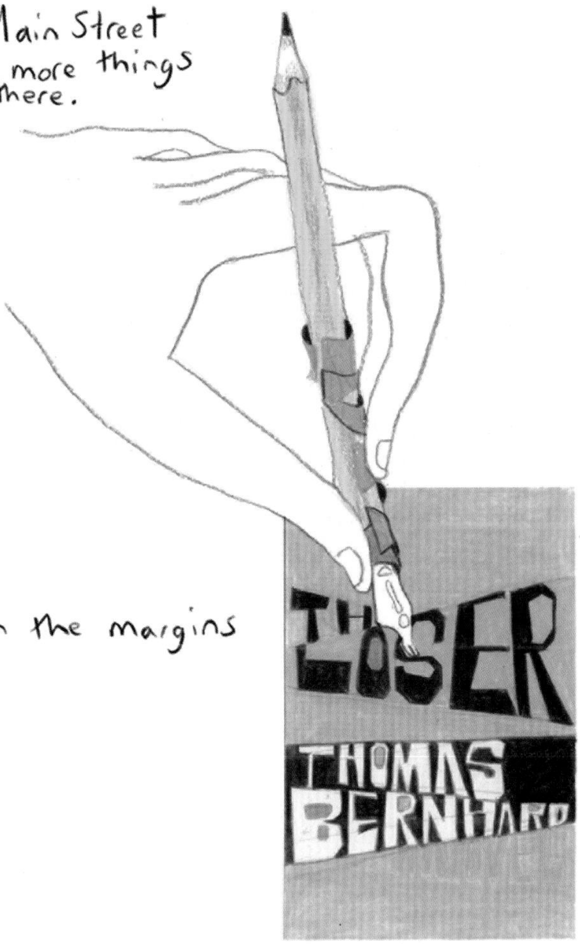
LOSER
THOMAS
BERNHARD

I write them down in the margins of a book.

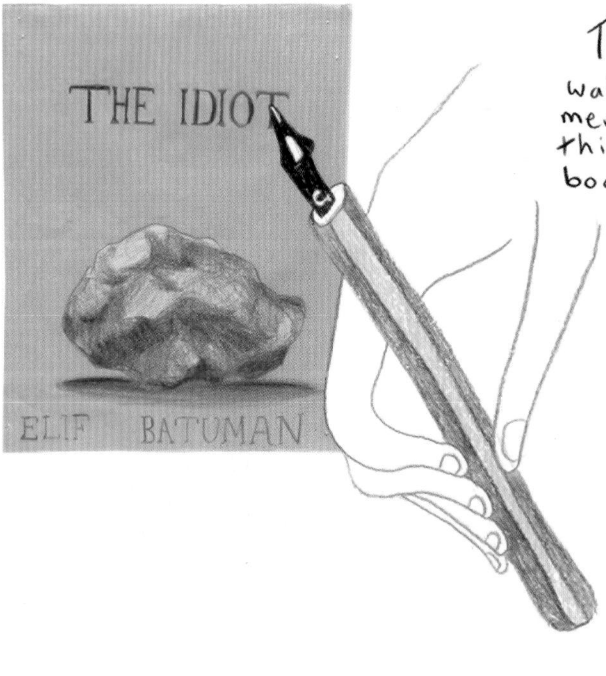
THE IDIOT
ELIF BATUMAN

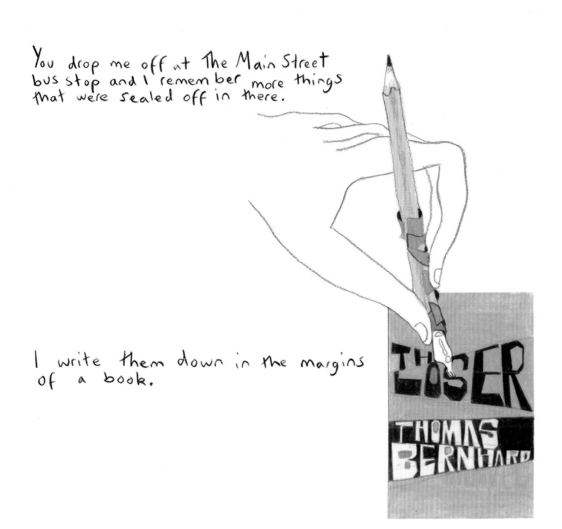

The next day, I wake up with the memory of one more thing, but I forget what book I wrote in.

The attic we left behind
is populated with more and
more things I seem to
remember.

There is almost no room
left in it for all the
things I collect at the
foot of my dreams.

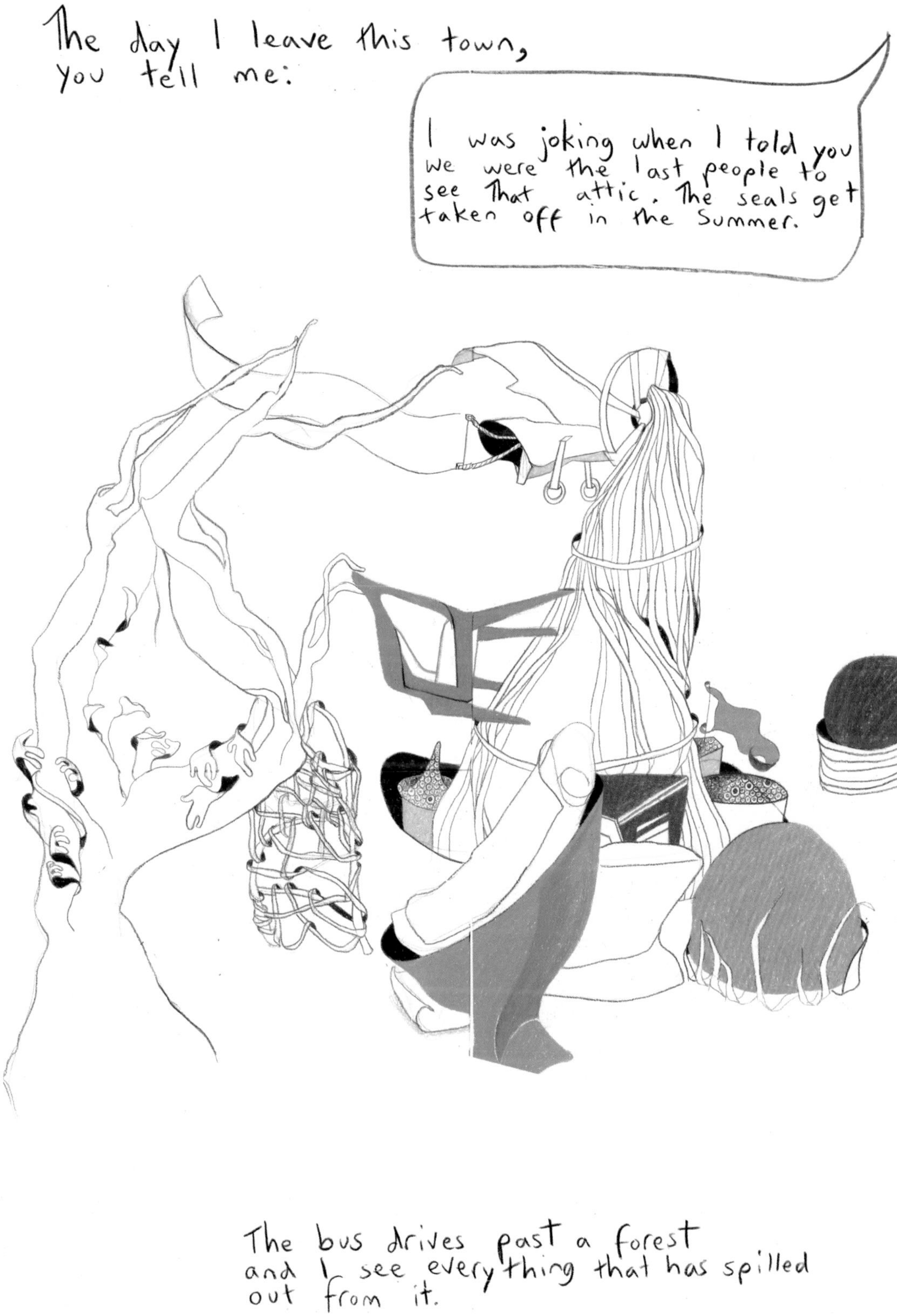
The day I leave this town, you tell me:
I was joking when I told you we were the last people to see That attic. The seals get taken off in the Summer.
The bus drives past a forest and I see everything that has spilled out from it.

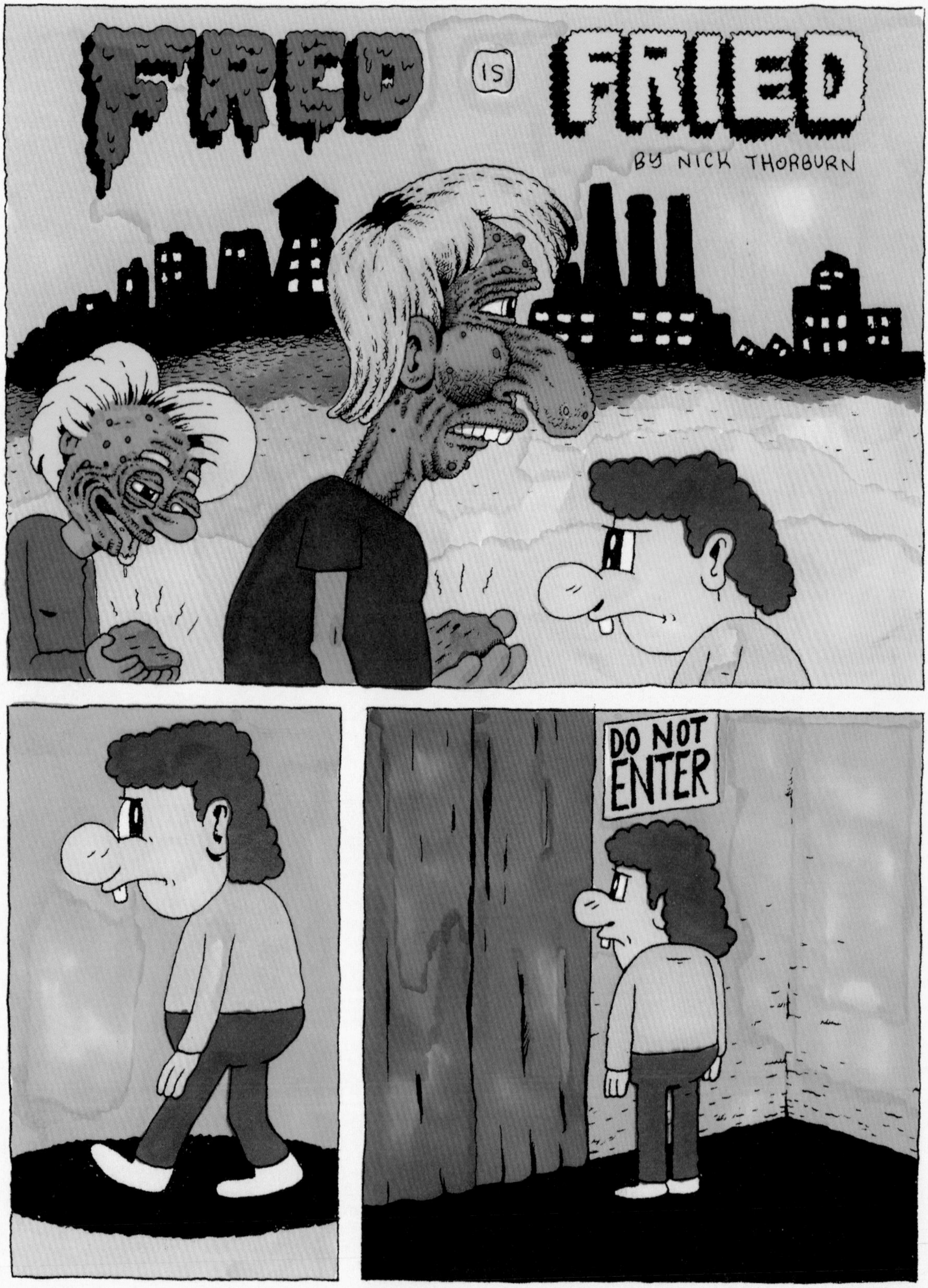
FRED IS FRIED
BY NICK THORBURN
DO NOT ENTER

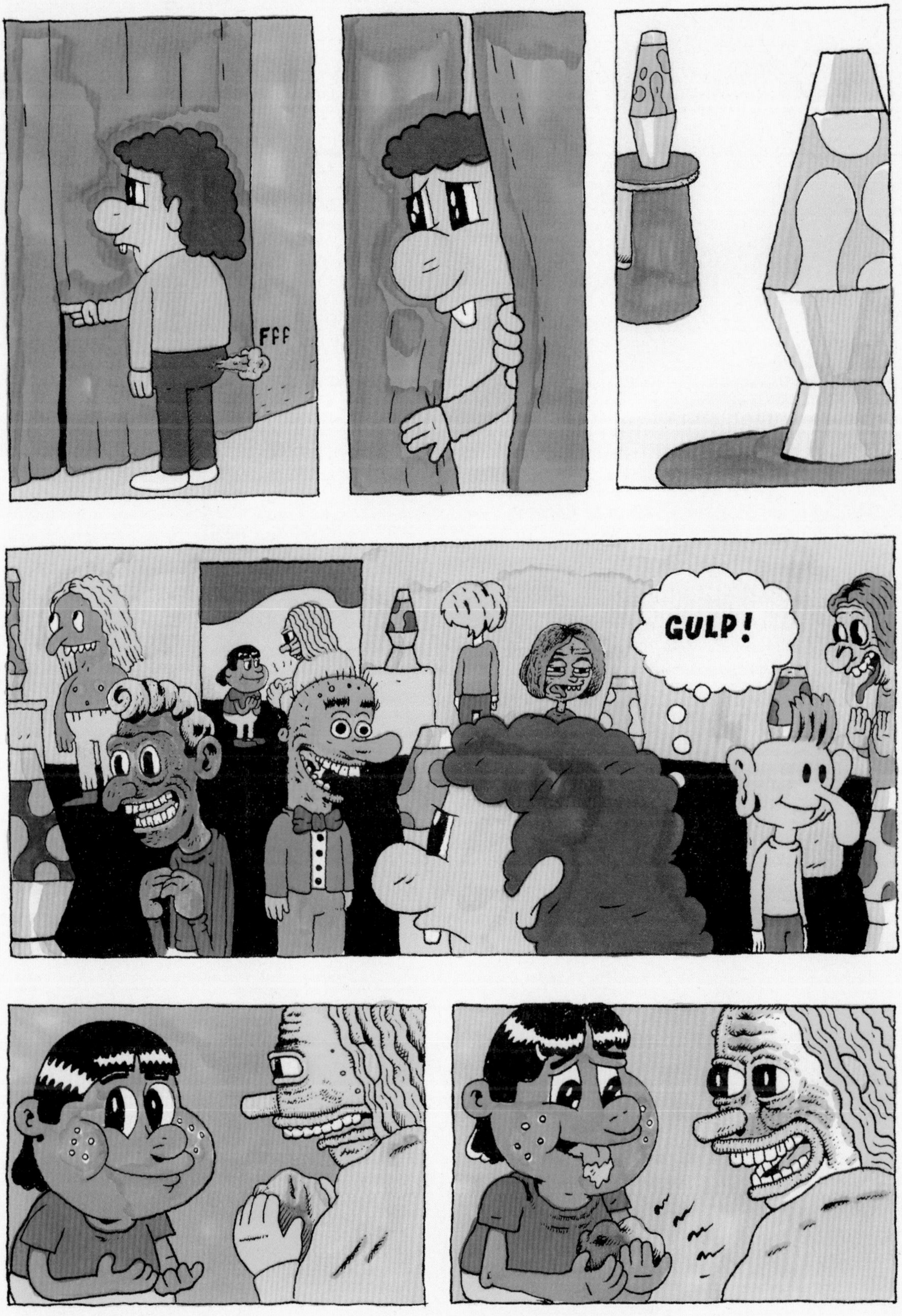
FFF
GULP!

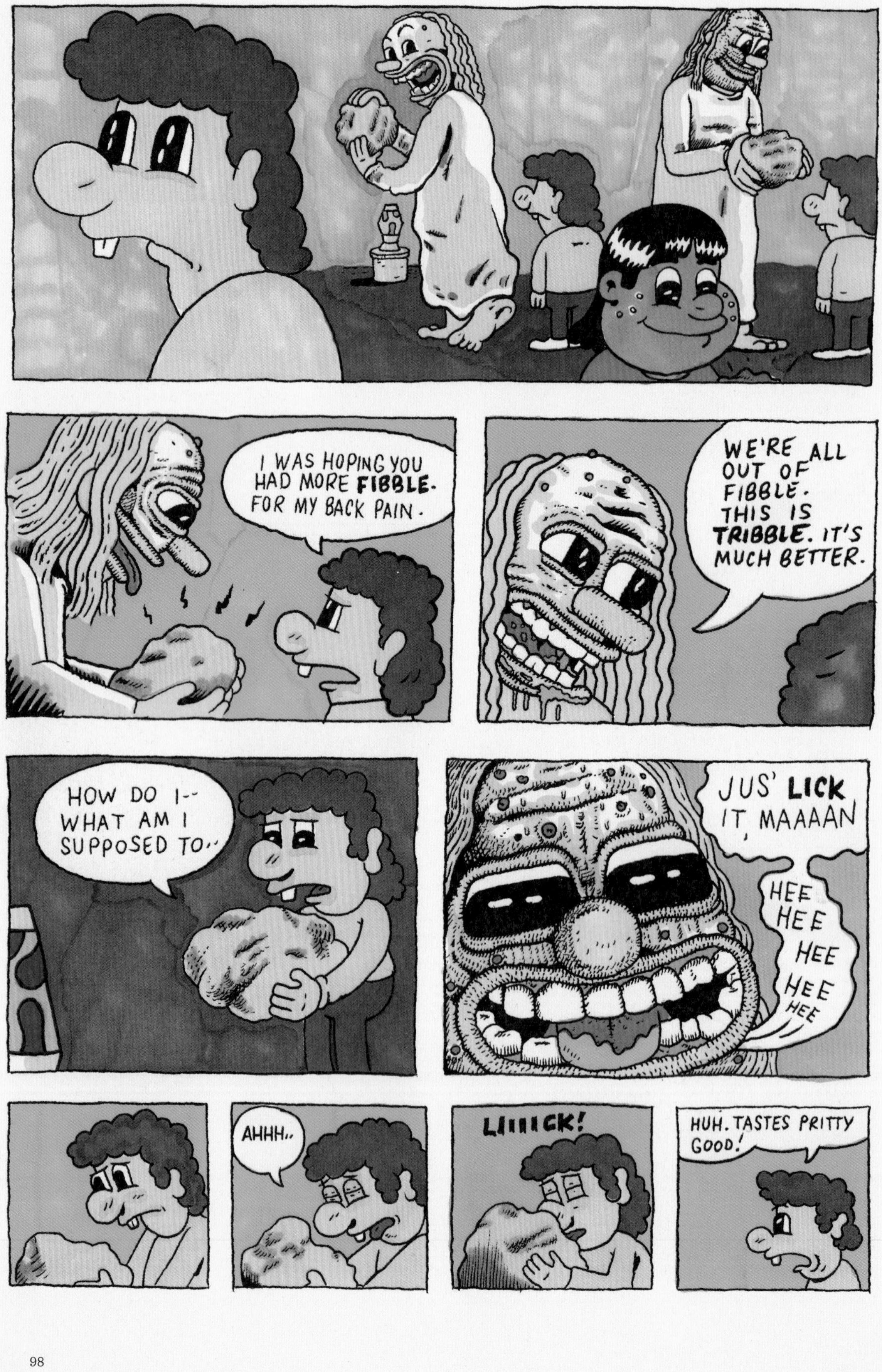
I WAS HOPING YOU HAD MORE FIBBLE. FOR MY BACK PAIN.
WE'RE ALL OUT OF FIBBLE. THIS IS TRIBBLE. IT'S MUCH BETTER.
HOW DO I-- WHAT AM I SUPPOSED TO..
JUS' LICK IT, MAAAAN
HEE HEE HEE HEE HEE
AHHH..
LIIIICK!
HUH. TASTES PRITTY GOOD!

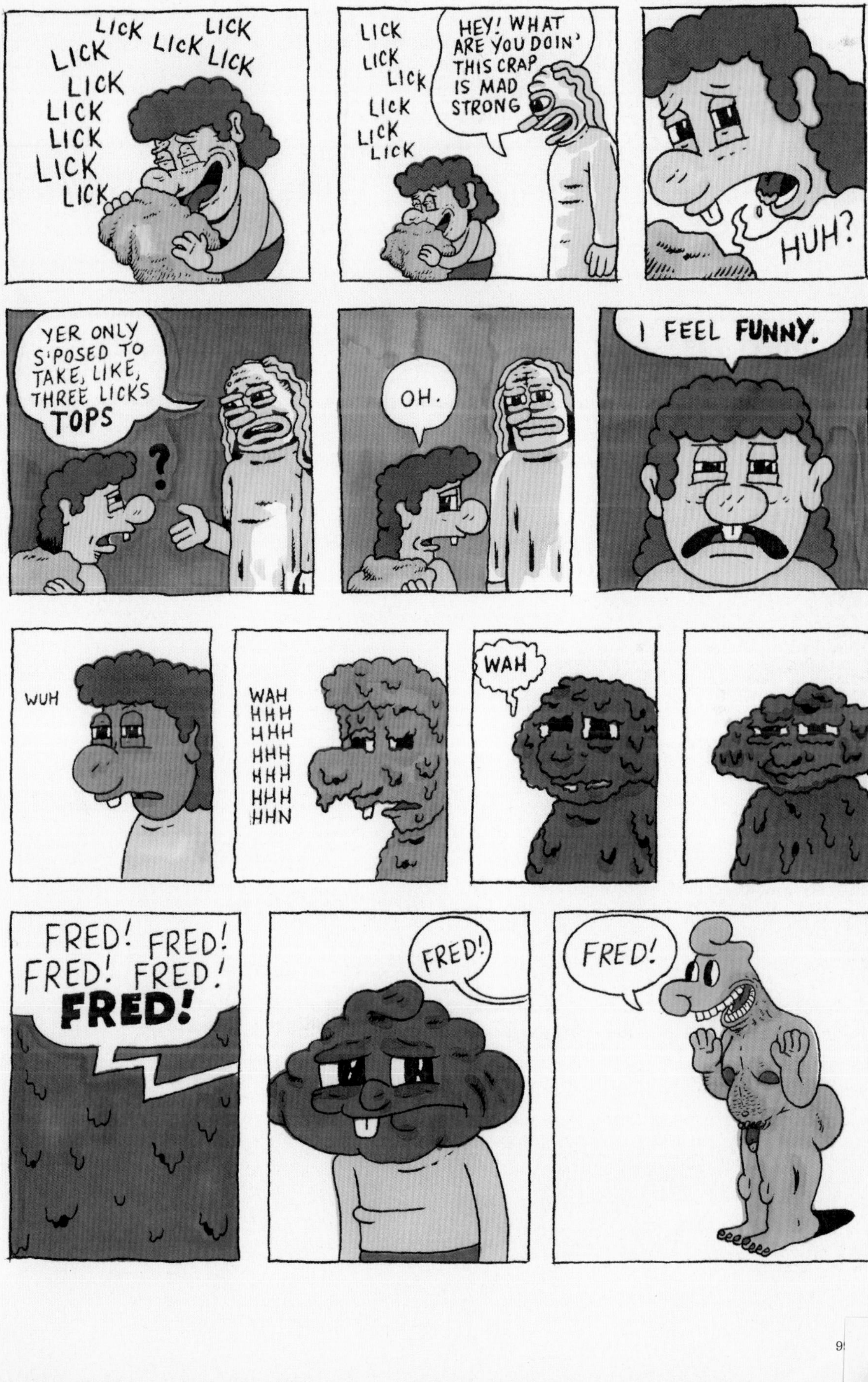
LICK LICK LICK LICK LICK LICK LICK LICK LICK LICK
LICK LICK LICK LICK LICK LICK
HEY! WHAT ARE YOU DOIN' THIS CRAP IS MAD STRONG
HUH?
YER ONLY S'POSED TO TAKE, LIKE, THREE LICKS TOPS
?
OH.
I FEEL FUNNY.
WUH
WAH HHH HHH HHH HHH HHH HHN
WAH
FRED! FRED! FRED! FRED! FRED!
FRED!
FRED!

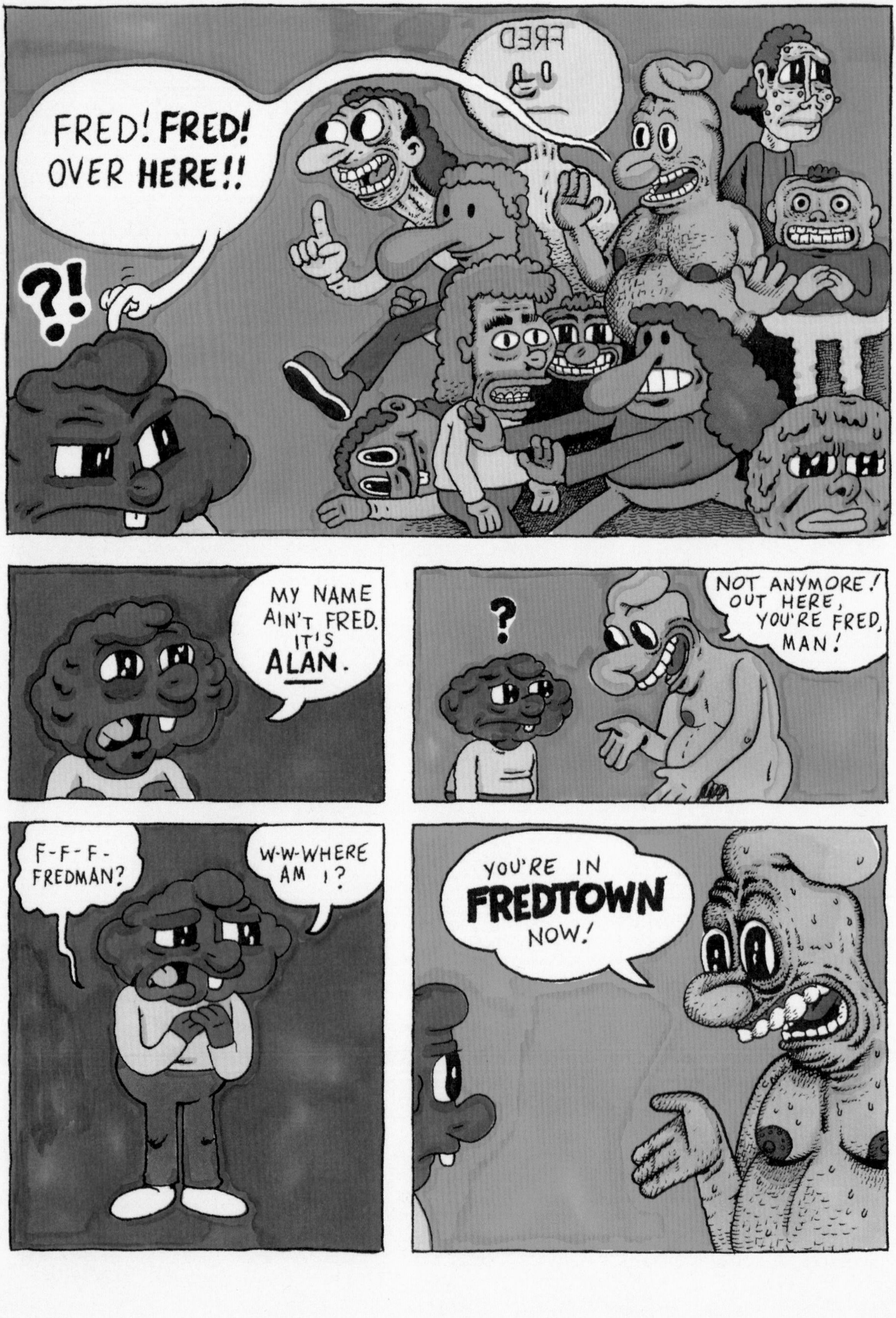
FRED
FRED! FRED! OVER HERE!!
?!
MY NAME AIN'T FRED. IT'S ALAN.
?
NOT ANYMORE! OUT HERE, YOU'RE FRED, MAN!
F-F-F-FREDMAN?
W-W-WHERE AM I?
YOU'RE IN FREDTOWN NOW!

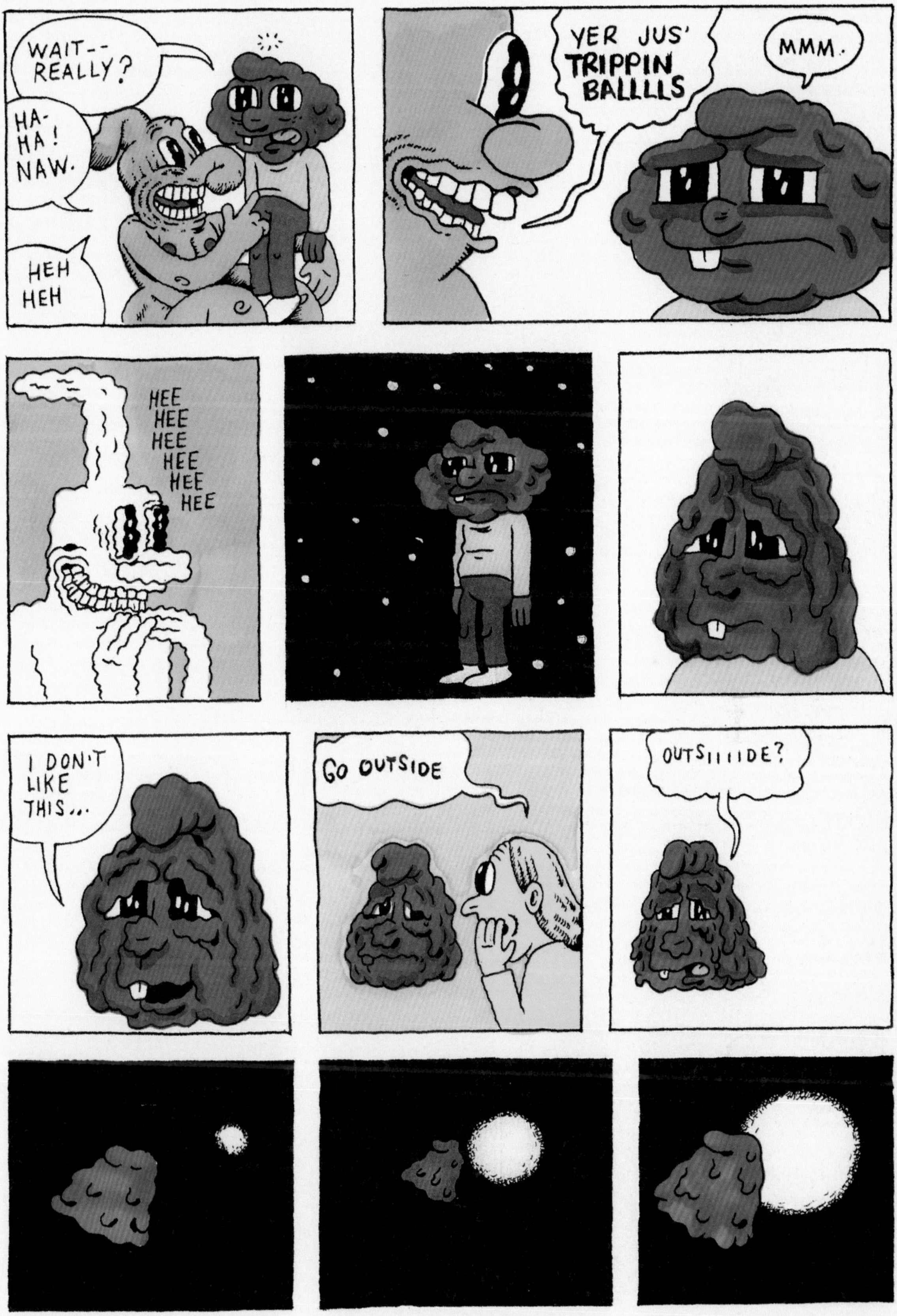
WAIT--
REALLY?
HA-HA! NAW.
HEH HEH
YER JUS' TRIPPIN BALLLLS
MMM.
HEE HEE HEE HEE HEE HEE
I DON'T LIKE THIS...
GO OUTSIDE
OUTSIIIIDE?

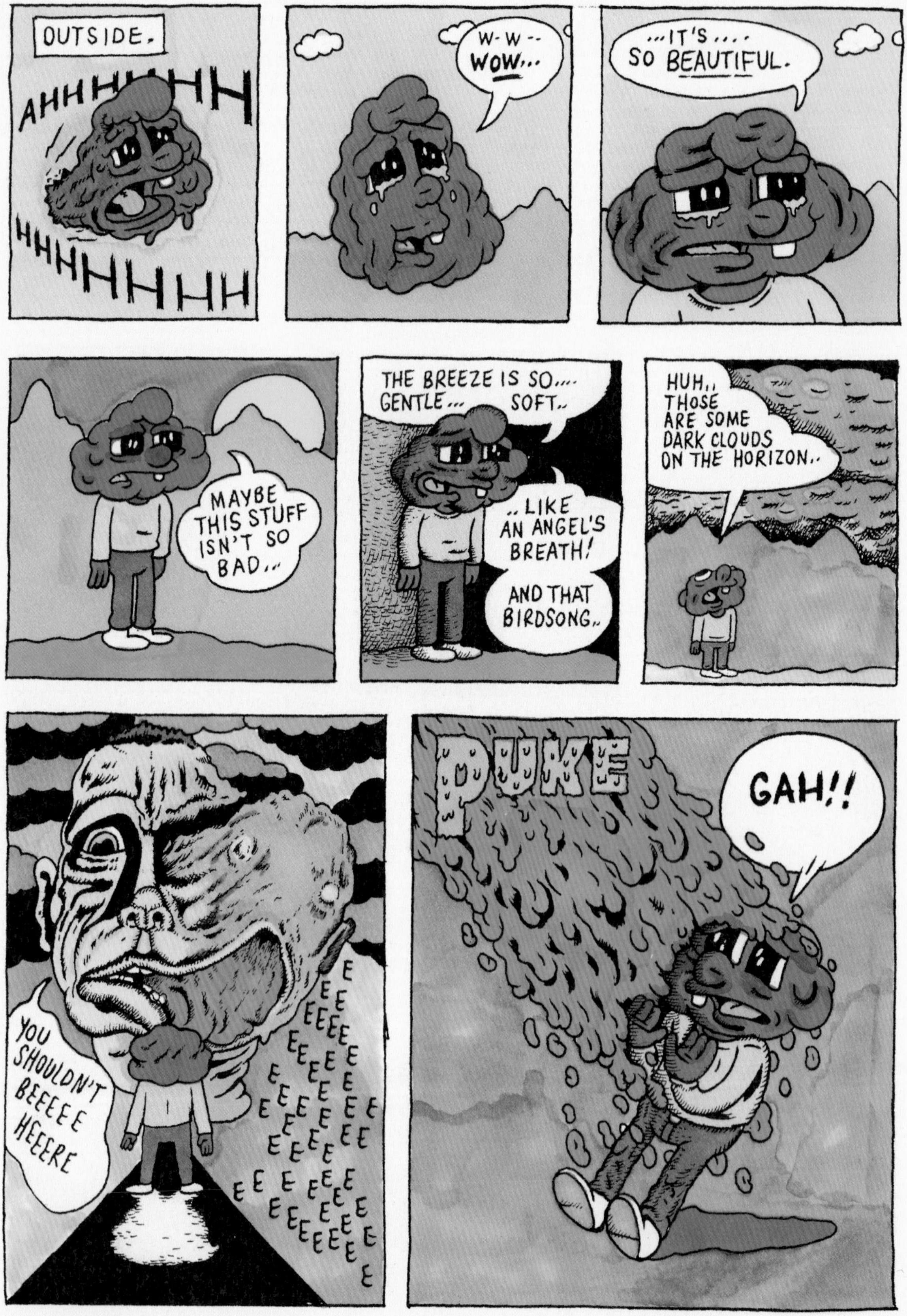
OUTSIDE.
AHHHHHHH
HHHHHHHH
W-W-- WOW,..
...IT'S.... SO BEAUTIFUL.
MAYBE THIS STUFF ISN'T SO BAD..
THE BREEZE IS SO.... GENTLE... SOFT..
..LIKE AN ANGEL'S BREATH!
AND THAT BIRDSONG..
HUH.. THOSE ARE SOME DARK CLOUDS ON THE HORIZON..
YOU SHOULDN'T BEEEEE HEEERE
EEEEEEEEEEEEEEEEEEEEEEEEEEEE
PUKE
GAH!!

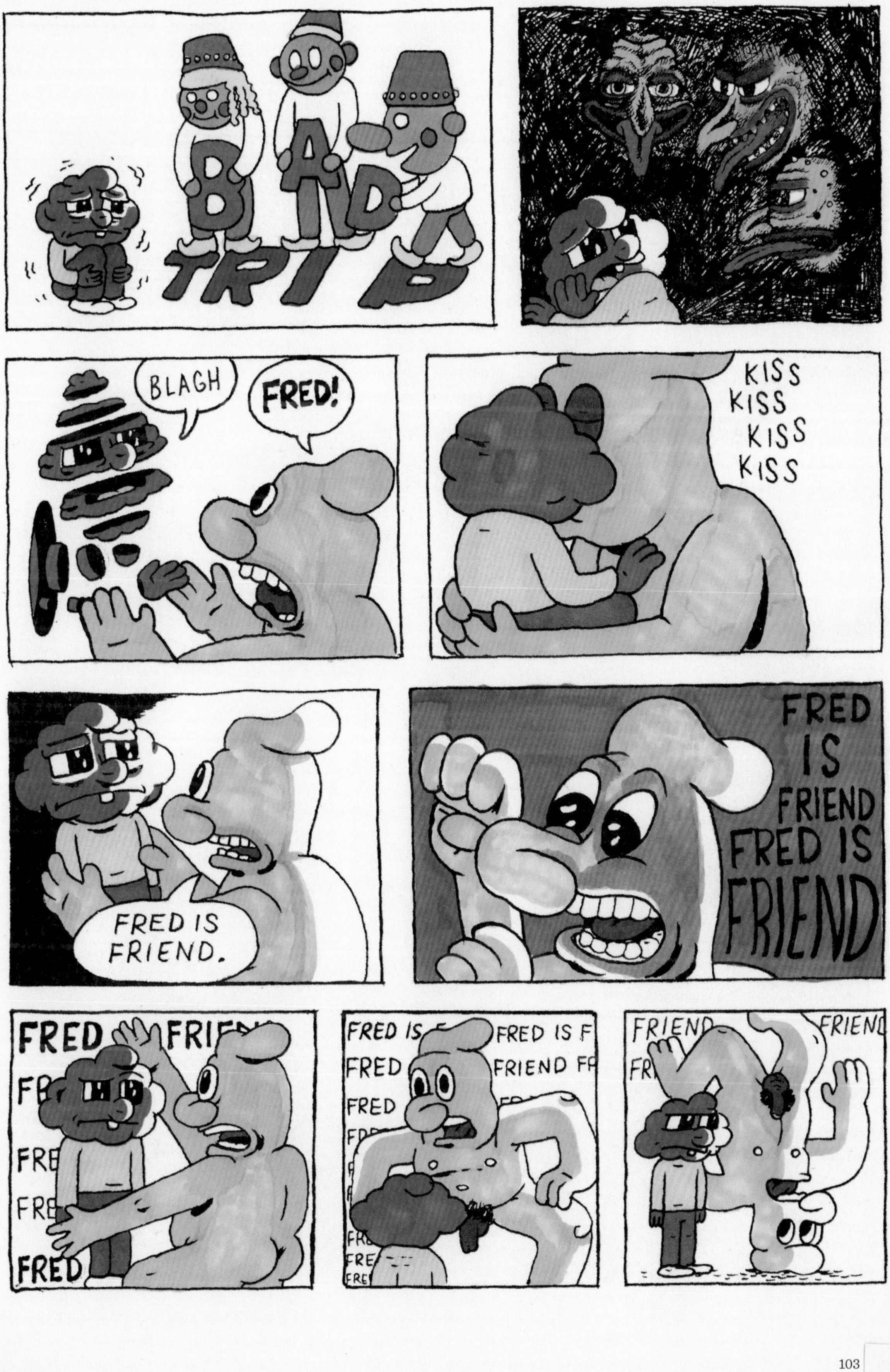
BAD
TRIP
BLAGH
FRED!
KISS
KISS
KISS
KISS
FRED IS FRIEND.
FRED IS FRIEND FRED IS FRIEND
FRED
FRED
FRED IS
FRED
FRED
FRED IS F
FRIEND
FRIEND

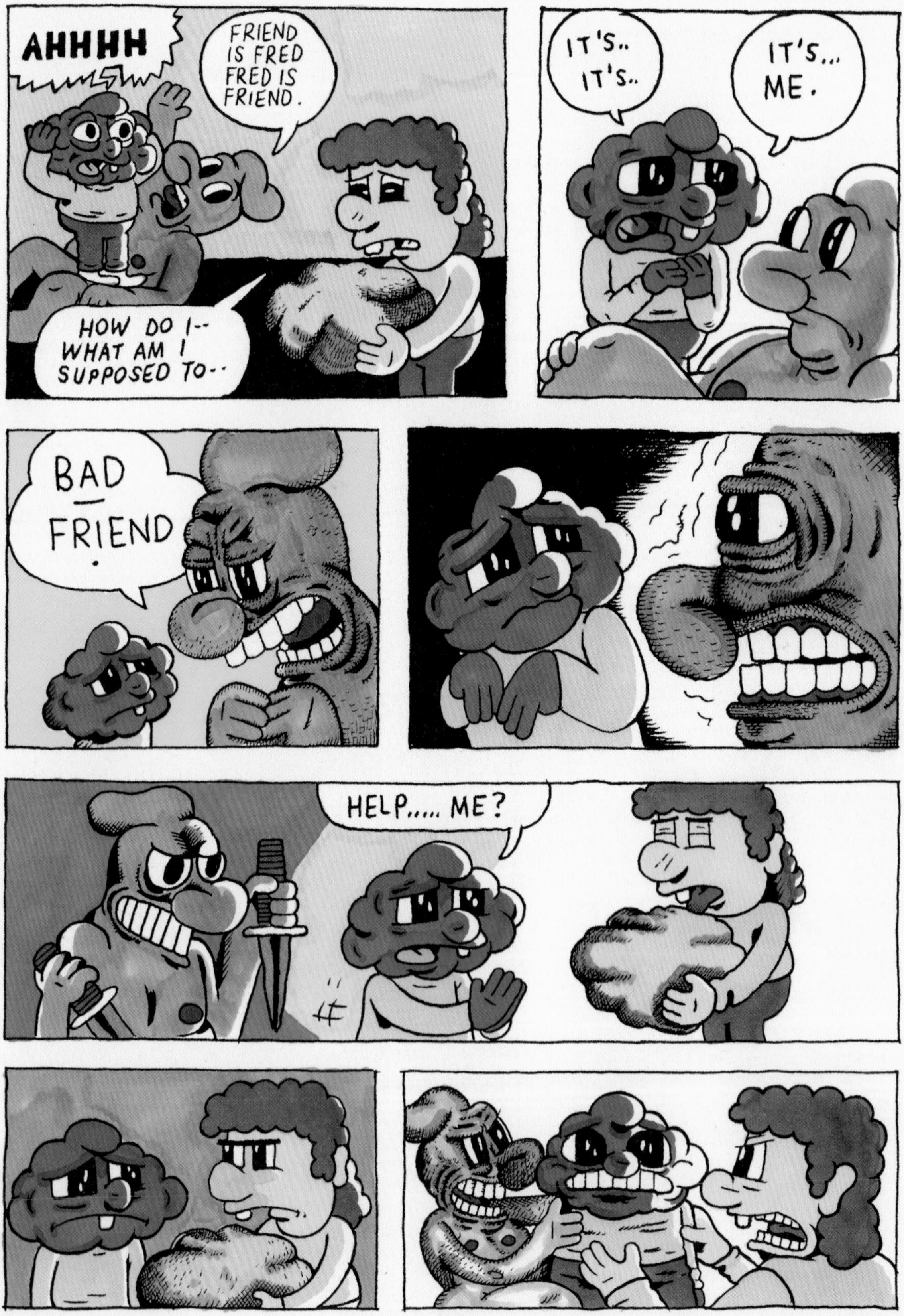
AHHHH
FRIEND IS FRED FRED IS FRIEND.
HOW DO I-- WHAT AM I SUPPOSED TO--
IT'S.. IT'S..
IT'S... ME.
BAD FRIEND.
HELP..... ME?

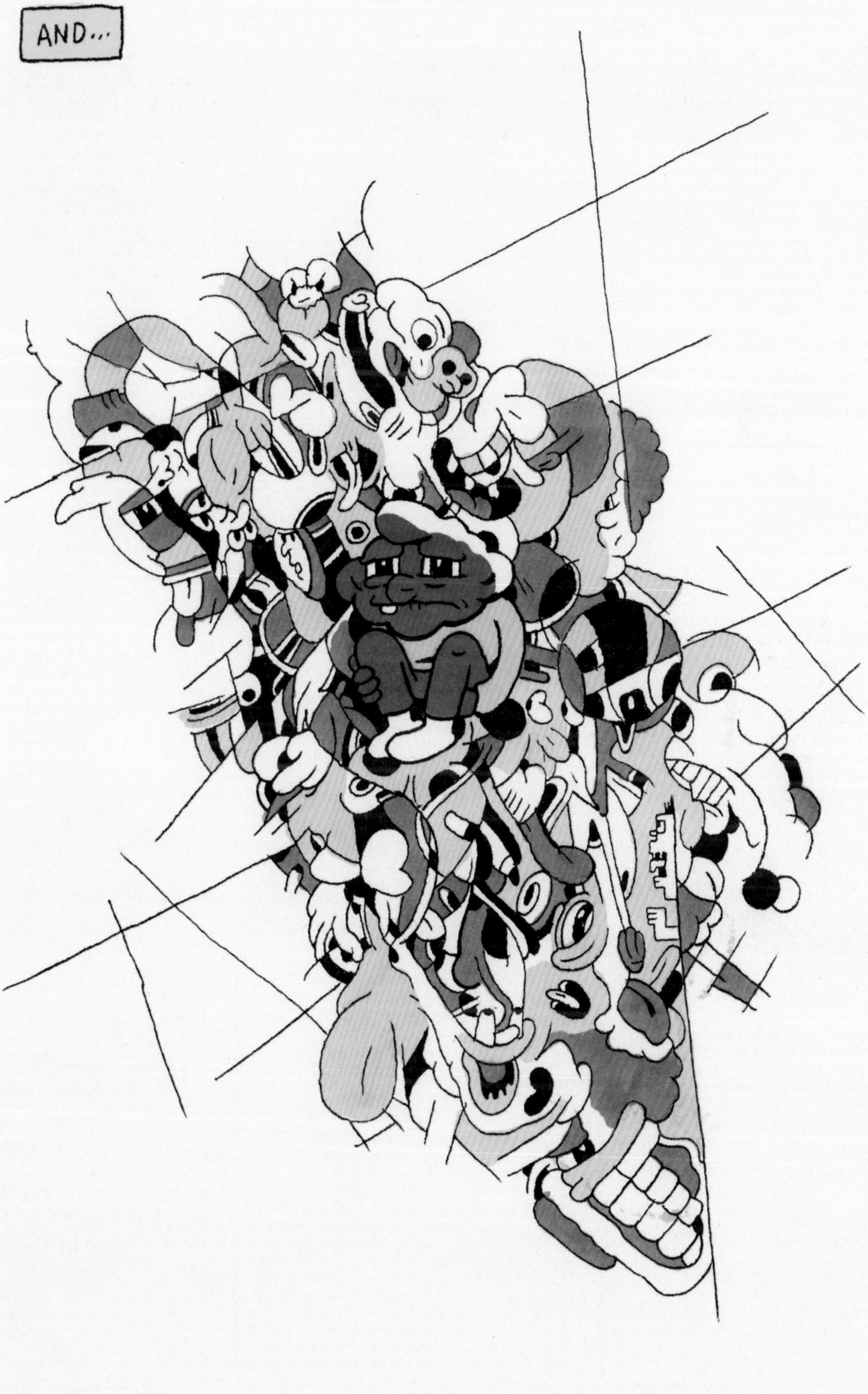
AND...

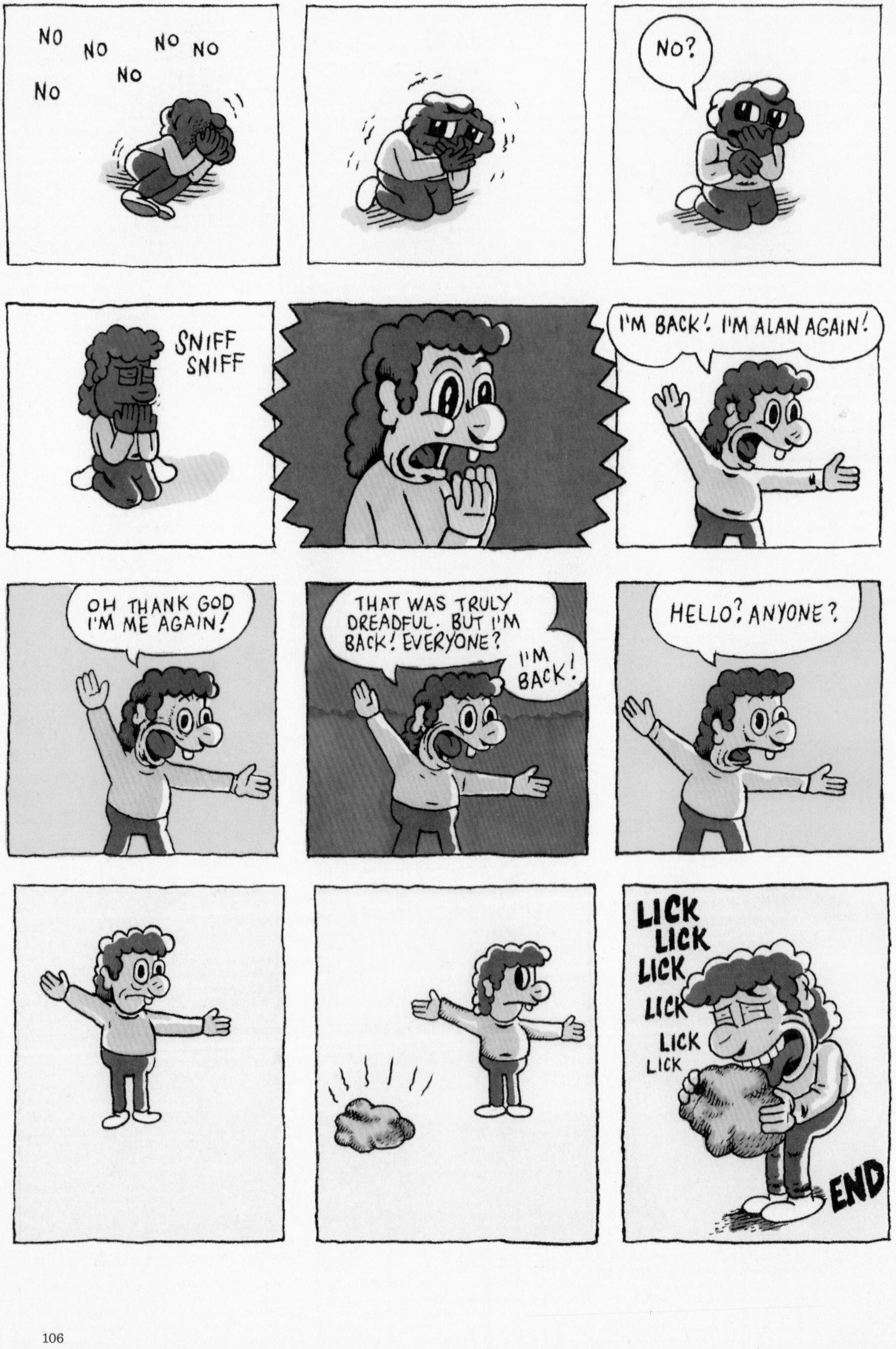
NO NO NO NO NO NO
NO?
SNIFF SNIFF
I'M BACK! I'M ALAN AGAIN!
OH THANK GOD I'M ME AGAIN!
THAT WAS TRULY DREADFUL. BUT I'M BACK! EVERYONE?
I'M BACK!
HELLO? ANYONE?
LICK LICK LICK LICK LICK LICK
END

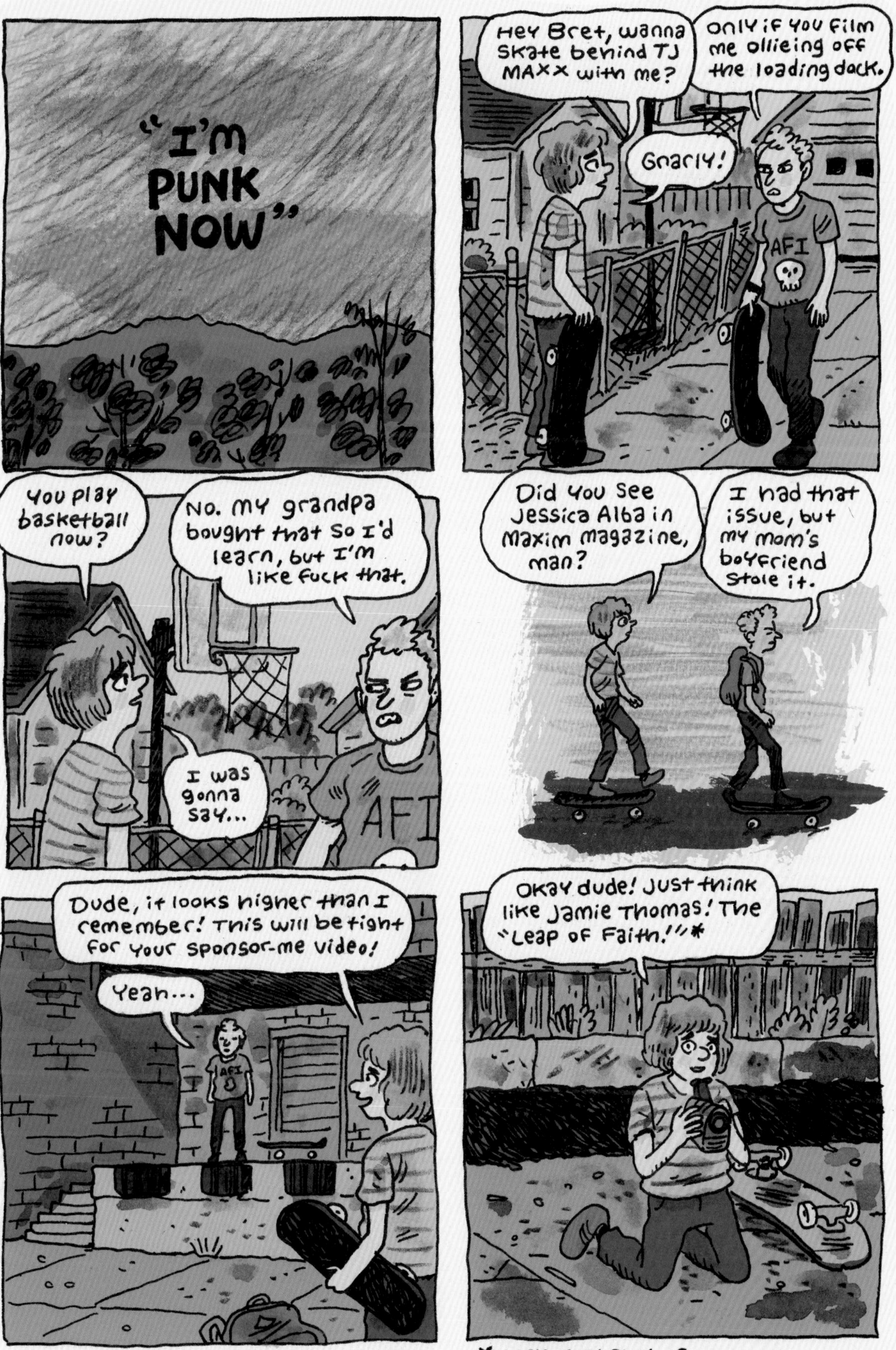
"I'M PUNK NOW"
Hey Bret, wanna skate behind TJ MAXX with me?
Only if you film me ollieing off the loading dock.
Gnarly!
You play basketball now?
No. My grandpa bought that so I'd learn, but I'm like fuck that.
I was gonna say...
Did you see Jessica Alba in Maxim magazine, man?
I had that issue, but my mom's boyfriend stole it.
Dude, it looks higher than I remember! This will be tight for your sponsor-me video!
Yeah...
Okay dude! Just think like Jamie Thomas! The "Leap of Faith!"*

* Look that shit up, homies

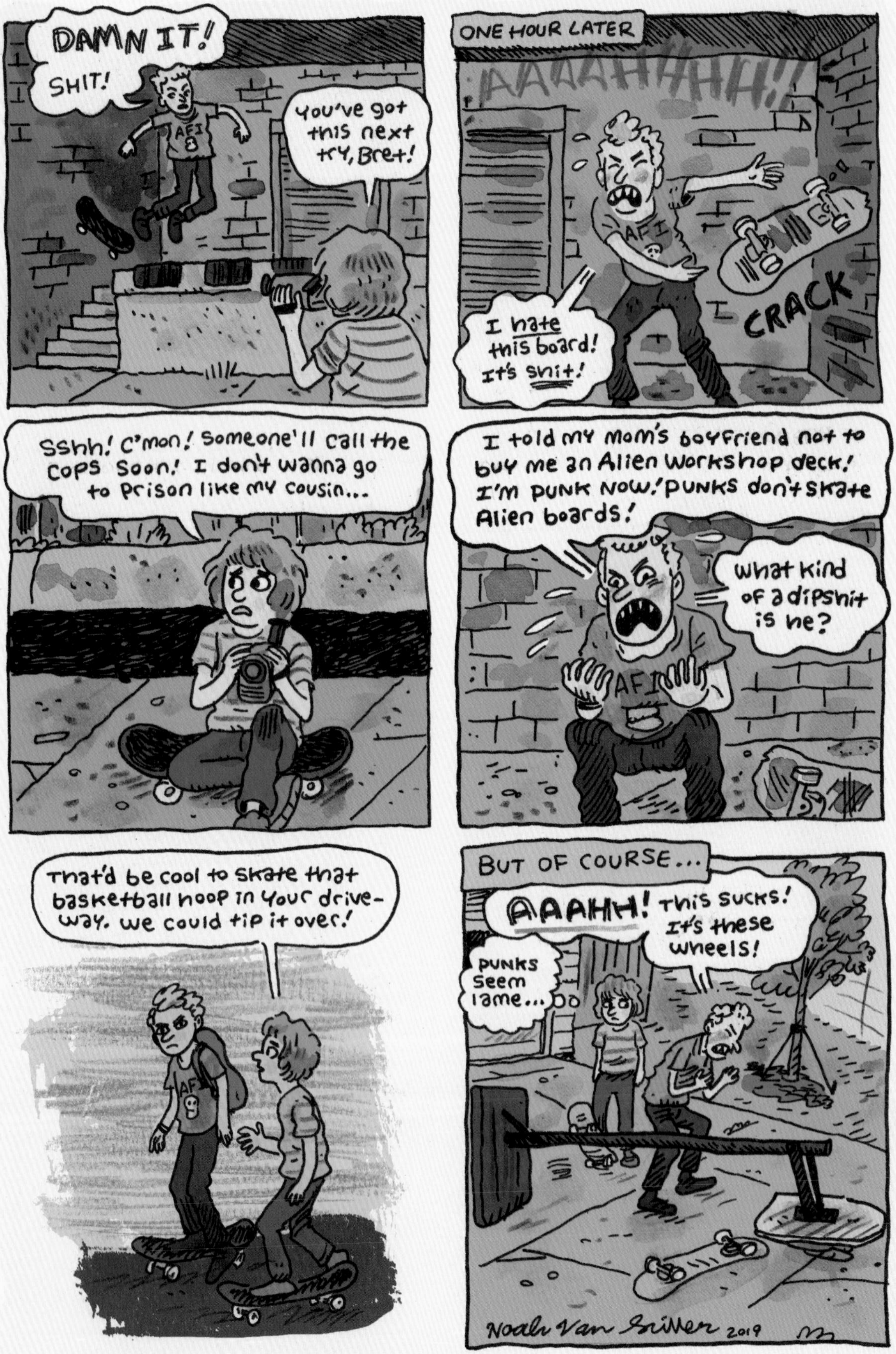
DAMN IT!
SHIT!
You've got this next try, Bret!
ONE HOUR LATER
AAAAHHHH!!
I hate this board! It's shit!
CRACK
Sshh! C'mon! Someone'll call the cops soon! I don't wanna go to prison like my cousin...
I told my mom's boyfriend not to buy me an Alien Workshop deck! I'm punk now! punks don't skate Alien boards!
what kind of a dipshit is he?
That'd be cool to skate that basketball hoop in your drive-way. we could tip it over!
BUT OF COURSE...
AAAHH! This sucks! It's these wheels!
punks seem lame...
Noah Van Sciver 2019

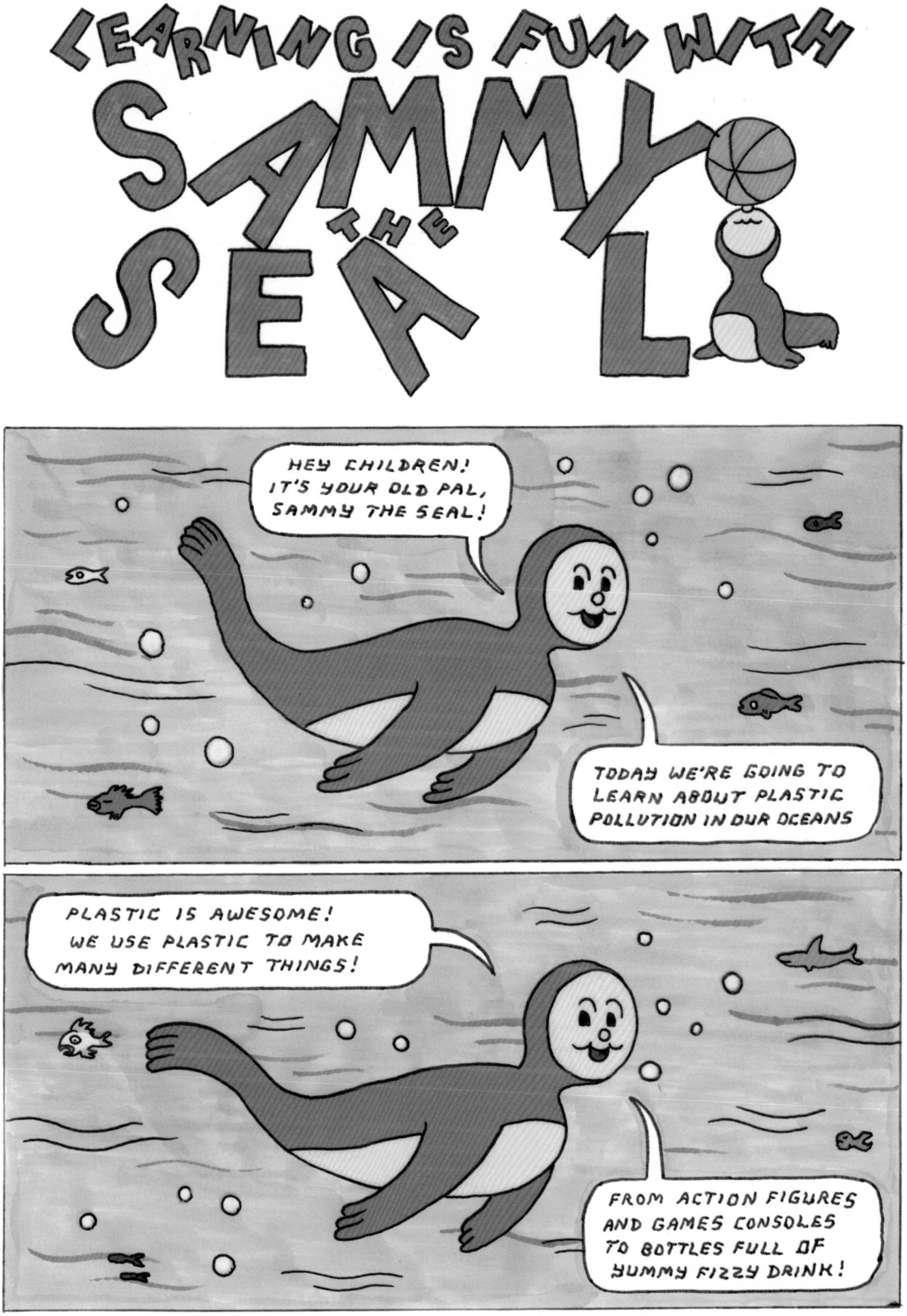
LEARNING IS FUN WITH
SAMMY THE SEAL
HEY CHILDREN! IT'S YOUR OLD PAL, SAMMY THE SEAL!
TODAY WE'RE GOING TO LEARN ABOUT PLASTIC POLLUTION IN OUR OCEANS
PLASTIC IS AWESOME! WE USE PLASTIC TO MAKE MANY DIFFERENT THINGS!
FROM ACTION FIGURES AND GAMES CONSOLES TO BOTTLES FULL OF YUMMY FIZZY DRINK!

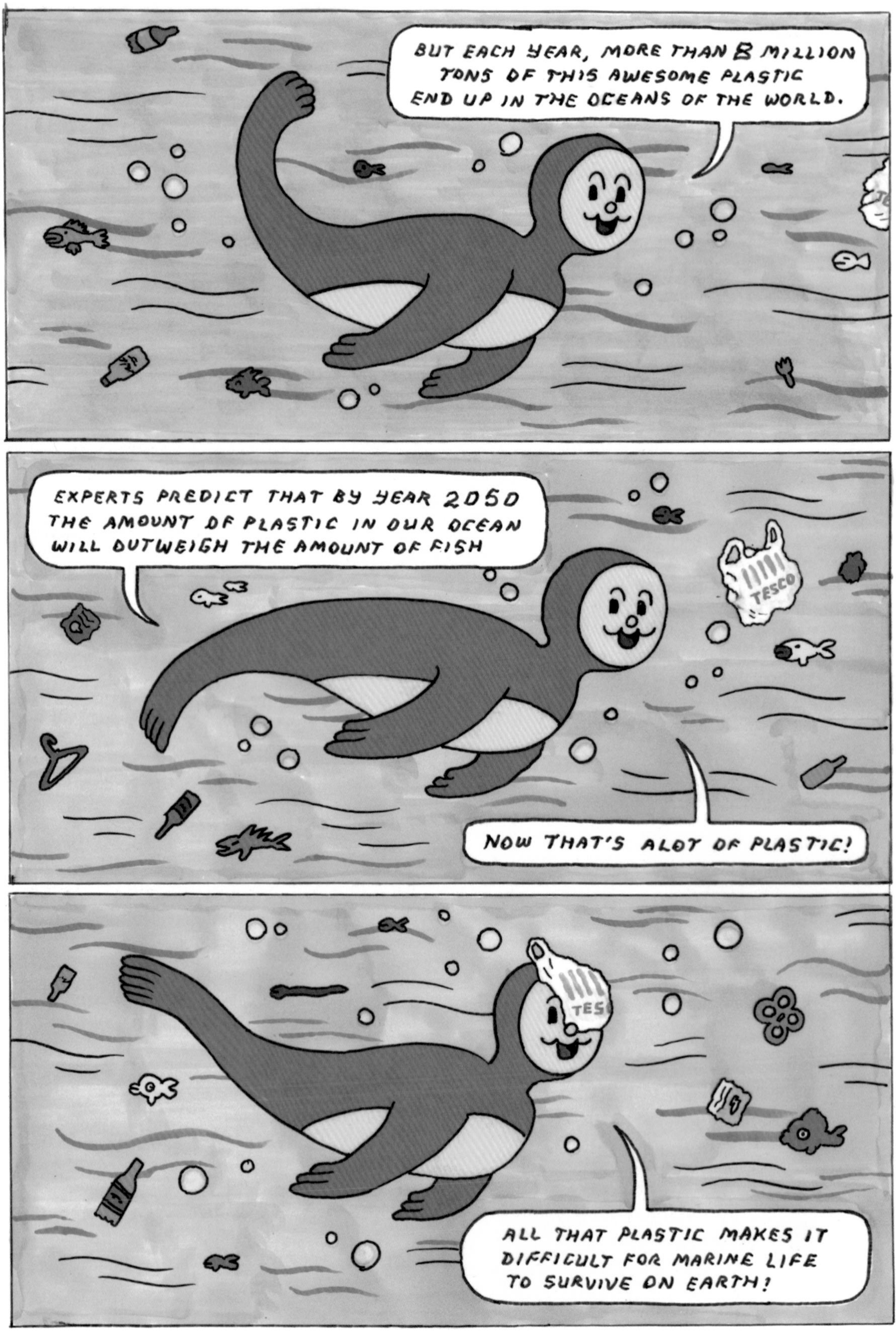
BUT EACH YEAR, MORE THAN 8 MILLION TONS OF THIS AWESOME PLASTIC END UP IN THE OCEANS OF THE WORLD.
EXPERTS PREDICT THAT BY YEAR 2050 THE AMOUNT OF PLASTIC IN OUR OCEAN WILL OUTWEIGH THE AMOUNT OF FISH
TESCO
NOW THAT'S ALOT OF PLASTIC!
ALL THAT PLASTIC MAKES IT DIFFICULT FOR MARINE LIFE TO SURVIVE ON EARTH!

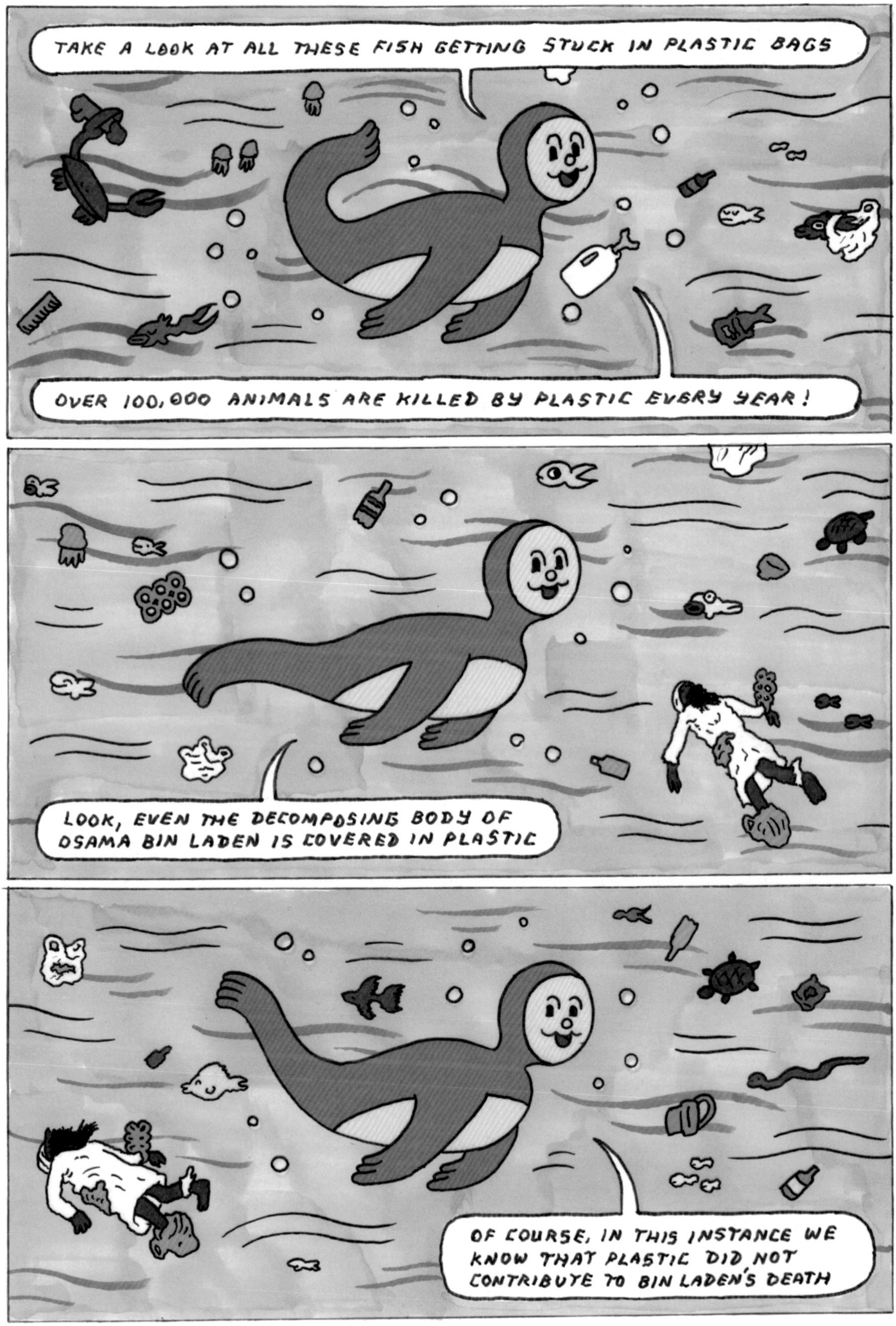
TAKE A LOOK AT ALL THESE FISH GETTING STUCK IN PLASTIC BAGS
OVER 100,000 ANIMALS ARE KILLED BY PLASTIC EVERY YEAR!
LOOK, EVEN THE DECOMPOSING BODY OF OSAMA BIN LADEN IS COVERED IN PLASTIC
OF COURSE, IN THIS INSTANCE WE KNOW THAT PLASTIC DID NOT CONTRIBUTE TO BIN LADEN'S DEATH

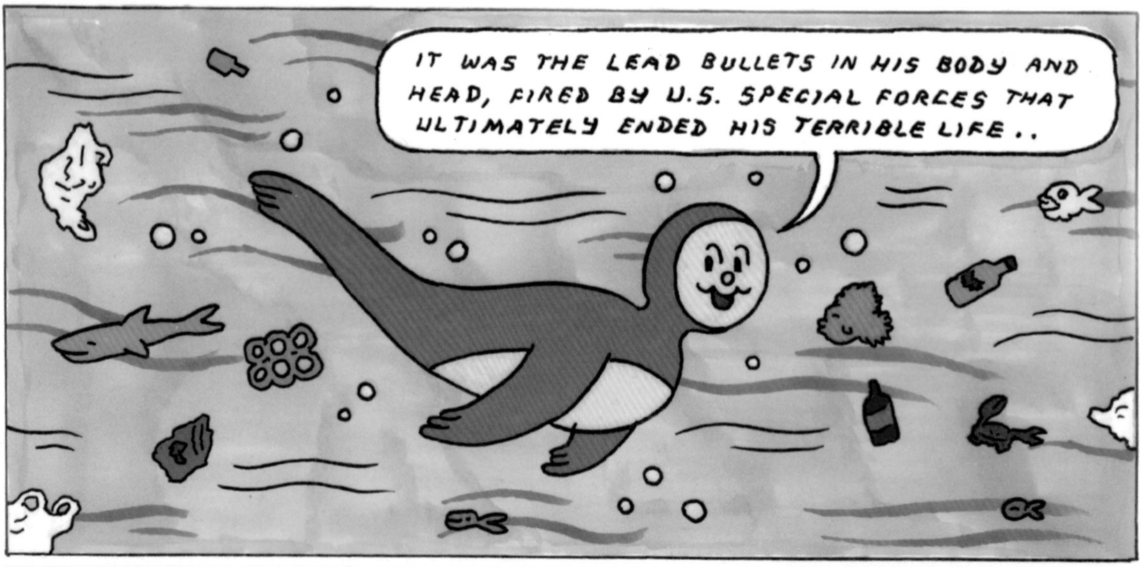
IT WAS THE LEAD BULLETS IN HIS BODY AND HEAD, FIRED BY U.S. SPECIAL FORCES THAT ULTIMATELY ENDED HIS TERRIBLE LIFE ..

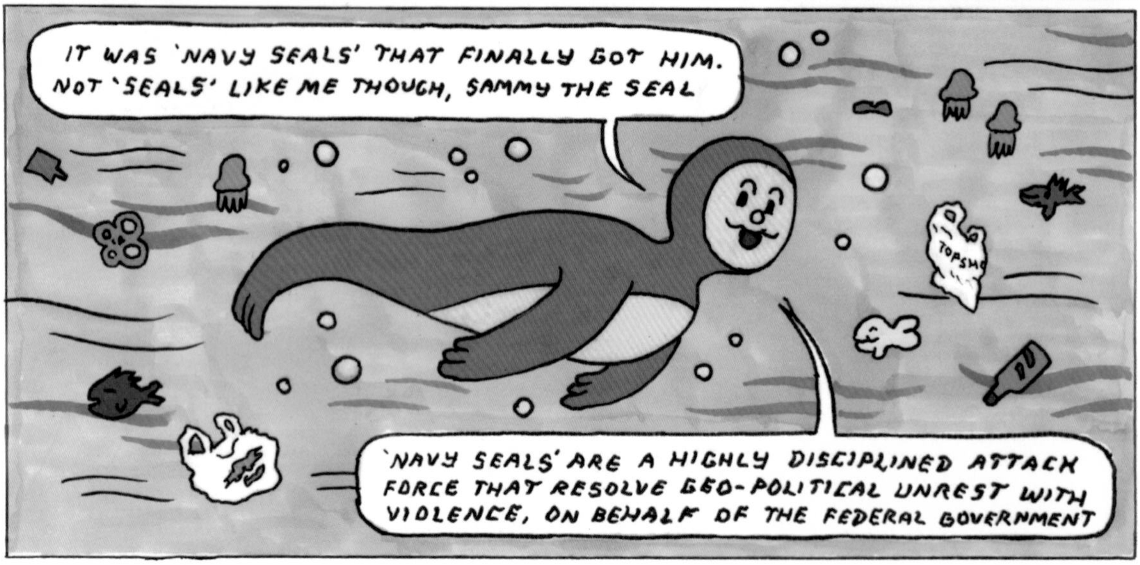
IT WAS 'NAVY SEALS' THAT FINALLY GOT HIM. NOT 'SEALS' LIKE ME THOUGH, SAMMY THE SEAL
'NAVY SEALS' ARE A HIGHLY DISCIPLINED ATTACK FORCE THAT RESOLVE GEO-POLITICAL UNREST WITH VIOLENCE, ON BEHALF OF THE FEDERAL GOVERNMENT

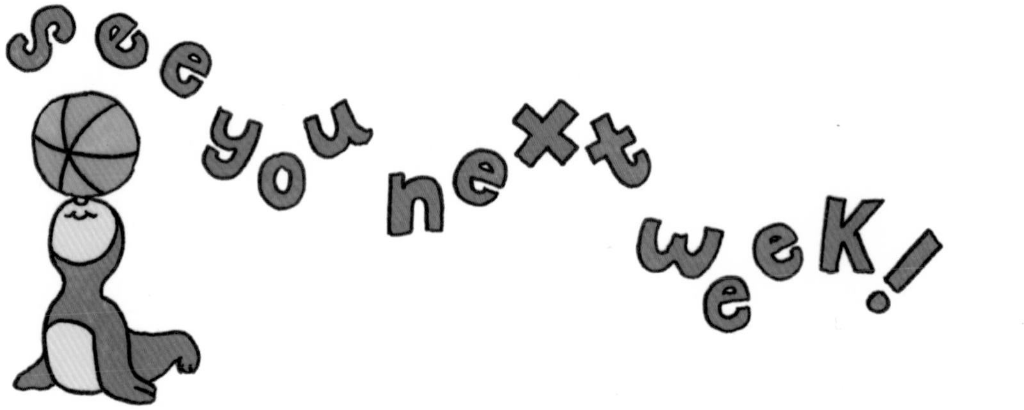
See you next week!

NEXT WEEK: CLIMATE CHANGE AND THE CHINESE